CRAVING CHARLOTTE

The Aces' Sons

By Nicole Jacquelyn

Craving Charlotte
Copyright © 2022 by Nicole Jacquelyn
Print Edition
All Rights Reserved

No part of this book may be reproduced or transmitted in any form or by any means, electronic or mechanical, including photocopying, recording, or by any information storage and retrieval system without the written permission of the author, except for the use of brief quotations in a book review.

This is a work of fiction. Names, characters, businesses, places, events, and incidents are either the products of the author's imagination or used in a fictitious manner. Any resemblance to actual persons, living or dead, or actual events is purely coincidental. The author acknowledges the trademarked status and trademark owners of various products referenced in this work of fiction, which have been used without permission. The publication/use of these trademarks is not authorized, associated with, or sponsored by the trademark owners.

Dedication

To my big kids
who took care of my little kids
so I could finish this story.

Prologue
CHARLIE

NOTHING HAD BEEN moved. Draco's running shoes were still in a pile next to Kara's carefully placed ones by the door. A towel from someone, probably Draco, was still hung over the banister of the stairway. The entryway still smelled like cinnamon from the little scented plugs I'd bought from a store at the mall and a little like the sprinkling of rain we'd had the night before. Everything was the same, it was the exact tableau that I'd left that morning, but something was *wrong*. The minute I walked into the house, I could feel it.

My scalp tingled and the back of my neck itched. Closing the door quietly behind me, I reached for the baseball bat we stored just inside, the handle resting against the corner just left of the doorframe. I let my bag slip gently down my arm and set it on the doormat as I slowly moved forward, raising the bat to my shoulder.

My dad teased me about the bat. Hell, nearly everyone at the clubhouse teased me about it. A baseball bat wasn't the best form of home defense because much like a knife, you had to be pretty damn close to someone in order to use it. So, yeah, they gave me shit.

They gave me shit, but they also didn't give me grief. There was a difference. They thought it was funny, and they made it known, but the members of the Aces MC knew better than to try and convince me that a bat would do no good. None of them would make that mistake. They'd watched me swing it, practicing hour after hour, from the time I was five years old. I'd played softball for fifteen years. The force of my swing was enough to put someone in the hospital, no matter where I hit them. I liked to call it the great equalizer since pretty much everyone I met was bigger than I was.

Stepping forward, I moved around the creaky floorboard and looked into the living room. Nothing there, but the tingle hadn't stopped.

I made my way through the kitchen and the downstairs bathroom, but everything was in its place. The back door in the laundry-slash-mudroom was still locked. Kara and Draco's room was empty.

As I made my way up the stairs I loosened my shoulders and readjusted my grip on the bat, rubbing my thumb along the grip tape the way I'd done a thousand times before. There were three bedrooms upstairs, but we only used two. I glanced inside the first one, but there was nothing. The entire room was empty, there weren't even curtains on the windows. The next room was neat and I couldn't see anything out of place. The bathroom upstairs was tiny with Jack-and-Jill doors that were both currently closed.

I took a deep breath as I stepped into my bedroom. It had originally been two bedrooms when the house was built, but some time over the last fifty years had been converted into one large room. I had twice the windows and twice the space as the other two bedrooms upstairs and I made good use of it. My bed sat in the center, made just the way I'd left it that morning. The pile of folded clothes I'd set on the small couch off to the right side under the windows were still where I'd put them. My yoga mat was still lying on the floor to the left side of the bed, my free weights still lined up by size against the wall. I braced my feet and threw open my closet door. Empty.

Oh, for fuck's sake.

I let out a little laugh as I walked over and dropped onto the foot of the bed, laying the bat across my knees. Kara was going to find it hilarious when I told her how bad I'd freaked myself out. Since we'd moved in, I'd had a hard time getting used to all the noises the old house made as it settled. After living in the same house my entire life and then in a tiny apartment with Kara, the new place was a little creepy. It had been updated, but it was still old. People had lived and died there long before my cousin Tommy bought it and I was pretty sure there were ghosts. Okay, maybe *pretty sure* was pushing it. Let's just say I hadn't ruled the possibility out yet.

I snickered and glanced toward the TV.

In an instant, my laughter cut off with a choking sound.

The bat fell from my hands and rolled onto the floor as I stared.

I could have missed it. I could have walked into my room and seen nothing wrong. It was plausible for anyone else. The way I'd hung the mural of framed photos above my TV hadn't looked like there was any pattern. I liked it that way. I thought it looked cooler if they looked like they'd been hung haphazardly over time. But they hadn't—I'd painstakingly found each photo by pouring through my mom's old boxes and albums and phones and thumb drives. I knew where each photo came from, when it was taken, and precisely where it hung on my wall.

The photos weren't in the right spots. I scanned the wall until I found it. The picture that didn't belong.

Someone had been in my goddamn room and I had a pretty good idea who it was.

Moving slowly, I crouched down and picked my bat up. As I rose to my feet, I heard the sound of someone stepping unknowingly onto the creaky floorboard downstairs.

Chapter 1
CHARLIE

"Remind me again why we're moving," I groaned, pulling another box of stuff out of the back of my best friend Kara's Jeep. "We had a perfectly good apartment."

Kara laughed. "Because the walls were thin," she replied slyly.

"Oh God," I muttered. "Couldn't you have said something about how small the apartment was?"

"It was," my nephew Draco said, coming up the driveway carrying a dresser. "Too small for all of us." He paused and grinned. "Especially when Kara and I want to get down."

"Maybe you shouldn't be so goddamn loud," I called after him as he walked away.

"You're one to talk," Kara said as we made our way into the house. "You're louder than both of us."

"But I'm not fucking a member of your family," I pointed out. "I mean, I'm glad you're together, obviously."

"Obviously," she agreed.

"But it's cruel and unusual to hear just how *together* you two are."

Kara snorted. "Point taken. But hey, we're on completely different floors now. Problem solved."

"God Bless America," I said, dropping my box in the center of the living room.

"That goes in our room," Kara said as she kept walking.

Sighing, I stared at the box I'd just put down. "Draco can move it later."

The house was bustling with people that were helping us move and thank God for that, because we were also consolidating two apartments. Draco and his twin Curtis had shared an apartment in the same complex as Kara and me, but now we'd all be in the same house. Well, almost all of us. Curtis was off doing some shit for the club and no one was saying when he'd be back. Either they didn't know, or they weren't willing to tell us. We just had to go along with it and make sure there was a room for him at this new place, whenever he graced us again with his presence.

"You're dawdling," my mom said, coming through the front door with grocery bags in her hands and dangling from her arms. "The faster we get this shit unloaded the faster we can all sit down. Get moving."

"Easy for you to say," I replied. "You're carrying groceries."

"I just cleaned out the boys' fridge," she said with a laugh. "Be glad you're moving boxes."

"I'm ordering pizza in about fifteen minutes," Kara's stepmom Rose hollered as she carried a box inside. "If anyone has any requests, keep it to your damn self!"

"You're such a sweetheart," I joked as I passed her.

"They can eat what I order and smile while they're doing it," she called to me over her shoulder.

"Rose is getting pizza," I told Kara as she moved around me, her arms wrapped around a random pile of shit that hadn't fit into a box.

"Good, I'm starving," she replied. "I want pepperoni and olive."

"Make sure you tell her that," I said with a snicker.

"Grab the keys out of my pocket, would you?" she asked, jutting out her hip. "Move my Jeep onto the street so they can move one of the trucks into the driveway."

"Aye, aye, captain," I said, pulling the keys out of her jeans.

"Move your ass, Charlotte," my dad said as he carried a coffee table inside. "I'm tired of movin' this shit from the street."

"Not my fault that your logistical team is a nightmare!" I said, hurrying toward Kara's Jeep.

"Don't run anyone over," my cousin Tommy ordered, pointing at me. "I don't want the neighbors pissed at me."

"Ha," I shouted. "The neighbors are going to fucking love us!"

Tommy glanced over his shoulder at the family a couple houses down that paused in their basketball game to stare at me. "Yeah, looks like they're impressed," he drawled.

I reached up and scratched my nose with my middle finger.

After moving the Jeep down the street I walked back toward the house my cousin Tommy was renting to us. I liked it, especially after living in an apartment for the last few years. Two stories, a big back yard, a big garage and huge driveway for all of our cars. Most importantly it was within our price range. Tommy swore he wasn't giving us any type of family discount, but I wasn't so sure. He'd flipped so many houses, keeping some to rent and selling others at a profit, that renting to us on the cheap wouldn't hurt his bottom line. Of course, he'd never admit to it.

"Charlie!" one of my favorite voices in the world called out behind me.

I spun around. "When did you get here, Rebel without a cause?"

Reb wrinkled her nose at the nickname and threw her arms around me in a tight hug. "Me and mom just got here. We had to park on the next street over."

"Oh," I said, looking up to meet her mom Molly's eyes. "You're here."

"I'm always an afterthought with you guys," she joked. "You know, I was popular once."

"Were you, though?" I asked dubiously.

"Like a hundred years ago," Rebel said at the same time, rolling her eyes. I laughed and grabbed her hand, wrapping my fingers firmly around hers.

"You two are the absolute worst," Molly complained with a smile.

"Show me your house," Rebel said, squeezing my hand. "Do you have your own room?"

"Of course," I replied. "I have one of the biggest rooms. Draco and Kara have the other one."

"Because they're in love," Rebel said simply.

"Yep. Gross."

Rebel giggled. "When I get married, I'm still going to have my own room."

"Interesting choice," I said, looking over my shoulder to meet Molly's eyes for just a second. "Don't you want to share with your husband?"

"I'll sleep with my husband," Rebel replied with a grin. "But all my stuff is going to be in my own room so nobody touches it."

"You know, you may be onto something," I said. "You thinking about getting married soon?"

Reb scoffed. "No way. I like to keep my options open."

"Oh, Jesus," Molly muttered behind me.

"That's what my dad said to do. He said not to even think about getting married until I'm thirty because there are tons of fish in the sea and I need to keep fishing."

"I'm going to kill Will," Molly said with a grimace.

We paused in the front yard and looked at the house, letting Molly pass us as she headed inside.

"It looks like all the other houses," Reb said evenly.

"I know, right," I replied. "Hopefully I don't forget which one is ours." Now that I was thinking about it, I couldn't deny that the possibility of coming home from a night out might be a problem if I couldn't tell which house was mine.

"I'll get you a flag."

"A flag?" I asked curiously, turning to look at her.

"Yeah," she said, pointing at the bracket to the right of the garage door. "You're supposed to put a flag right there."

"Huh. Good eye."

"I'll get you a rainbow flag," she said, giving my hand a squeeze. "Since you find men *and* women sexually attractive."

I stared at her for a moment. "You're the best, Reb. You know that?"

"You told me that before," she said with a smile.

"And I'm going to keep saying it."

"I'm going to marry Wes," she said conspiratorially, her smile growing wider. "But my dad starts to breathe really heavy whenever he comes over and he's always coming into the living room when we're watching TV or playing a game."

"Oh yeah?" Wesley was Reb's boyfriend, and I really liked the dude, but I had no idea that they'd been talking about marriage. I tried to hide the fact that it felt a little like I'd been hit with a sledgehammer.

"I don't think dad wants me to get married."

"No dad wants their little girl to get married," I replied.

"I don't think he's ready."

"They never are," I said dryly.

"That's okay," she said with a shrug. "I'm not ready either."

"Good," I said grinning. "We can be single girls together."

"Okay. But someday I'm going to marry him and then you'll have to be single alone," she replied simply as she started toward the house. Ouch.

"Does he know you want separate bedrooms?" I asked, following her.

I trailed Rebel around the inside of the house, pointing out where everyone was going to sleep and showing off the rooms like a game show host. No one bothered us or hassled me for not helping move the boxes. They knew how important those few minutes of showing Rebel around were.

There were five of us that were close in age and had grown up together. My nephews Draco and Curtis, my cousin's stepdaughter Kara, me, and Rebel. We'd done almost everything together until we'd reached an age that things had started to change. Rebel had Down syndrome and while we'd moved out and started our adult lives, she wasn't ready for that. She was still at home, and she was just getting to the part where she dated and started to venture out more on her own.

It was important to all of us that Reb felt comfortable in our new place. She was putting on a brave face about it all, but she'd liked our old apartments and she hated change. The fact that we were clear across town, not to mention that Curtis was gone God knows where, was throwing her for a loop. The longer I showed her around, the more tense she became.

"This is my room," I said, throwing my arms out wide.

"It's bigger than my parents' room," she said, walking around. She peeked into the closet and ran her hand across the windowsills.

"Right? It's huge. I'm thinking the bed goes right in the middle and then we'll put our old couch by the windows."

"Your couch is going in your bedroom?"

"Well, yeah," I said, grinning. "Then you'll have a place to sleep when you stay the night."

Rebel's smile was slow to emerge, but it was there.

"Unless you want to share the bed with me?" I asked.

"You're a bed hog," she replied seriously. "It's like sleeping with an octopus."

"Slept with many octopi?"

"Haha. Funny," she replied, completely straight faced.

"It's a cool place, right?" I said, suddenly kind of nervous.

"I like the windows," she replied.

"Me too."

"And there are two ovens so you can make two pizzas at the same time."

"Good point."

"Your bedroom is really big."

"Way bigger than the last one. So much room for activities."

"And it's closer to my house."

"It is?"

"By three minutes," she confirmed. "I timed it."

"Hot damn," I said with a smile.

Kara poked her head in the room, her face red and sweaty. "You like our new house?" she asked Rebel.

"It's three minutes closer to Reb's house," I said.

"Duh," Kara said, smiling at Rebel. "Why do you think we chose it?"

"No way," Rebel said, practically lighting up.

Kara shrugged. "Come on guys, no more screwing around. We need to finish unpacking so Rose will order the damn pizza."

"I'm hungry," Reb said, following her into the hallway.

"Go tell Rose," I said as I hurried after them. "And tell her you want beer too."

"I don't like beer," Rebel replied easily.

"Fine, tell her *I* want beer."

LESS THAN AN hour later, the house was full of boxes and we'd all collapsed on the floor of the living room, eating pizza off of paper plates.

"What are you going to do about furniture in here?" my dad asked, taking a sip of his beer.

"Beanbags," I replied immediately.

"Plannin' on finding something this week," Draco answered, ignoring me. "We need somethin' bigger than the girls' old couch."

"Which is now all mine," I said with satisfaction.

"I'm going to sleep there when I spend the night," Rebel told her mom.

"Perfect," Molly replied.

"I'm thinking a sectional," Kara said. "We never have enough seats for everyone. Especially when Curtis finally gets home."

The room grew quiet.

"A sectional is a good idea," Kara's dad Mack said, ignoring the implied question of *when* Curtis would get home. "You should try that discount place where we found our bed. They had some sectionals. What's that place called Rosie?"

"Notice how he changed the subject?" Kara murmured to me. "Classic Jacob Mackenzie dodge."

"It was impressive, really," I murmured back.

"No parties," Tommy said out of nowhere.

We laughed.

"I'm not kiddin'," he griped. "You wanna party, come to the clubhouse. I don't want the neighbors callin' at all hours of the night bitchin' at me."

"Why are you so sure the neighbors won't like us?" I asked innocently. "Maybe they'll come to the parties."

"Don't," Tommy ordered. "Don't do it."

"Can he really tell us who we can have in our house?" I asked, looking around the room. "Someone help me out here."

"Stop being such a stick-in-the-mud, Thomas," Rose said, laying on the carpet with her head on Mack's legs. "It's not like they're going to throw a rager."

"I don't know about that," Draco's friend Bishop said as he stepped inside the open door. "Give a guy a little bit of freedom and…." His words trailed off.

"Nice of you to show when the work is over," my dad joked.

Bishop said hello to everyone and conversations moved on, but I just stared. Why in God's name did I find the man so attractive? I'd been with plenty of people, some that I shuddered to think about now and some that I remembered more than fondly, but there had never been anyone else that I was so overwhelmingly attracted to. Everything from his voice to his stupid feet turned me on. I hadn't found a single thing that I didn't like, and that pissed me off.

"Shut your mouth," Kara whispered. "You're drooling."

"Fuck off," I replied, automatically wiping at my face.

"Just bang him and be done with it," she said with a sigh. "Maybe he sucks in bed."

"He's Draco's best bud," I hissed. "Shouldn't you be telling me to steer clear so I don't ruin their friendship when things go south?"

Kara snorted. "You're friendly with all your exes. I'm not worried about that." She hummed. "I am a little worried that all the sexual tension is going to spontaneously combust our new house, though."

"Fine, I'll bang him and get it over with."

"Seriously?"

"No, not seriously, you fucking lunatic." I reached over and pinched her leg. "I'm going to bang someone else and pretend it's him."

"You're a head case."

"I am intelligent and have a healthy sense of self-preservation," I replied quietly as I met Bishop's blue eyes from across the room. I was ready when the familiar feeling of falling, like the downhill slide of a roller coaster, ran through me.

"Right," Kara said, her words thrumming with amusement. "Maybe you should tell Bishop your plan. See what he thinks about it."

"Maybe you should mind your own beeswax," I said, looking away from him before I did something stupid. "I have a date tomorrow."

"With who?"

"A woman that came to the shop a few days ago," I said, finally looking at Kara again. "Green eyes, chiseled cheekbones, and legs that'll wrap around me twice."

"Let me know how that goes."

"Oh, I will," I said. "In detail."

"Please, no."

"We're gonna head out, baby," my mom said, strolling in from the kitchen. "I got all of your food put away, so at least that's done."

"Thanks, ma," I said, tilting my head back to look at her.

"No one should have that much instant ramen, Charlotte," she said, shaking her head.

"Who says it's mine?" I asked with a fake gasp. "That's all Kara's. She can't get enough of the stuff."

"Have you forgotten that I raised you?" mom asked, reaching down to pinch my cheek. "You have the eating habits of a raccoon."

"Thank God for your genes, am I right?" I asked, patting my belly.

"Someday it's going to catch up with you," mom warned with a laugh as she walked over to help pull my dad to his feet.

"Yeah right," he said, slapping my mom's ass. "When's it going to catch up to *you*?"

"No parental ass-slapping in this house," I ordered, pointing at them. "Get that shit out of here."

"We'll go too," Rose said, climbing off the floor with a groan. "I need a bath and a massage."

"I can handle that," Mack replied seriously.

"Oh, for God's sake," Kara snapped.

"You're such a prude," I said, elbowing her in the side.

Kara sputtered and I made the mistake of looking at Bishop. I could never keep my eyes off him for long. He was already looking at me, laughing. Jesus, that man needed to be put in some kind of museum so people could pay to see the perfection.

"You gonna stay and hang, Reb?" Draco asked as Tommy, Will and Molly made moves to leave.

"No, Wes is coming over at seven o'clock," she replied, shaking her head.

"That's a little late, isn't it?" I teased, glancing between her and her parents. "You guys okay with that?"

"It's not late," Rebel argued. "It won't even be dark yet!"

"Better they're at our house," Will muttered.

"We like when Wes comes to visit," Molly said, shooting her man a look that told him to shut it.

Reb made the rounds, giving each of us a hug, and I watched closely as she got to Bishop. He didn't open his arms for her, or do anything really, but smile.

"Good to see you, Reb," he said softly, his eyes on her. He held out his hand.

"A hug this time," Rebel said firmly. She stepped forward and wrapped her arms around his waist and I bit my cheek at his expression of surprise and delight. It was so fucking cute I could scream.

"I finally get a hug," he said happily, looking across the room at Draco.

"She likes tight hugs, man," Draco said, grinning. "None of those half-assed ones."

"Noted," Bishop replied, tightening his arms around her shoulders.

"Okay, that's enough," Reb said, pulling away. "Bye!"

I laughed as Bishop quickly dropped his arms and waved as the group filed out calling their goodbyes over their shoulders. Tommy turned at the door and pointed two fingers at his eyes and then at each of us in an *I'm watching you* gesture. I flipped him off.

"I'm gonna start putting the kitchen away," I said, getting to my feet.

"You're choosing the kitchen because your mom already did most of it," Kara accused, grabbing at my ankle as I sidestepped her. "Cheater."

"Obviously," I said, pretending to step on her hand.

"Fine," she griped. "I'll do the bathrooms."

"Don't steal my shit," I said as I walked away.

"Yeah right," she called back. "I have my own stuff, thank you!"

The guys stayed in the living room as we puttered around, unpacking boxes, and though I'd never admit it, I liked hearing the low hum of their voices in the house. It was kind of comforting.

It was weird as hell having Curtis gone. I knew he was okay, out there doing whatever for the club, but I resented the fact that he wasn't with us. After years of Draco being in prison it had felt like everything was getting back to normal, the five of us all finally together. Now shit was all lopsided again.

"We need music," I muttered, pulling out my phone. I searched through the box of odds and ends from our kitchen and found the speaker that we'd kept in our old place. "Gotcha."

As soon as I'd turned on some tunes, the unpacking seemed to go faster. I had an ulterior motive for unpacking the kitchen—I could put everything away where I wanted it. Cooking in a kitchen was a pain in the ass when you didn't know where everything was, and it was going to drive Kara crazy for weeks until she figured it out. I grinned as I shook my ass, putting silverware away in one of the drawers.

"Goddamn," Bishop said from somewhere behind me, making me freeze in place. "Please, don't stop."

"Ha," I said, spinning to face him. "No free shows in this house."

"I'll pay," he replied, lips twitching as he reached for his wallet.

"I don't know what you're paying for and I don't wanna know," Draco said as he strolled into the kitchen. "Just getting another beer."

"Hey, why aren't you unpacking?" I asked.

"I am," he replied, saluting me with his beer. "Makin' the bed right now."

"Wait," I said, frowning. "You already rebuilt your bed?"

"Kara's pops helped me when we moved it in."

"Well that's bullshit," I replied, waving the handful of forks at him. "No one built my bed."

"Should've asked," Draco said simply, flicking the cap of his beer at me as he walked away.

"You don't have a maid just because you moved in with two women," I yelled at him, bending down to grab the bottle cap so I could throw it at him. "Don't throw shit on the floor."

Draco just laughed.

"I'll help ya build it," Bishop said easily.

I stared at him, debating the merits and pitfalls of having him in my room, that close to my mattress, *building shit*. Using tools. Looking like a fucking Greek god. While I wasn't sure if I could keep my goddamn hands to myself, I also needed somewhere to sleep that night.

"I accept," I said finally, tossing the forks into the drawer. "Come on."

"Let me grab my tools out of the truck," he said. "You're upstairs?"

I nodded. "The only room with anything in it."

"I'll find you," he said with a grin.

Well, shit.

While he went outside, I jogged up the stairs to my room. There were boxes everywhere, with no rhyme or reason to their placement, and I started moving them against the walls to make room for my bed. I couldn't believe my dad hadn't built it when they'd carried it upstairs, but I knew Draco was right. I should have fucking asked him to. There were so many moving parts, my dad probably just figured someone else had done it.

"Damn," Bishop said as he stepped inside the room. "How did you score the big room?"

"It's actually smaller than Kara and Draco's," I said with a huff, setting a box down against the wall by my closet. "Their room is downstairs and it's massive."

"This house is the shit."

"I know, right?" I said with a laugh. "We got lucky when the old renters moved out. They didn't trash the place and Tommy barely had to do anything before we were able to move in."

"This is one of Tommy's houses?"

I snorted. "Uh, yeah," I said, brushing my hair out of my face. "We probably couldn't afford it otherwise, especially with the college kids downstairs only working part time."

"Aren't you a college kid, too?" he asked, setting his tool belt down by the door. I wondered for a split second if he'd put it on for me and do a little turn around the room. Just for entertainment sake. And, you know, so I could think about it later when I was alone.

"I'm almost done," I said, stuttering a little at the picture I'd painted for myself. "Plus, I work full time."

"Busy," he commented.

"I like it," I replied with a shrug. "I've never been one to sit around."

"Same," he said. He was watching me and it was irritating as hell because I had to fight the urge to fidget.

"So," I said, a little too loudly. "That's the bed." I swung my hand toward where the pieces rested against the wall.

"Really?" he asked, his eyes crinkling at the corners. "You sure?"

"Oh shut it," I replied, the spell broken. "I want it right here with the headboard against this wall."

"Alright," he said. He leaned down to undo the laces of his boots.

"What are you doing?" I asked accusingly.

"Takin' my boots off."

"Why?"

"Because I'm gonna be crawlin' around on your floor and I don't know what's on 'em," he answered easily.

"Oh."

"You don't have to be so jumpy around me," he said as he padded over to the bed pieces. "I'm not gonna attack you."

"I don't think you're going to attack me," I argued. Then as an afterthought, "And I'm not jumpy."

"You're jumpy as fuck," he replied dryly. "We slept together once—"

"With our clothes on!"

"And I wouldn't mind doin' it again," he continued, ignoring my interruption. "But that's up to you."

"You *wouldn't mind* doing it again?" I sputtered.

"Oh, come on," he said, sorting through the pieces. "You know what you look like. Can't imagine you're short on people who want to see you naked."

"You haven't seen me naked."

He licked his lips, still not looking at me. "Unfortunately, true."

"And you're one to talk," I said, unsure why I was even trying to argue with him. "You look like that."

"I look like what?" he said, turning his head to meet my gaze.

"Like sex on two legs," I said accusingly. "Like a fucking exotic dancer or something."

"A stripper?" he said with a confused laugh. "That's a new one."

"You fucking ooze it!"

"Ooze what?"

"Sex!"

"Ah," he said, turning away again. "Maybe that's just you."

"How am I responsible for it?" I asked with a huff.

"'Cause every time I'm around you I'm practically pantin' for it," he said ruefully.

"We should just do it and get it out of our systems," I blurted. I came a hair's breadth from slapping my hand over my mouth, but stopped myself, planting my hands on my hips and raising my chin. I wasn't some nervous virgin. Maybe Kara was right, maybe I could get over this crush or desire or whatever if I just fucked him. Then we could be friends. Move on.

"Do it?" he asked slowly, rising to his feet.

"Fuck," I said with a shrug, like it was no big deal.

Bishop smiled and walked toward me.

"Maybe not right this minute," I said as he got closer. "I'm sweaty and dusty from moving and I probably have pizza breath—"

I held my ground until he was just inches away and then took an involuntary step back.

"Baby," he said, his hands coming up to tangle in my hair. I felt the scrunchie holding it back loosen as his fingers tunneled in. "I don't think once is gonna get anything out of our systems."

"It will," I said, reaching up to grip his forearms. The muscles there were firm and shifted as his fingers tightened.

"We've been doin' this dance for months," he said, leaning down to run his nose along my jawline. "By the time I get you into a bed, I'm not gonna stop at once."

"Fine, twice," I said, shuddering.

Chapter 2
BISHOP

Fuck. Fuck. Fuck.

I finally had my hands on her, and I wasn't sure how to proceed. I knew exactly what I wanted to do—take her up on the offer, strip her ass naked and fuck her into oblivion right there on the floor—but I wasn't sure that was a good idea for a variety of reasons. I wanted her in a goddamn bed, with sheets and no interruptions. I wanted her to be showered—not for me, I thought she smelled fucking great and I was salivating at the thought of licking the sweat from her skin—but for her. Because I knew if we went down that road now, she was going to be, if not self-conscious then at least aware of the fact that she'd been doing physical labor all day.

The first time I had her, I wanted her to be primped and feeling sexy. Holding nothing back because she knew she looked like a fucking goddess and smelled like one too. No hesitation. No reservations. Exactly how I knew she'd be when we eventually got down to it. I wanted Charlie all in—anything short of that would be doing us both a disservice.

"Not sure twice is gonna be enough," I murmured, lightly running the tip of my tongue over her throat. Hell, if I didn't pull back soon all my good intentions were going to fly out the window.

"You're pretty sure of yourself," she said, tipping her head back further to give me more room to work.

"I'm pretty sure of you," I said, my words coming out like gravel.

"Holy hell, woman."

I tipped her head back down and practically dove toward her mouth. She was right, she tasted like pizza and beer and I didn't give a single fuck. She knew what she was doing, her tongue sliding against mine, and I struggled against going after her like some overeager puppy. The kiss made my fucking hands shake.

I'd known that it would be that way. I knew that she would tilt my world on its fucking axis if she ever let me in there, but I don't think I'd had any idea just how quickly or irrevocably that would happen. The thought was almost enough to make me pull away.

"Charles, Draco said they didn't build your bed. Do you guys need any help—oh!"

Kara's voice behind me hit Charlie like a bucket of cold water. In a split second she had pulled away, her cheeks rosy and her lips gorgeously swollen.

"Whoops," Kara said sheepishly.

"They need any help?" Draco called from somewhere in the house.

"Uh, no," Kara called back, still standing in the doorway.

"You have shit timing," Charlie griped as she stepped around me.

"Sorry," Kara replied, grimacing. The sound of footsteps coming up the stairs behind her made Charlie sigh.

"What's up?" Draco asked. "You sounded weird."

"You're so fucking nosy," Charlie said. "But now that you're here, help Bishop put the bed up."

"Sure, Charlie," Draco said easily, glancing between us. "Since you asked so nicely, I'll help build your bed."

"Thank you," she said primly.

"Might need to give Lover Boy a minute, though," Draco said jokingly.

"I'm fine," I said, turning toward the bed so I could discreetly adjust the most uncomfortable erection I'd ever had. Fuck.

"Why do you call him that?" Charlie asked as she gestured for Kara to help her reposition the couch.

Draco laughed. "Have you seen him?" he asked. "Prettiest man I've ever met."

"Well, thank you, sweetheart," I said dryly.

I'd been hearing the same thing for most of my adult life. Hell, I'd been pretty as a kid too. I'd never had an awkward stage. When other kids were dealing with permanent teeth that were too big for their faces, mine had just looked even more charming than the baby teeth had. As a kid who'd grown up in the system, I couldn't say that had worked to my advantage. I shrugged off the memory and moved toward Charlie's headboard.

"This thing is easy," Draco said, grabbing one of the bedrails. "But it's heavy as fuck and takes two people."

We made short work of building the bed and sliding the box spring and mattress into place.

"Okay, now you two leave so we can make it," Charlie ordered, her arms full of bedding.

Draco laughed. "Fuck off." He strode to the couch and dropped onto it.

"This is my haven," Charlie said dramatically, setting the bedding on the mattress. "My own special oasis where I can be alone."

"Cool," Draco replied, patting the other seat on the couch so I'd sit with him.

I hid my smile as I went to take a seat.

"I'm getting a lock on my door," Charlie said in exasperation. "A deadbolt."

"Probably a good idea," Kara said, looking over at me.

I laughed.

"You remember what I told you?" Charlie said to Draco, her gaze moving pointedly toward me. "I bet it's going to get loud, too."

"Oh, for fuck's sake," he said in disgust. "I don't want to know."

"I bet he's a screamer," Charlie said with relish, snapping the sheet out over the bed.

"I'm not a screamer," I mumbled, unsure about what she'd told Draco before, but sure she was talking about me now.

"We'll see," she replied, giving me a smug smile.

"I was right about washing the sheets this morning before we moved," Kara said loudly, deliberately and awkwardly changing the subject. "Right? It's so nice to sleep on clean sheets."

"Do you like clean sheets, Bishop?" Charlie asked me, unwilling to let it go. "Wanna climb on in?"

Now that there were other people in the room, all her reservations were gone. I wasn't surprised. Charlie was full of piss and vinegar when she knew it would go nowhere. It was the moments we had alone when she was jumpy.

"You're trouble," I replied as Draco scoffed.

"I'm fucking fantastic in bed," she replied as they continued making the bed. "You'll scream."

"Is that a promise?" I asked in amusement.

"Please don't encourage her," Draco said, his face still screwed up in disgust.

"It's a guarantee," Charlie said, grinning.

"You'll scream first," I replied quietly.

"Challenge accepted."

"Okay, now *I'm* getting uncomfortable," Kara muttered, throwing a pillow at Charlie's head. "And I've heard most of your conquests through the wall. Quit it."

"It's just a little light flirtation to pass the time," Charlie said, throwing the pillow back as she winked at me.

"More like foreplay," Kara countered. "I'm going to get a drink. Anyone want one?"

"I'll help," Charlie said. "Maybe we should all go?"

"I'm good," Draco replied, grinning as he made a show of getting more comfortable on the couch.

"When are you going shopping for living room furniture?" Charlie asked Kara as they left the room. "He needs a couch *downstairs*."

"You three should take this show on the road," I murmured. "The shit slinging is actually kind of impressive."

"We've been doin' it since we were kids," Draco replied with a smile. "We bicker, but we're tight."

"You're lucky," I said quietly.

"I'm aware," Draco said with a nod. "How's things? I wasn't sure if you'd show up today."

"Things are good," I replied, leaning forward to rest my elbows on my knees. "This crew I'm working with is good. No fuckwads in the mix and everyone gets along so we're runnin' like a machine. Got a raise already."

"Workin' your way up that ladder," Draco said with a grin.

I laughed. "Yeah. Give me another week and I'll be runnin' the place."

"Don't doubt it for a second," Draco replied, still smiling. "How's the house?"

"Smells like fuckin' cabbage," I said, tilting my head to smell my shirt. "Feel like I can't escape it. I smell?"

"I'm not gonna smell you."

"Fair enough."

"When do you get outta there?"

"Whenever," I replied with a shrug. Draco had been fortunate. When he'd gotten out of prison he'd had a place to go. I hadn't. When I got out, my parole officer had set me up in a halfway house. He was a good guy and I knew that he was doing me a solid, but the place sucked. "I gotta get a security deposit together before I can get a place, though. Couple more months, maybe."

"Hell, you should just move in here. We've got the room. Even when my brother gets back, we'll still have extra space."

I considered it.

"I don't know," I hedged. "That might not be a good idea."

"What might not be a good idea?" Charlie asked as she came back into the room. She handed me a beer before climbing onto her bed, sitting cross-legged with a pillow on her lap.

"Told Bishop he should move in," Draco said, taking his own beer from Kara. "Thanks, baby."

"Draco," Kara scolded, glancing at Charlie. "You can't just ask someone to move in with us without talking to us first." She looked at me, embarrassed. "No offense, Bishop."

"None taken," I replied, waving her off. "Like I said, probably not a good idea."

"We're talkin' now," Draco said defensively. "Havin' a whole ass conversation, in fact."

"He's literally sitting right there," Kara said out of the side of her mouth, pointing her thumb at me. "What if I didn't like him or something?"

"If you didn't like him, you would've said somethin' by now," Draco replied.

Charlie was unusually quiet.

"I do like you, by the way," Kara said to me. "It's just the principle of the thing."

"No worries."

"He should move in," Draco said stubbornly. "It'll split the rent even more, there'll be another man in the house when I'm not, and I've lived with him before."

"Mentioning that we shared a cell might not be the recommendation you're goin' for," I said dryly.

"The house he's livin' in smells like fuckin' cabbage," Draco continued, like it was the most important factor to consider. "Cabbage, Kara. The BO of vegetables."

Charlie's silence ended then. She snorted once. Then again. Then she was full out laughing, and falling back on the bed, her beer held out above her to keep it from spilling.

"It's not funny, Charlie!" Draco snapped. "He fuckin' hates it there."

"I don't hate it," I said calmly. "It's alright."

"Baby, I love you," Kara said, sitting on Draco's lap as she fought a smile. "You're the best."

"It's a fuckin' good idea and you know it," Draco replied.

"I'm not the only one with a vote," Kara said quietly.

Draco stared belligerently at the bed, where Charlie still giggled.

"Charlotte," he said sharply.

"What?" she asked.

"Is it cool that he moves in?"

"Aw, hell," she said with a sigh as she sat back up. She stared at the ceiling for a moment before meeting my eyes. "Wouldn't want you smelling like vegetable BO."

"Good," Draco said, leaning back into the couch. "It's settled."

I turned slowly to look at him. "I didn't even say I wanted to move in here."

Charlie started laughing again, and this time it was infectious. Within seconds, we were all doing the same damn thing.

When we'd finally calmed down, Kara stood.

"I'm going to work on some more boxes," she announced, she pointed at me. "Go pick which room you want."

"I'll help," Draco said, getting off the couch with a sigh. "I need to get the dressers set up."

"Bye," Charlie sang, waving her fingers at them. "I'm going to work on my room."

"Come down when you want and I'll give ya the grand tour," Draco told me, slapping me on the shoulder as he passed. "The back yard's huge. Thinkin' of getting' a smoker."

"You're such an old man," Charlie teased as he walked away. "If I catch you wearing socks and sandals I'm moving out!"

"Great. I'll buy some tomorrow," Draco yelled back from the hallway.

"So you're moving in, huh?" Charlie said, sliding off the bed. "This relationship got serious fast."

My jaw dropped and I struggled to find a response. I couldn't tell if she was serious or just fucking with me, and I sputtered for a minute before she took pity on me.

"I'm joking," she said, setting her beer on a windowsill. "It would've been fun as hell, but we obviously can't fuck around if we're going to be living together."

"We can't," I repeated, almost a question, but not quite.

"I'm all for friends with benefits or whatever," she said, smiling at me. "But living together while we're doing it is a bit too far, I think."

"Alright."

"I mean, I have a date tomorrow—"

"You have a date tomorrow?" I asked incredulously.

"Yep," she said, lifting a nightstand and carrying it over next to her bed. "And you can see why that would be weird. You know, bringing dates back here to hang out and having the other person you're screwing around with just…watching. Sounds messy."

"You're plannin' on bringin' them back here?" I asked, still trying to catch up.

"Well, maybe not tomorrow, but it'll happen eventually, right?" she asked, stopping to look at me. "Not just me—you too. I mean, it'll be your place, too, so you could potentially be bringing dates home?"

"Yeah, I guess," I replied.

"See?" She shrugged.

"So, if I move in here, I'm not gonna see you naked," I said, walking toward her.

"Bingo," Charlie replied, putting her hands on her hips. "If you haven't noticed, I'm not about that kind of drama."

"Then I won't move in," I said simply.

"Don't be stupid."

"Not bein' stupid," I replied through clenched teeth.

"Well, don't get mad," Charlie said in exasperation. "It's not like I'm being unreasonable."

"Don't like bein' called stupid." I reached up and rubbed the back of my neck. It had already been a long ass day of work and I wasn't really interested in arguing with her.

"Oh," she said quietly. She must have seen something in my expression because hers immediately softened. "I'm sorry. I wasn't calling you stupid."

"I know that," I replied, shaking my head.

"I won't say it again."

"It's no big deal."

"Still," she said, tilting her head to the side. "You don't like it so I won't say it. Easy."

"You're not really makin' a convincin' argument that I should give up seein' you bent over the bed takin' my cock when you're bein' all sweet like that," I told her seriously.

Charlie jerked in surprise and her eyes widened. "You've got a dirty mouth." She chuckled. "I'm starting to rethink my position."

I waited.

"No," she said, scrubbing her hands over her face. "You should move in. Get out of the cabbage house. We can keep our hands to ourselves."

"I'm not so sure about that," I replied.

"I have superior self-restraint," she said cheerfully.

"I do not."

"You'll have to learn, then," she said, wiggling her finger at me. "Now make yourself useful, would you? I need that dresser against the wall."

I nodded and moved the dresser, helping her with the other pieces of furniture as she pointed to where everything should go. Some of it she could've easily done herself, but I didn't mind doing it for her. If I was honest with myself, I would've painted her fucking toenails if she'd asked me. There was something about Charlie that just made me feel good. When I was around her, shit just felt lighter.

"So, you're almost done with school, huh?" I asked as she tore open a box.

"Yep. I have to finish this term and then I'm home free."

"You got plans for after?"

"Yes."

I waited but she didn't say anything else.

"Care to elaborate?"

Charlie glanced at the door to her room like she was making sure no one was there.

"I'm gonna buy the coffee cart," she said conspiratorially. "But it's not a sure thing so don't repeat that."

"The place where you and Kara work?" I asked in surprise.

"That's the one," she said happily. Her whole energy changed as she spun toward me. "So, I've done the numbers, right? And I can buy Mal out. I've already talked to her about it and since she's ready to retire she's considering it." She tiptoed toward the door and quietly closed it. "I've been saving as much as I can and I got lucky on some investments. I think if I can up the revenue at the shop by just fifteen percent, I'd have enough in a year to open another cart. I'd have to do some cool events, make some specialty drinks for holidays, that sort of shit. But I could start a whole brand, you know? Maybe even have a whole bunch of carts eventually or roast my own coffee."

"Damn," I replied, impressed.

"Sorry," she said, grinning. She threw her hands up in the air. "I've just been dying to tell someone! I even have the second location all picked out. Tommy just bought this small commercial property less than a mile from the club. It's an old corner store that he's hoping to lease and the parking lot would be *perfect*."

"You're fuckin'—" I just shook my head. I didn't even know what to say. She was just so goddamn gorgeous all lit up the way she was. Talking about her plans and sharing her secret with me.

"What?" she said, deflating a little. "Does it sound stupid?"

"Hell, no," I replied instantly. "You sound determined and fuckin' brilliant. You know those boys like their coffee, and if you're right down the road they'll stop brewin' the shit themselves and buy from you in bulk."

"That's what I was thinking, too," she replied excitedly. "Plus, think of the traffic in the summer! If I can make some exceptional smoothies and iced drinks, people will stop by on their way to the river and the park and shit!"

"Absolutely," I said firmly.

Charlie sighed happily. "I think it's really going to work. The cart I'm trying to buy now is in a really good spot and does great business already. I don't think that it'll be that hard to increase the sales just fifteen percent."

"You can do it."

"Yeah?"

"I don't think I'm gonna be able to move in though," I said regretfully.

"What?" she asked in confusion. "Why?"

"Cause seein' you all fired up when you get this whole thing started?" I shook my head solemnly. "No fuckin' way can I keep my hands to myself."

"Funny," she said flatly.

"I'm not jokin'," I replied, moving toward her. "Jesus, when you're into somethin' you fuckin' *glow*."

"When I get excited about something I have a hard time hiding it," she joked with a shrug.

"It's beautiful," I said honestly.

"You're charming, too?" she said, throwing up her hands in frustration. "You're not supposed to be charming when you look like that."

"Sorry, honey," I said with a laugh, catching her hands. I pulled them down and around to the base of her spine, holding them lightly. I wanted her to know that she could pull away if she wanted, but she didn't.

"I wanna be your friend," I said, our noses just inches apart. "And I'll be your roommate, help you save some more for the big purchase."

"Well, that's kind of you, friend."

"But I want you in my bed," I said, leaning closer.

"Not a good idea."

"Maybe not, but I have a feelin' it'll happen."

"Then we'll just make sure it doesn't."

"Can't promise that. Can you?"

She didn't answer.

I let go of her wrists and gripped her waist. She wasn't skinny in the traditional sense, she had an ass on her that made my mouth water, and she was muscular in a way that you knew she worked at it.

I slid my fingers just under her t-shirt.

"Shit," I muttered. "May as well know what we'll be missing."

Charlie must've agreed with me because before my mouth hit hers, she'd wrapped her fingers around the back of my head and pulled me toward her. The kiss from earlier had been staggering, but this one was like lightning striking. We both went nuts.

My hands roamed frantically, sliding up her sides and down her hips, tangling in her hair and wrapping around her throat. Hers were just as busy. She traced my arms from wrists to biceps, scratched her nails along the back of my neck, smoothed her palms down over my ass and over the fly of my jeans. Before long, my fingers were spread wide over her ass and I barely had to boost her up as she gave a little hop and wrapped her legs around my waist.

I didn't bother trying to get her on the bed, I couldn't even think that far in the future. Protecting the back of her head with my hand, I braced her back against the wall for leverage as her hips rolled.

Charlie tore her mouth from mine. "Holy hell," she whispered with a groan. Her legs tightened as she jerked her hips harder against mine.

"Jesus, you're pretty," I mumbled, watching as she tilted her face toward the ceiling. I put my mouth against her throat and sucked, making her gasp.

"Please tell me you have a small dick," she said, startling me.

"Say what?" I asked, pulling back.

"There has to be something wrong with you," she said, tipping her head back down to look at me. She laughed. "A tail? Anything?"

"Sorry, no tail," I replied. "And you can feel me." I pressed her harder against the wall. "That feel small to you?"

"Well, shit," she muttered, grinning.

"You're a fuckin' trip," I said, my mouth twitching.

"And you, *friend*, are quite possibly the hottest man I've ever seen." She sighed and dropped her head against my shoulder.

"You say that like it's a bad thing," I replied. As her legs loosened around my waist, I knew the moment was over.

"It's not a bad thing," she said, gently kissing my neck before shifting so I'd set her back on her feet. "It's just going to make you hard to resist."

"Then why are you fightin' it so hard?" I asked seriously as I dropped my arms to the sides and stepped back. "It's not about the roommate thing. You've been keepin' your distance for months."

She laughed a little and walked around me, reaching up to fix her hair. As I turned to watch her, she strode toward the middle of the room, first letting her long blonde hair fall in waves around her before pulling it up with both fists and wrapping it into a knot on top of her head.

"You're gonna be a problem," she said to me easily, shrugging her shoulders. "And I knew it from the first time I saw you eye fucking me across the parking lot at the apartments."

"Eye fucking you?" I asked, remembering that first day when I'd come to find Draco and found her, too.

"I was carrying a bag of garbage, for fuck's sake," she said with a huff, still smiling. "And you were still looking at me like you were starving."

"I'm not seein' the problem."

"I've got plans," she said almost apologetically. "Big ones."

"I'm not gonna stop you," I replied, seriously. "Shit, Charlie. I want you to succeed. I wanna *watch* you succeed."

"I believe that," she said, nodding. "But if I get all caught up in you, I'm going to lose focus."

"Bullshit."

"Have you ever heard the saying, right person, wrong time?"

I just looked at her.

"You're fantastic," she said quietly.

I wanted to walk out right then and there. I was all for knowing that we were trying to keep our hands to ourselves so things didn't get awkward in the house, but this was different. This felt like she was trying to let me down easy or some shit and I didn't want to hear it. It was a fucking break-up and we weren't even together.

"Message received," I said. I moved over to the tools I'd set by the door.

"Are you mad at me?" she asked in confusion.

"Hell no," I replied. "Just disappointed."

"Yeah, me too," she said with a sigh.

"I'm gonna head out. I gotta work tomorrow and I'm beat." I lifted the tools and my boots and gave a little wave with my full hands.

I was a few steps down the hallway when she called my name. When I turned to look at her, she was standing in the doorway of her room, her arms crossed over her chest.

"You understand what I'm saying, right?" she called softly. "We'd be fantastic together. It's just the wrong time."

I nodded and kept moving. She was right, we'd be fucking great together—but it didn't really matter if she wasn't willing to give it a chance.

Chapter 3
CHARLIE

We'd been in our new place for two weeks and I'd slept like shit every single night. I couldn't get the thermostat set to a comfortable degree, I didn't have time to get blinds on the windows yet so the sun woke me up early as hell on the days I wasn't working, and there were too many sounds all the time. Creaking and groaning happened all through the night as the stupid house settled. If I accidentally left the bathroom door open, it would swing open with the hinges squealing, startling the hell out of me right as I was about to fall asleep. Plus, I felt so fucking alone upstairs. After living in such close quarters with Kara, having her so far away was weird.

Don't get me wrong, I loved the extra space and privacy—most of the time. It was just late at night when I'd finally finished my schoolwork and was climbing into bed when shit started to feel dodgy. Even going out to my car in the dark on my random early days at work creeped me out.

Thankfully, everything else in my life seemed to be going forward as planned. I was barreling toward graduation, getting shit done early so the last few weeks would be a breeze, and Mal had finally agreed to sell me the coffee shop. If I thought she'd give me some kind of a deal, I'd been sadly mistaken. She wasn't stupid and it was making good money—but we'd finally come to an agreement and I was completely stoked. By the time I graduated, all the paperwork would be done and I'd be able to jump into my venture with both feet.

Well, I could jump in with both feet once I got today's conversation over with. What I really wanted to be doing was sleep all day, but instead, I was driving over to my parents' property. They'd been living in a trailer since their house burned down in the wildfires we'd had last fall, but from what I could see when I turned into their long driveway—they wouldn't have to be there much longer.

"Look at my house!" my mom yelled, walking toward my car as I parked behind a white truck with some kind of logo on it. "It's gorgeous!"

"It is," I agreed as I climbed out.

Where once there had been a beautiful old two-story house there was now a brand spanking new ranch with workers doing their thing all around it. Smaller, but just as gorgeous in its own way. I had no doubt that they would've lived in the old place until they died, but fate had other plans and they'd decided if they were building something new they were going to have a new place that fit them as they got older. There were no stairs for them to climb, only two bedrooms since all their kids were out of the house, and eventually, my mom would have the wraparound porch she wanted.

"Come see," Mom said excitedly. "There's still a lot to do—"

"Really?" I asked sarcastically.

"Yeah," she said with a laugh. "It's all framed in, though, so we can see where all the rooms are."

"Are you sure it's cool that we go in there?" I asked as a man strode by carrying a window. "We won't be in the way?"

"We're old friends by now," she replied, waving me off. "I come in every day to see how far they've gotten."

"I'm sure they love that," I muttered.

"Please," she said, scoffing. "Everyone digs me."

"Harry," my mom called, waving at a guy in a hardhat a few feet away. "We're gonna take a look around!"

"Put a hard hat on," he ordered, pointing at the floor near our feet. "You know the rules."

"I look like a goober with it on."

"You look gorgeous as ever and you know it," he replied, still pointing. "Hardhats. Both of you."

"Oh, all right," Mom said with a sigh.

She handed me a hardhat and gave me a wink.

"Dad know you're in here flirting with the builders every day?" I asked dryly.

"Ha!" She laughed. "Harry knows dad. No one in here would dare flirt with me."

"He just called you gorgeous," I pointed out.

"That's just the truth," my mom said simply. She reached out and grabbed my hand excitedly. "Come on."

She tugged me through the "rooms" one by one, pointing out where she was going to put her new furniture and where she wanted to hang pictures. Using her hands, she shaped where the counters would be and where she'd decided to put her appliances in the kitchen. The excitement was infectious, and by the time we'd reached the master bathroom, I was chattering as much as she was, discussing the claw foot tub she wanted and what kind of mirror she should hang.

"Thought I'd find you two in here," my dad said, stepping over a pile of lumber. Even he didn't escape the hardhat rule and I looked at him dumbly for a moment. He looked completely home in the thing while me and my mom looked like a couple of dorks.

"Just showing our baby around the new place," my mom replied happily.

"It'll look better once there's walls and shit," my dad pointed out.

"It looks glorious now," my mom corrected. "I cannot wait to get out of that trailer."

"Gonna have to wait a bit longer," a voice I recognized joked from somewhere behind me.

I spun to face Bishop, the hardhat I was wearing sliding over my eyes and disorienting me for a minute.

"Harry's wonderin' if he can have a word," he said to my parents, leaning through a gap in the framing.

"Sure!" My mom patted my back. "Stay right here. I want to tell you about the tile we're putting in. The floor is going to be heated!"

"Fancy," I mumbled, nodding as she walked away.

I hadn't seen Bishop since he'd left my bedroom the night we'd moved in, and time seemed to have made things awkward between us. We stared at each other for a moment.

"Your boss made me wear a hard hat," I blurted eventually. It was the only thing that came to mind and I wanted to slap myself for calling attention to the stupid thing.

"You look cute as a button," Bishop replied, grinning.

He didn't. With a hard hat on, he looked exactly as I'd described before—like a stripper. Half of me was waiting for the music to start and his hips to begin undulating.

My gaze traveled the length of him and I swallowed.

"You're wearing a tool belt," I croaked.

Bishop looked down. "You've seen my tool belt before," he reminded me.

"You weren't wearing it," I argued, my eyes glued to his hips. The belt hung heavy, pulling his jeans down slightly and framing the fly like a damn neon sign. God, my mouth was watering.

"You keep lookin' at me like that and I'm gonna be walkin' around with somethin' I can't exactly hide," he warned, making my eyes snap up to meet his. "Normally I wouldn't mind, but I don't wanna hear shit about it for the next five years."

"Sorry," I stuttered. "I just—" My gaze wandered again.

"Woman," Bishop snapped. "My eyes are up here."

"Sorry," I said again, laughing a little.

"You really want your dad walkin' back in here when my dick's standin' at attention?" he asked in exasperation. "Stop it."

"I won't do it again," I promised, raising my right hand like I was taking an oath. It took everything in me not to glance down again.

"Jesus," he muttered, reaching down to adjust himself. "Charlie!"

"I'm sorry," I said, throwing up my hands. "You were calling attention to it!"

"Just keep your eyes up here," he grumbled, annoyed.

"Hey, I thought you were moving in," I said accusingly, eager to change the subject to anything other than how mouthwatering he looked in his work gear. "You haven't even been to the house again."

"I've been there," he replied gruffly. "You weren't there."

"Oh," I said, his words taking the wind out of my sails. "Are you avoiding me?"

"Not at all," he replied firmly. "I think you were workin' last time I was there."

"Are you still moving in?" I asked, nervous about his answer.

While I figured it would probably be torture having him right down the hall all the time, I also really wanted him there. I didn't like having the upstairs to myself. Plus, I just genuinely liked him and even if we weren't bumping uglies, I'd still like to see him more often.

"Plannin' on it, yeah," he said, looking over his shoulder as my parents came back toward us. "Probably this weekend," he told me before lifting his chin in goodbye and walking away.

"Everything okay?" I asked my parents.

"Yeah, just delays on some stuff," my mom said with a frustrated sigh. "No big deal."

"All part of the process, Ladybug," Dad said consolingly, patting her ass. "Things have been smooth sailin' for too long, had to hit a snag at some point."

Mom smiled and nodded, then kicked a beam. "Okay, I feel better now."

Dad chuckled.

"So, you said something about heated flooring?" I asked, raising my eyebrows.

We spent almost an hour in the house, talking about every little detail, and by the time we walked back into the yard, I was practically bursting with the urge to bring up why I'd come.

"Come have some coffee," my dad said, throwing his arm around my shoulders as he led me to the trailer. "It's not as fancy as that shit you make, but it'll do."

"Put some hair on my chest?" I asked jokingly.

"Shit, I hope not," my dad replied in fake alarm, pulling out the neck of his t-shirt as if to check his own chest.

"Funny you should bring up coffee," I said, drawing out the words as we went inside. "That's kind of what I wanted to talk to you about."

"Are you leaving the coffee cart?" my mom asked in surprise. "Did you already get a new job? Don't quit unless—"

I cut her off by shaking my head. "Nope," I said, sitting down at their little table. "Actually kind of the opposite."

"Clue us in, baby girl," my dad said as he poured us all some coffee. "Ya got us on the edge of our seats."

Mom slid in across from me and waited.

"Okay, so I like making coffee. I like the whole thing. And I know that you guys helped me with college and I'm so thankful. Like, I can't ever repay everything you've done for me—"

"Slow down," my dad said calmly. "You're ramblin'."

"I've been thinking about it a lot, and I've run the numbers." I grinned. "That college education was good for something."

Mom laughed, but dad just watched me, waiting for me to get to the point.

"I'd like to buy the coffee cart from Mal," I said quickly. "And then, I'd like to grow the business and if I can do that, not even a lot, just like fifteen percent, I think I could open another cart."

"Really?" my mom said in surprise, sitting back in her seat.

"Really," I confirmed.

I waited for my dad to say something. I wasn't really worried that he'd think it was a bad idea, I was just trying to figure out if I had to gear up to convince him that it was a good one.

He set the coffee cups down in front of us, poured one for himself, and sat down next to my mom.

"Alright," he said easily. "Tell me your plan."

I broke down everything, how much I was paying for the original cart, how much money it was currently bringing in and how much more I'd have to make in order to open a second location. I explained my ideas for promotion and marketing, how I'd bring more customers in, and why I thought we weren't currently reaching as many people as we could be. By the time I was finished, my parents were nodding along, their excitement for me evident in every gesture and question they asked.

"Okay then," my dad said with a chuckle. "You've been workin' on this a while."

"Yeah," I replied. "I mean it started as just a vague idea, because I really like working there, you know? But I can't be just a barista forever."

"Why not?" my mom asked, wrinkling her nose.

"Okay, I could," I amended. "But I don't want to. I want to build something and I want to be in charge."

"That's fair," she replied.

"So, what do you need from us?" my dad asked. "Money?"

"No," I replied immediately, shaking my head. "I'm not here for funding."

"Okay, Ms. Moneybags," my mom said, smiling. "I don't even want to know where you got that much money—"

"I saved and invested in that shit Tommy was talking about all last year. I got in right before it went crazy and got out before it started dropping. I made a shit ton."

"Knew I shoulda listened to his crazy ass," my dad mumbled, shooting my mom a disgruntled look.

"Yeah, yeah," she said to my dad before looking at me. "So you don't need anything from us?" she asked, sounding almost disappointed.

"I'm sure I will at some point," I joked. "But right at this moment, no." I shrugged. "I guess I just wanted your opinion."

"Our opinion?" my dad asked in mock confusion. He looked at mom. "Our youngest is asking for our opinion."

"Will wonders never cease?" my mom replied, raising her hands and staring at the ceiling.

"You two are hilarious," I replied, deadpan.

"I say, do it," my dad said, reaching across the table to give my hand a squeeze.

"Yeah?"

"Hell yeah," my mom said. "If your numbers are right—and I don't doubt they are, it's a fantastic idea."

"Yeah?" I asked again, happily.

"You knew that before you ever came in here," my dad said proudly.

"I just—" I shook my head. "I mean, I just wanted to make sure that you thought it was feasible. You're the money guy."

Dad laughed.

"Well, you are. You know more about this shit than anyone else I know."

"I think it's a good plan, Charlie," he said, nodding. "You bring me over any paperwork before you sign it though. I'll take a look."

"Absolutely," I replied.

"Well, this was a relief," my mom said cheerfully. "When you said you wanted to talk to us I figured you were pregnant or something."

"Mother!"

"Sorry," she said, laughing. "When one of my children ask to talk to me and dad together, it always sounds ominous."

"I'm not pregnant," I replied, rolling my eyes. "And I won't be at any point in the near future."

My dad reached out to knock on a piece of wood, but all they had inside was fake paneling. "Eh, it'll do," he said, knocking anyway.

I laughed.

"I gotta get over to the garage," my dad said, getting to his feet.

"I'm gonna go, too," I announced. "I need to do a bunch of laundry and take a nap."

"A nap?" my mom asked, frowning.

"I know," I groaned. "Today is full of surprises."

"You haven't napped since you were two years old. Are you getting sick?"

"No," I replied, standing. I reached my arms over my head and stretched. "I'm having a hard time sleeping at the new place still."

"Do you want to take a nap here?" she asked. "I need to grocery shop and stop by Callie's, so you'll have the place to yourself."

"That's okay," I said with a smile. "Laundry, remember? Plus, I doubt I'd be able to sleep with that racket."

We were quiet for a minute, listening to the sound of power tools and hammering going on outside.

"I'll walk you out," my dad said, gesturing for me to go out ahead of him. He leaned down and kissed my mom goodbye, murmuring something quietly in her ear before he followed me.

"Bye ma," I called, waving over my shoulder.

"You're about due for an oil change," my dad reminded me as we walked toward my car.

"I know," I said with a sigh. "I'll come in as soon as I have some time."

"Don't wait too long."

"I won't."

"I'll have Cam do it," he said. "Since he was conveniently out of town when we moved you guys into the new place. He owes me one."

"So lazy," I joked. "The worst."

We paused by the driver's door.

"This coffee cart thing is a good plan," he said, nodding. "I'm proud of you."

"Be proud after I actually execute the plan," I replied with a laugh. "I'm scared shitless."

"Nothin' is worth havin' unless it scares you a bit," he said, grinning.

I SPENT MOST of the day doing laundry in the quiet house. It was kind of a pain in the ass lugging piles of clothes up and down the stairs, but I didn't really mind it. I'd been so busy lately that I hadn't had a chance to work out and I was starting to feel the effects. A few runs up and down the staircase at least made me feel like I was moving my body. As soon as the last piece of clothing was folded and put in my dresser, I stripped, leaving a trail of clothing on the floor to my bed. Even with the afternoon light shining into my windows, as soon as I'd crawled into the blankets, I passed right out.

When I woke up it was dark outside and I had no idea what time it was. Hell, for a minute I wasn't even sure what day it was. I stumbled out of bed and threw on a t-shirt and some old running shorts and made my way downstairs.

I was still so groggy from the nap that I didn't think to check who was home as I zombie walked to the kitchen for a glass of water.

"Good evening, sunshine," Draco greeted from the kitchen table. "Nice of you to join us."

"Water," I croaked, waving lazily at him, Bishop and Kara.

"We got Chinese food for dinner," Kara said as I shuffled toward the sink. "If you want some."

It wasn't until after I'd grabbed a glass, filled it at the sink, and drank the entire thing that it finally clicked that I'd just come downstairs in my rattiest pajamas, with my hair doing God knows what, drool probably dried onto my face, and Bishop was sitting at our kitchen table.

"I could eat," I said, deciding in a split second to just brazen it out. I mean, he'd already seen me. The damage was done.

"Have a good nap?" he asked as I sat down.

"It was glorious," I replied, reaching for the plate Kara had set out for me. "As soon as I'm done eating, I'm going right back." I looked at him. "What are you doing here?"

Bishop laughed. "You're so nice when you're tired."

"I just mean—" I waved the serving spoon in my hand around. "Are you moving in tonight or just hanging out?"

"I brought a load of stuff," he replied. "But I don't have a bed yet, so I'll probably head back tonight and start stayin' here tomorrow or Sunday."

"You're goin' back to the cabbage house?" I asked, wrinkling my nose.

"It's got a bed."

"You should just stay here," I said confidently, filling my plate. "You can sleep on a couch."

"We don't have a couch yet, Charles," Kara reminded me. "It's not being delivered until Monday."

"Oh, right," I said with a sigh. I stuffed a piece of sweet and sour chicken in my mouth. "You can sleep on the couch in my room if you want."

The table was silent.

"What?" I asked, glancing around.

"You sure?" Bishop asked. "I don't want to put you out."

"Eh," I said, taking another bite. "I don't mind. I'm seriously going to crash as soon as I get back up there. You're free to use it."

"Thanks," he said, watching me closely.

"If there's anything in your way, just throw it on the floor," I said easily. "You can sleep there but I'm not cleaning up for you."

"Fair enough," he said with a laugh.

"I am truly impressed by you sometimes," Kara said dryly, sitting back in her chair while she stared at me. "You just held an entire conversation with food in your mouth—"

"I'm hungry and tired, give me a break."

"And you were both welcoming and kind of an ass at the same time—"

"I'm welcoming as hell."

"And somehow, you look like shit but you don't really because you're so gorgeous that even your shit looks better than half the population."

"Good genes," I replied, my mouth full of food. I was pretty much shoveling it in at that point. I hadn't realized how hungry I was. I hadn't had anything but coffee all day because I'd been so focused on getting shit done so I could sleep for a while.

The conversation went on, but I didn't contribute. I was still so exhausted that I focused on eating so I could go back to bed. The early morning shift at the coffee cart loomed large just hours away. Plus, I was hoping that if I didn't completely wake myself up and could keep the hazy feeling, I would actually be able to sleep through the night in my new room.

"You're the best," I said to Draco as soon as I'd finished. "Good idea on the Chinese food."

"Hey, maybe it was my idea," Kara joked.

"It wasn't," I replied as I brought my plate to the sink. "Draco always chooses Chinese. You always choose diner food or tacos. I'm going back to bed. Love you."

"Love you, too," Kara and Draco said at the same time.

I patted Bishop on the back as I passed him. "I'll throw a pillow and a blanket on the couch for you. Just come in whenever."

"Thanks, honey," he said quietly.

Within minutes I was back in my little bedding cocoon and completely dead to the world. Unfortunately, it didn't last.

"Motherfucker," I whispered, checking the time on my phone.

It was one in the morning and I was wide awake, the wind blowing outside was making the house creak and groan yet again. Turning over in bed I stared into the darkness, finding Bishop's sleeping shape on my couch.

Maybe if I could hear him or something, the noise of the house wouldn't bother me so bad—but the man breathed so quiet I was tempted to go check if he was alive. Normal people snored, okay? Like, maybe they didn't snore loudly, or maybe they only made intermittent noises, but I'd slept around tons of people and all of them made noises in their sleep. Not Bishop, though. What a freak.

"You alright?" he asked, making me nearly crap myself.

"Holy shit," I gasped. "You're awake?"

"You've been thrashin' for the past half an hour and woke up swearin'," he said with a smile in his voice. "Yeah, I'm awake."

"Well, you could've said something," I replied, pressing my hand to my heart. It was beating so fast it felt like it was going to escape my chest.

"I did," he said with a quiet chuckle.

"Sorry, I woke you," I said, curling onto my side.

"It's alright," he replied. "If you hadn't, I would've woken up anyway. I don't sleep real well."

"Because of prison?" I asked without thinking. "Shit, sorry. None of my business."

Bishop laughed and rolled onto his side so he was facing me. "I've never been a good sleeper," he said, his voice low. "I can't remember, even when I was a kid, falling asleep and staying asleep for the whole night."

"That would drive me nuts," I replied. "I've always been the person who can sleep anywhere. Well, except *here* apparently."

"Why is *here* a problem, you think?"

"I don't know," I said with a sigh. "Maybe just because it's a new place? I'm not used to all the noises."

"This house settles a lot," he agreed. "Everything squeaks."

"I'm also not used to sleeping alone," I confessed.

He coughed.

"Okay, yes, I sleep alone most of the time," I continued. "But I'm used to there being someone just down the hall. Having Kara and Draco downstairs and me the only one up here is weird."

"Problem solved," he said simply. "I'm here now."

Chapter 4

BISHOP

"Go to sleep," I murmured. "I'm not goin' anywhere."

Charlie sighed and shifted, pulling the bedding up over her shoulder. After a few moments she shifted again, rolling to her back. Then again, back onto her side facing me.

"I think that nap may have fucked me," she said ruefully. "I'm wide awake now."

"Maybe if you close your eyes," I replied dryly.

"How do you know they're not already closed?"

"Because I can feel you looking at me," I answered.

"Oh yeah?" she asked, her words quiet. "What does it feel like?"

For a moment, my mind went blank. At first I thought she was flirting with me, but then I realized she was really asking.

"It feels like someone's watchin' me," I replied jokingly.

Charlie scoffed.

"It feels like electricity," I said seriously, my voice as quiet as hers. "Like you just reached out and shocked me."

She was silent.

"But it also feels warm and kind of relaxing," I continued. "Like a heavy blanket or that night you slept with me and I could feel your breath on my neck all night."

"Oh," she whispered.

We were quiet for a while and I waited to hear the sound of the little huff of breath she let out every few seconds after she'd fallen asleep, but it never came.

"You're still awake," I said finally.

"Why do you call me honey?" she asked.

"What?"

"You call me honey."

"Okay," I said, confused. "You want me to stop?"

"No," she replied. "I like it, actually." She let out a quiet laugh. "It's just not something you hear people our age say very often."

"Really?" I hadn't really thought about it.

"Baby," she said. "Babe. Nicknames. Whatever. You just don't hear honey very often."

"Ah," I said, finally seeing where she was going with her question. "I think I've called you baby."

"You use honey more often," she replied stubbornly.

"I had an uncle," I began, scratching the side of my head as I got more comfortable on the couch. It was too small for me and if I straightened my legs they'd fall off the edge, but it smelled better than where I'd been sleeping for the past couple years, so I wasn't about to complain. "I lived with him for a while. Draco tell you I grew up in foster care?"

"Yeah, he told me," she replied.

"Well, I was in and out. My mom died when I was six—"

"I'm sorry," she said.

"It's alright. I mean, it shifted my entire world on its axis, obviously. But I'm good now."

"I can't imagine losing my mom," she said roughly. "I love both my parents, but my mom is it, you know? She's my person."

"Yeah, honey," I replied. "I get it."

"Sorry, keep going. You had an uncle?"

"Yeah, he was my mom's uncle, actually. So, when my mom died I went into the system. Spent a couple years bein' shuffled around—

nothin' surprisin' there. But I was one of the rare cases that had family come lookin' for me. Can't tell you how surprised I was when my caseworker showed up—his name was Mr. Dangle, by the way, no fuckin' joke."

Charlie laughed.

"Anyway, he showed up one day and said, 'Let's go, your uncle's pickin' you up.' Drove me across town to his office with my bag of stuff and there's this old man standin' in the lobby. I mean, I swear to God, he looked older than dirt, but he'd really churched it up for the occasion, hair slicked down, flannel shirt tucked into his jeans, the whole deal."

"Aw," Charlie said. "I like this story."

It was my turn to laugh.

"Uncle Beau," I said, still smiling. "He was a tough old dude. He looked me up and down, said, 'You're a hard man to find,' grabbed my bag and my hand—I was almost ten and way too big for hand-holdin' by then—and walked us straight out of the office to his beat-up old Bronco. Drove straight to McDonalds for lunch."

"So he was your favorite person, obviously."

"He was," I replied with a laugh. "Beauregard Augustus Bishop. I was named after him. I guess he'd been looking for me for a while. He hadn't found out about my mom's death for more than a year after she was gone, but he started searching as soon as he knew. Gettin' a kid out of foster care isn't easy—even if you're family—and he'd had to jump through a lot of hoops. Took a while."

"But he found you," she said happily.

"He did. Took me in and I lived with him in this little trailer park until I was fifteen. There was a lady next door that was always outside in her garden, I called her Dottie, but her name was Dorothy. She and my uncle had been together for more years than I'd been alive, but they never lived together. I never asked why."

"She was a strong independent woman," Charlie said. Even in the dark I could tell she was smiling.

"She was," I confirmed, thinking back to the little old lady who'd patched up my scrapes and cooked me dinner and waved from her front porch every day when I stepped off the bus.

"Uncle Beau called her honey," I said finally.

Charlie was quiet.

"So, that's probably where it comes from."

"Bishop," Charlie said, leaning up on her elbow. "Why did you only live with him until you were fifteen?"

I'd known when I started the story that the question would come but I hadn't anticipated the way it would make my chest ache with memories. I thought about Uncle Beau a lot. Daily. He'd taught me everything he thought I'd need to know as a man. How to shave, change a tire, fix a leaky sink, dance with a woman, tie a tie, sew on a button, shoot a rifle, use any handheld tool ever made, drive, stand up for myself, the list was endless. But even though he popped into my head constantly throughout the day, I always cut the memories off before they got painful.

"When I was fifteen he had a stroke," I said, clearing my throat. "Went into the hospital and never came back out."

"Oh my god," Charlie whispered. "I'm so sorry."

"Dottie took me in for a while, but she had her own health problems and since I was already in the system, they said I couldn't live with her. Back to foster care I went."

"That's bullshit," Charlie said, sniffling.

"They were just tryin' to do the right thing."

"Well, it wasn't," Charlie snapped.

"No argument from me," I replied. "I loved that old lady and it killed me knowin' that she needed me and I couldn't help her."

"I want to punch something."

"Don't," I said with a chuckle. "Believe me, I punched enough shit back then for the both of us. It turned out all right. The house I went to was close enough that I could hop on a bus and check on her a couple times a week."

"Is she still there?" Charlie asked softly.

"Nah," I replied and cleared my throat again. My eyes started to burn at all the shit I'd willingly dredged up. I was a fucking idiot. "She passed away in her sleep when I was nineteen."

Charlie didn't say anything as she threw back the blankets and got out of bed. Without a word, she came to me. I scooted back a little as she sat on the edge of the couch, her hip pressed against my stomach.

"I'm sorry," She whispered, draping the top half of her body over mine, her arms wrapped around me. "I shouldn't have brought it up."

"Hey now," I said, running my fingers through her hair. "Nothin' to be sorry for. I coulda told you that you tasted like honey or some shit."

I laughed as she pinched me.

"I would've known you were bullshitting me," she said with a huff.

"I'm pretty convincin,' you woulda ate that shit up," I teased.

Charlie let go of me and leaned back, but she didn't stand up.

"You're named after your uncle?" She asked, smiling.

"Yes," I replied, propping my head on my bent arm so I could see her better.

"Your first name is Beauregard?"

"Where you goin' with this?" I grumbled.

"Beauregard Augustus Bishop?" Her voice was wobbling with suppressed mirth.

"You got a problem with my name?"

"Your name is Beauregard Augustus Bishop," she repeated.

"You sayin' it fifty times ain't gonna change the fact."

"And you go by Bishop?" She hit my shoulder lightly. "Why the fuck would you go by Bishop when you have that epic fucking name?"

"Well, I wasn't gonna go by Beau," I said with a laugh. "One Beau was enough for our tiny trailer. Went by Gus growin' up."

"You don't look like a Gus," she said immediately. "Did your mom call you Gus?"

"You know, I can't really remember," I said, thinking back. "My memories of her are bits and pieces, ya know? I remember her calling me son and baby and buddy, that type of shit."

"Huh," she said.

"She called me her sunshine boy," I said, remembering the woman with soft hands and the perfect shape for curling into when I was tired.

"That's really sweet," Charlie said softly.

"She was a good mom," I replied. "I remember that much."

"She must have been to give you that incredible name."

"Hell, she copied it," I replied with a laugh. "So, you know, good mom—but no imagination."

"She must've really loved your uncle."

"From what he said, they were tight when she was growin' up. He and my grandpa were best friends and since my uncle was a bachelor, he was always at my grandparents' place hangin' out."

"I can understand close knit families," Charlie said dryly. "You can't pick your nose in my family without every single person making fun of you for it by dinnertime."

I laughed. "You pick your nose a lot?"

"Wouldn't you like to know," she said, pretending to stick her finger in her nose.

"You're gonna be tired as fuck in the mornin'," I said, rubbing her back.

"I should probably try to sleep," she said with a sigh. She stood and stretched then looked down at me. "You comfortable all curled in a ball like that?"

"I'm good," I assured her. "Slept in worse places."

"Come on," she replied, jerking her head toward the bed. "You can sleep with me."

"Charlie," I said, drawing her name out in warning. If she was expecting me to keep my hands to myself, inviting me to share a bed with her wasn't a good idea. Could I keep to my side of the bed? Yes. Would it be torture? Also, yes. Not my idea of a good time.

"Beauregard Augustus Bishop," she said, climbing back into her bed. "We're adults. We can sleep in the same bed and keep our clothes on."

"You're blurrin' the lines here."

"It's too late to go round and round with you," Charlie said easily, snuggling into her pillow. "Come to bed."

I laid on the couch for a few more minutes. Finally, when she flounced onto her back dramatically I stood up and rounded the bed.

"It alright if I take off my jeans?" I asked, my hands on my belt. "Who knows what shit's on them from bein' out today."

"You wearing boxers or boxer briefs?" she asked.

"A thong, actually," I replied deadpan.

In a split second a pillow came sailing at my face.

"I just wanted to make sure no one would come popping out to say hello," she said with a laugh. "Boxer briefs keep wardrobe malfunctions to a minimum."

"Then it's your lucky day," I replied, dropping my pants.

Charlie hummed. "It *is* my lucky day," she said hoarsely.

"I feel like a piece of meat," I replied jokingly, getting in beside her. "So, I'm keepin' my shirt on."

"If you must," she teased.

I laid down on my back and stared at the sloped ceiling. I was far more comfortable in Charlie's bed, but I probably would've had better luck actually sleeping if I'd stayed on the couch.

"Good night, Beauregard Augustus Bishop," Charlie said softly, reaching out to touch my shoulder before retreating back to her side of the bed.

"Goodnight, honey," I replied.

At some point the impossible must've happened and I'd dozed off because when I woke up a few hours later, Charlie had moved to my side of the bed and was wrapped around me like a piece of ivy. Her face was in my armpit, her arm wrapped around my chest, and one of her legs was thrown over mine, her knee perilously close to my balls.

"Hey," I said, reaching down to put my hand on her knee in case she woke up with a jerk. "Honey, your alarm's goin' off."

"What?" Charlie asked, her head popping up as she looked around blankly.

"Your alarm's goin' off," I repeated. "You gotta get up?"

"Fuck," she muttered, dropping her head back down.

I was pretty fastidious about personal hygiene—another thing Uncle Beau had instilled in me—but I was still fighting the urge to push her head away from my damn armpit.

"You got work?" I asked.

"Yes," she replied, her breath tickling me so bad I jerked in response.

"You think you should maybe get up?" I asked in amusement.

"Need a second," she mumbled.

I waited.

A minute or two later, Charlie lifted her head and went about untangling her body from mine.

"Just wanna point out that I stayed on my side of the bed," I said, as Charlie got out of bed and switched on the lamp next to it.

"Reb called me an octopus the other day," she responded oddly as she moved around the room grabbing clothes. "Sorry about the light, but I need it to get ready."

"It's your room," I replied. "Do what you need to do."

I wondered if I should get up and get moving. If it was any other situation where I woke up in a woman's bed and she had to leave for work, I would've already been out the door. Unless, of course, she wanted to share a shower first. I wouldn't turn that shit down.

I grit my teeth and readjusted the pillow beneath my head, trying and failing not to imagine Charlie in the shower I'd just heard come on. Glancing down, I glared at the erection making its presence known under the quilt. Before I could get my body to relax, Charlie was walking back into the room fully clothed, her wet hair slicked back in a fancy braid.

"Sorry," she said with a grimace as she turned on the overhead light, making me flinch.

"You get ready quick," I said as she sat down on the floor in front of a full-length mirror.

"Only in the mornings," she replied with a rueful smile. She reached for the zipper of the toiletry bag on the floor in front of her. "If I'm going all out, it takes forever. But this early? Pfft. I go the easy route."

I rolled toward her and braced my head on my hand so I could watch her.

"I've tried going into work with no makeup on," she said as she went about her routine. "Because I always forget to turn the stupid fan on and the mirror gets all fogged in the bathroom. But I can't do it. I feel naked without makeup. Like I forgot to put my pants on or something. I blame my mother."

"I like your mom," I said, fascinated by the efficiency and grace of her movements as she dropped a little tube of something and picked up a tiny brush.

"I like her, too," she said, glancing at me for a second. "But she's always done up, and I guess it was just programmed into my psyche. I can't go out barefaced. It feels too weird."

"You're beautiful either way," I replied honestly.

"Too charming early in the morning," she said, waving a brush at me. "Tone it down a notch."

"I can install a switch in the bathroom that turns your fan on automatically when you turn on the light," I said as she went back to what she was doing.

"I kind of like getting ready on the floor," she said, wrinkling her nose and smiling at me. "It reminds me of when Kara and I lived in the apartment."

"I get that," I replied quietly. "Once you're all settled in, let me know if you want that switch. Not good to steam up the bathroom like that, it could cause mold issues."

"Yes, dad," Charlie replied, leaning close to the mirror to run a brush along her eyelid.

"Never been called daddy," I said, watching her. "But if you're game, I'm up for anything."

It took her a second to catch on, and I knew the instant she did. Her eyes widened and quick as a flash she'd thrown a little squishy thing shaped like a teardrop at my face.

"That is not happening," she shot back, laughing and glaring at the same time. "I have a dad and thinking of him or dear God, *calling his name* during sex is pretty much the absolute last thing I'd ever want to happen." She made a fake vomiting sound.

"Noted," I said, throwing the squishy thing back onto her lap.

"I need to get my eyelashes done again," she muttered.

"The hell do you do to your eyelashes?" I asked, leaning closer. They didn't look out of the ordinary.

"They're fake," she said, batting them at me. "Well, not all of them. Just some."

"You have fake eyelashes?" I'd seen fake eyelashes. They were long and fluttery and well, they didn't look like Charlie's.

"Yep. Semi-permanent," she said, amused. "They glue them on and then they fall off eventually, just like regular eyelashes, but these ones obviously don't grow back so I have to have them re-done."

"What's wrong with your normal eyelashes?" I asked curiously.

"Nothing," she said with a shrug as she got to her feet. "But I like it when they're fuller."

She studied my blank expression.

"I bet you use the same soap for your body and your hair, don't you," she accused.

"It's made for that," I replied.

"No," she shook her head laughing. "It's not."

"It says it right on the bottle."

"While I hesitate to change your habits because whatever you're using smells fucking fantastic and I'd hate to change what you've got going on—" She gestured to me, waving her hand in a circle. "You should really be using actual shampoo. You know, for hair."

"Why the hell would I buy something else?" I asked, crossing my arms behind my head. "One bottle of shit and I'm good to go."

"When you take a shower, use my shampoo," she said merrily. "It'll change your life."

"I'm not goin' around smellin' like you," I replied.

"Ouch!"

"I'm workin' on your parents' house," I said with a chuckle. "And your pop notices every-fuckin'-thing. If he smells you on me, I'm actually gonna have done somethin' worth having my ass handed to me."

Charlie burst out laughing. "That's fair."

"You better get to work, honey."

"Yeesh," she said, jerking into movement. "You're right. I'll see you after?"

"I'll be around at some point," I confirmed. "Might come in and grab a coffee from you."

"I'd love that," she said, slipping on her shoes. She opened her bedroom door before pausing to look at me over her shoulder. "Sleep as late as you want, but as soon as the sun comes up you may want to face in the other direction because the sun will shine directly into your face."

"Thanks for the tip," I said, grinning. "Have a good day, dear."

Charlie dramatically blew me a kiss and closed the door behind her. I jumped in surprise when she opened it again.

"Sorry," she said hurriedly as she raced over to turn out the lamp. She smiled at me. "Now you don't have to get up to turn them off!" She hit the overhead light switch as she swept out the door again.

I laughed and threw my arm over my eyes. She was so goddamn cute and I was so fucking fucked. Relaxing into the bed, I decided to get a few more hours of shut eye before I went to get some blinds for Charlie's bedroom windows.

Chapter 5
Charlie

Saturday mornings at the coffee cart were never as busy as weekdays so I found myself cleaning and reorganizing and daydreaming of the changes I'd make in order to pass the time. Of course, leaving a warm, rumpled, sleepy, Beauregard Augustus Bishop in my bed that morning could have had something to do with the way time seemed to drag. The more I got to know him, the more I liked him. I couldn't say it was a problem, because how could meeting someone you clicked with ever be a problem? But the timing was so bad it made me want to scream. I didn't have the mental capacity or enough hours in the day to spend with him the way I wanted, and that sucked.

I wasn't about to start something up just when I needed to focus on other shit.

Of course, none of that mattered when he pulled up to the shop an hour before my shift ended.

"Let me guess," I said, leaning toward him. "Something super sweet that doesn't actually taste like coffee?"

Bishop shot me a look. "Americano," he said. "With room for cream?"

"Dang," I joked. "I'm usually really good at guessing."

"You've been servin' me coffee for months," he called as I went about making his coffee. "You know what I like."

"I do know what you like," I affirmed, the words instantly sounding like an innuendo even though that hadn't been my intention.

It was quiet for a moment.

"So, I got a call this mornin'," he said.

"Oh yeah?" I carried his coffee back to the window, exactly how he liked it.

"Yeah," he said, watching me closely as he took the cup. "Brenna said she was gettin' rid of the bed in her guestroom and asked if I wanted it."

"Imagine that," I said with a smile, resting my elbows on the counter between us.

"I have you to thank for what sounds like a free and nearly new bed?"

"She's been talking about turning that room into a craft room for ages," I said, smiling. "So I just let her know that if she wanted that bed hauled away—" I shrugged.

"Thanks, honey," he said, taking a sip of his coffee. He reached out and put a twenty in the tip jar, knowing without asking that I wouldn't take payment. "This means no more sleepovers."

I swallowed hard. "You'll be just down the hall," I replied, trying to hide the twinge of disappointment.

Okay, that's a lie. It wasn't a twinge, it was more like a gigantic wave of disappointment.

"You're welcome to come crawl in any time you can't sleep," he said, his eyes on mine. "Yeah?"

"I'll keep that in mind," I said, holding his gaze.

"What time you get off?"

"I should be out of here by noon if Mary shows up on time," I replied. "Which she never does."

"She know you're gonna be her boss soon?" he asked in amusement.

"Nope," I said with a laugh. "It's kind of nice to get everyone's measure without them knowing that you'll be in charge soon."

"Oh shit," he said with a laugh.

"Oh, shit, is right," I said. "I know exactly who's staying and who's going."

A car pulled up behind Bishop and he glanced in the rearview mirror.

"I'll see you later."

"Sounds good," I replied. I watched as he pulled away, then turned back to the car who'd come up behind him.

It was a struggle to keep the smile on my face.

"What can I get you?" I asked the man.

"A vanilla latte," he replied. "And your number."

"A vanilla latte I can deliver," I said, keeping my voice pleasant. "But I told you before, I like women."

"I bet I can change your mind," he called as I moved into the back of the cart where he couldn't see me.

"I wouldn't touch you with a ten-foot pole, former Officer Asshole," I mumbled quietly to myself as I made his coffee. I hated the guy. Not only had he hassled Kara for years, but he was also just a giant asshole, always making comments about how he'd turn me straight. I'd decided when he'd started the innuendos that I'd just tell him flat out that I was into women. If he had any clue that I preferred partners of both genders equally it would only encourage the garbage he spewed. I had no idea why he thought for a moment that I'd ever go out with him after the shit he'd done, but I was a bit nervous that eventually he was going to stop taking no for an answer. I glanced at the door, making sure I'd locked it when I came in that morning.

"That'll be four bucks even," I said evenly as I leaned down in the window again.

"Keep the change," he said cockily, handing me a five.

Whoa, big spender. Internally I rolled my eyes, but outwardly I smiled and thanked him, handing over his coffee.

"You change your mind, you know where I'll be," he said, his fingers trying to brush mine as we exchanged the cup.

I just nodded. He'd told me all about the jewelry store where he was working security.

"Yeah," I muttered as he drove away. "I know exactly where you won't be—the police station, you fucking douche."

When the guys at the club found out he'd been harassing my best friend, they'd put an immediate end to it. A few quiet words placed in the right ears and Officer Asshole had become civilian asshole pretty damn quick. His confidence had deflated when he'd lost the badge and Kara hadn't seen him once since then. Unfortunately for me, he must recognize my car because he'd started stopping by every day I was working, no matter which shift I was on.

The rest of my shift was so easy, I worked it on autopilot. A few friends and family came through, mostly because they also recognized my car and wanted to chat, but other than that I didn't do much business. That was going to have to change if I wanted to increase profits enough to open the new cart.

At twelve forty on the dot, Mary whipped into the parking spot next to mine.

"You're late," I snapped as I threw open the door.

"Doesn't my shift start at twelve thirty?" she asked innocently, walking toward me slowly.

"It started at noon," I replied flatly. "Even if it started at twelve thirty you'd still be late."

"Ten minutes," she replied, rolling her eyes. "I'm here, you can go."

I grit my teeth and grab my bag, slinging it over my shoulder. It was going to be a pleasure to fire her ass when I bought the cart.

"Bye," she called cheerily as I walked toward my car.

I pulled my phone out as soon as I'd closed myself inside.

"Hey sister," my older sister Cecilia answered.

"What are you doing right now?" I asked.

"Nothing," she replied with a laugh. "Kids are at Lily's, Mark's working, and I don't have any appointments today."

"I'm coming over," I said, turning on the car.

"Cool."

"You should make us lunch."

"Well, aren't you needy today," she said. "What if I've already eaten?"

"Then make me lunch," I said with a huff. "I need to bitch, but I'm also starving. I might be hangry and the bitching won't be necessary after I eat."

"Oh fine," she said in mock irritation. "I'll make you lunch."

It only took a few minutes to get over to my sister's. She and Mark had bought the property right next to my parents and even though I liked having some space between me and Farrah, I was a little jealous that they were so close. The kids roamed free between the two properties and sometimes it just felt like one giant compound.

"I made you a sandwich," Cecilia called from the porch. "And some chips. Anything more than that and you'll have to cook it yourself. It's my day off."

"That's perfect," I said as I climbed the steps.

She was sitting on an Adirondack chair and waved me to the matching one.

"Let's hang out here," she said with a sigh. "Listen to that silence."

"The construction noise carries, huh?" I asked with a laugh.

"I cannot wait for them to finish," she said as I grabbed my plate of food from the tiny table between us. "I don't know how mom and dad can stand it."

"Are you kidding?" I asked, glancing at her. "Mom's so stoked I'm surprised she's not spending her days in a lawn chair watching them work."

Cecilia laughed. "I'm glad she's so excited. I don't know what I would've done if we'd lost this place."

"You guys got lucky as hell the fire didn't come this way."

"I know," she said. "Only the death house got destroyed."

"Don't let mom hear you call it that," I mumbled, taking a bite of my sandwich.

"I won't," she replied. "But I'm glad they're starting with something new. The whole back yard area is going to pretty much be a part of the house now. It won't even be recognizable back there."

"Our memories of the old place are different," I said with a shrug.

There had been a shooting at my parents' house the summer before I was born. My mom had actually been pregnant with me when it all went down. People had died. My older siblings had lived through it and dealt with the fallout, but I hadn't. I'd been too small to even realize the toll it had taken on our family. When I was finally old enough to actually understand what had happened, time had softened the edges of their trauma a little.

"I'm glad you have better memories," she said, smiling at me.

"You should come by our new place," I said, switching the subject. "Tommy really came through. The house is huge and nice and there's a big yard."

"You care about the yard?" she asked dryly.

"Not even a little," I replied, making her chuckle. "But Draco thinks it's the best thing ever."

"Let me guess, he's going to get a barbeque?"

"A *smoker*."

"Dudes are so predictable," she said. "You guys should do a housewarming party!"

"We didn't buy the place," I replied. "We're just renting it from our dumbass cousin."

"Still," she said, leaning back to put her feet up on the porch rail as it started to rain. "You just moved in and everyone loves a party."

"Good point," I conceded. "Plus, Tommy has told us like ten times not to have a party and that's reason enough to have everyone over."

"He's such a hypocrite," she said, shaking her head. "That manchild has thrown more parties than anyone else I know."

"He does like to host, doesn't he?"

"I think he just likes not having to drive home afterward," she said with a snicker. "He and Heather can get toasted and then crash in their own bed."

"Yeah, he likes that *Heather* can get toasted," I said, joining in on the laughter. "Poor thing has been the designated driver since they got married."

"To be fair, she was pregnant for most of their married life."

"Yeesh," I muttered.

"You think you'll have kids?" my sister asked curiously.

"I don't even have a partner," I complained, throwing a chip at her. "I am not having kids any time in the near future."

"You'd be a good mom," she said with a shrug, eating the chip I'd thrown. "I want some more nieces and nephews to snuggle. All the kids are getting too big."

"I have a feeling you'll have great-nieces and nephews before I have any kids," I said, stuffing the last of my sandwich in my mouth.

Cecilia dropped her feet from the railing and sat forward. "Do you know something I don't?"

I stared at her blankly for a few moments before it clicked. "No," I blurted, my eyes widening. "Kara isn't pregnant. She and Draco want to finish school and get married first."

Cecilia sighed and sat back. "She's such a square."

I snorted. "Smart, square, same thing."

"Seriously," she said, zipping up her sweatshirt as the wind began to blow. "I want a baby to snuggle."

"Then have one of your own," I replied in exasperation.

"That is not happening," she replied firmly. "This baby factory is closed for business. The kids are old enough to do their own shit now, go to their friends' houses and stay the night at their aunts and uncles. I'm not starting all over."

"No, you just want me to do the baby stage!" I shook my head and pointed at her. "Selfish."

"Yep," she said easily. "Hurry up and find someone great, alright? Geesh."

"Actually," I said, drawing the word out.

"What?" she said in surprise. "Tell me everything. Wait! Let's go inside, it's cold as hell out here." She got to her feet. "Then you can tell me everything."

I followed her inside and we got cozy on the couch. My sister's house looked like a magazine with everything in its place at all times, but she always had comfortable pillows and throw blankets easily accessible.

"You met someone?" Cecilia asked, curling up under a fuzzy blanket with the face of some crime show TV star all over it. "Boy or girl?"

"Boy, actually."

"Surprising," she said with raised eyebrows. "I always thought you leaned a little further the other way."

"It depends on the person," I replied. "I've just been more lucky with women in the past."

"For obvious reasons," Cecilia said with a laugh. "Men are a pain in the ass. So, who's the guy?"

"Draco's friend Bishop," I said, falling dramatically against the back of the couch.

"Oh, yum," Ceecee said, nodding. "Dreamy."

"Right?" I said, snapping back up. "He's the most beautiful man I've ever seen."

"Same," she agreed. "The eyes."

"And the fucking cheekbones," I added.

"And that smile?" she fanned herself. "Goodness."

"You know what his full name is?" I asked, leaning forward. "Beauregard Augustus Bishop."

"And he goes by *Bishop*?" she asked in confusion.

"That's what I said!"

"That's a seriously cool name."

"He's—" I shook my head and smiled. "He's great."

"I've been around him a few times at parties and stuff and I've always really liked him. Mark does too."

"He's genuinely likable," I said, raising my hands palms up. "He's just such a nice guy. Gets along with everyone."

"I've noticed."

"But it's not the right time—"

"Wait," she said. "Go back. We're talking about why you like him."

I laughed. "I like him because if I'm in the room, it's like I'm the only thing he sees. I like him because he treats Reb like spun glass but he's never once talked to her like she's a child. I like him because he touches me and I lose my goddamn mind. I like that he came looking for Draco the moment he got out because he wanted to make sure that his friend was okay. I like the way he fits with us."

"That's a lot of things to like."

"But it's not the right time," I repeated.

"Says who?" Ceecee asked.

"Says me."

"It's never the right time," she replied with a wave of her hand. "You can't plan falling in love. Look at Lily and Leo—she fell in love with him while he was still hung up on me for fuck's sake."

"I'm glad you guys can joke about that now," I said with a huff.

"It was a million years ago," Cecilia said easily. "I can't even remember what he looks like naked."

"Jesus."

Cecilia laughed. "No time is a good time to have your life completely upended, that's all I'm saying."

"Well, I have to finish school."

"People have been falling in love in college since colleges were invented," Cecilia countered.

"And I'm starting a business."

"Same applies."

"I can't shift my focus right now," I said, shaking my head.

"Back to the business," Cecilia said, raising her eyebrows. "What business?"

I couldn't have stopped the smile if I'd tried to. "So, you know the coffee cart where me and Kara work?"

We spent the next two hours talking about my plans for the coffee carts and spitballing ideas about promotion and marketing. My sister was a barber and a damn good one but she'd left her old shop years ago to stay home with the kids. Mark made serious money with his security business stuff but when she'd decided that she wanted to add some extra fun money into their accounts she'd had to get creative drawing in clients. She knew her shit, and some of the ideas she had blew my mind.

"I'm home," Mark called eventually, coming in the door from the garage. "Where you at?"

"Living room," Ceecee called cheerfully. "Just in here discussing my baby sister's new business."

"I don't own it yet," I told Mark as he came into view. "Soon though."

"Oh yeah?"

"Coffee carts," Cecilia said proudly.

"One cart," I corrected. "Hopefully more in the future."

"Very cool," he told me as he leaned down to give my sister a kiss. He looked at me as he stood back up. "Let me know when you're ready and I'll install some security. The shit they have at the place you work is a joke."

"Noted," I said with a nod. I looked at Ceecee. "I'm gonna head out."

"Tell me when you guys are having the housewarming party," she said. "We'll come."

"You bought a house?" Mark asked in surprise.

"Just renting," I replied.

"She should have a party anyway," Cecilia told him. "She did move."

"Never said otherwise," he replied, raising his hands in surrender as he left the room. "See ya later, Charlie!"

I waved and went to the door to put my shoes on while Ceecee watched me over the back of the couch. "I think you should give him a chance," she said, laying her cheek on her hand. "Bishop's a good guy and I haven't seen you this googly eyed before."

"Maybe," I said with a shrug. "I need to overthink it some more."

"Us Butler girls are good at that," she said with a smile.

I opened the door. "Love you! Thanks for lunch."

"Love you, too," she said. "Next time you're bringing *me* lunch."

When I got home, the house was surprisingly empty. I didn't like it. Dropping my bag by the door, I slipped off my shoes and jogged up the stairs. Now that Ceecee had planted the idea, I was beginning to think having everyone over to show off the new place might be fun. If we were going to do that, though, I wanted to have my room completely finished.

As soon as I walked inside, I knew something was different, but it took me a second to realize that it was dark. In the middle of the afternoon. I looked wide eyed at the freshly installed wooden blinds that covered all four windows. Holy shit.

I stood frozen until I heard the front door open.

"Who's home?" I called as I walked to the top of the stairs.

"Me," Bishop called back, looking up at me. He lifted a keychain and swung it from side to side. "Draco made me a key."

"Beauregard Augustus Bishop," I said, putting my hands on my hips as he started up the stairs. "Did you put blinds on my windows?"

"You like 'em?" he asked, stopping two stairs down from me. "I wasn't sure what color you'd want—black or brown woulda kept the room darker but white matches the trim so I went with that."

"You didn't have to do that," I replied.

"Do you like 'em?" he asked again.

"I love them."

"Good," he said, starting toward me again. He gripped my hips and pushed backward until we were both on the landing. "I put mine up, too," he said, walking toward his room.

I followed him, completely flabbergasted that he'd done something so sweet without even asking and stopped in his doorway.

"You've been busy," I said, looking around the room. What had once been an empty space was now filled with a bed, dresser, and two nightstands.

"When I got over to Dragon's place, Brenna decided that I should take the whole set," he said, throwing his hands in the air. "She wouldn't take no for an answer."

"Well, right," I said, my lips twitching. "What would she do with a random dresser and nightstands?"

"I tried to pay her—"

"Uh oh," I murmured.

"Yeah," he said in exasperation.

"I can't believe you haven't noticed this already," I said softly, watching his face as he looked over his new furniture. "But we take care of our own."

"This shit must've cost thousands of dollars," he replied, just as quietly. "I don't think the bed's ever been slept on."

"Probably just hundreds," I said, smiling. "Brenna's good at making inexpensive stuff look really good."

"That's still way too much," he replied.

"You said thank you?" I asked, knowing the answer.

"Of course," he replied instantly.

"That's all she expected."

"I also offered to remodel her craft room for her," he said ruefully, rubbing the back of her neck.

"I bet she'd love that," I replied. "Just as long as you know that she's not gonna let you pay her back in goods either. Dragon will buy and pick up all of the supplies."

"Oh, for fuck's sake."

"Just accept and enjoy the bounty," I said, waving my hand at his bed. "Now you just need some bedding."

"I know," he said, turning toward me. "I dropped all the bedding I had at the old place into a donation box."

"That's just cruel," I said, laughing. "Now some person is going to be all stoked about their new sheets until they realize they can't get the scent of cabbage to go away."

"Better them than me," he said, smiling. "Plus it was twin sized so it wouldn't have fit anyway."

"I cannot imagine you in a twin bed," I said, turning away. He followed me down the hall to my room.

"It was a tight fit," he murmured.

The words should have been innocuous, but they weren't.

"Too easy," I said, shaking my head.

"What?" he asked innocently.

I ignored him as I flipped on my light and looked at my fresh new blinds.

"You really didn't have to go to all this trouble," I said.

"No big deal."

"It must have cost you a whack," I replied, still marveling. They looked gorgeous and I almost laughed at myself for caring so much. Our apartment had cheap mini blinds and they'd gotten the job done so I'd never really thought about them, but these were nice. They complimented the trim and they were so clean and new and pretty. "I'll pay you back."

"Not happenin'," he said quietly, coming up behind me. "I take care of my own, too."

I inhaled sharply, turning my head a little to look at him.

"We don't have to be together for you to be someone important," he said, his voice still low. "Just say thank you."

"Thank you," I murmured.

"Feel better knowin' no one is lookin' through your windows at night, anyway."

"Ew," I blurted, my eyes widening. "I'm on the second floor!"

"That doesn't matter," Bishop replied, nonplussed. "You stand across the street and you've got a damn good view."

"You've been looking in my window?"

Bishop huffed. "No, I haven't. But I've seen inside plenty of second story windows in my lifetime."

"Well, now I'm creeped out," I said in disgust.

"I wasn't a peepin' tom," he replied defensively.

"I'm not creeped out by *you*." I laughed and shuddered. "I'm creeped out that someone could've been watching through my damn window."

"Problem solved now, yeah?"

"Thank you."

"Welcome." He paused. "Got a favor to ask."

"I knew I was going to pay for those blinds somehow," I joked.

"Come with me to the store to pick some bedding and shit?" he asked, looking embarrassed.

"What?" It wasn't even close to what I'd been expecting.

"I don't know what to get and that stuff Brenna gave me is so nice that I don't want to make it look like shit," he said, reaching up to rub the back of his neck.

I was beginning to realize that was Bishop's tell. When he was nervous or uncomfortable, his hand automatically went to the back of his neck every time. It made me want to find ways to make him do it.

"Sure," I replied. "Right now?"

"Are you busy? We could do it a different day and I could just borrow a blanket for tonight—"

"Not happening," I said, cutting him off. "You're sleeping on clean sheets and new pillows tonight, my friend. Let's go."

"You sure?" he asked as he followed me out of my room.

"I'm not a huge shopper—not really my thing. But I'm a magician at finding a good deal and making shit look nice. I mean, not at my sister Cecilia's level, but still."

"Never seen your sister's place," he replied as we went down the stairs. "But I liked your apartment."

"We'll find you something good."

"Honey, we're home," Kara called as she came in the front door with Draco trailing behind her. "We were at Poet and Amy's and you would not believe this painting she did. Like, she said she was just screwing around, but it's gorgeous. I made her promise she would let us hang it in our living room—what were you two doing upstairs?"

I snorted at the gleeful look on her face.

"Both of our bedrooms are upstairs, genius," I replied.

"Uh huh."

"We're leaving."

"Where are you going?" she asked nosily.

"Baby," Draco said to her in amusement.

"We're going to get Bishop some super spectacular bedding for his new bedroom furniture," I replied.

"Ooh, I wanna go," she said happily. She looked at Draco. "You want to?"

Draco looked like he'd rather go to the dentist for a root canal.

"Or you two could go?" Bishop said from the stair behind me.

"Nice try," I replied without even looking at him.

"Yeah," Draco said with a sigh. "Sure, I'll go."

"Honeymoon's over, pal," I told him, practically skipping down the stairs to pat him consolingly on the shoulder.

"I really want to get some canisters for the kitchen," Kara said as I put on my shoes. "And maybe some towels or something."

"Ceecee said we should have a housewarming party," I replied.

"Oh, that would be fun!"

"Look at you, out and doing shit." I glanced at Bishop. "Before Draco got out, she was a hermit."

"I wasn't a hermit," Kara argued.

"Shut-in, then."

"Ignore her," Kara said to Bishop. "She just can't understand why anyone would ever want to spend time by themselves."

"It's boring," I said defensively. "Why you'd want to just sit around by yourself is beyond me."

"Obviously," Kara said as Draco waved us out the door. "Let's take my Jeep. Your car is too small."

"Fine with me," I said happily. "Shotgun!"

"I'm drivin'," Draco said dryly.

"I don't care. Shotgun!"

"If you think I'm riding in the back, you're out of your mind," Kara said, racing me to the Jeep. As we reached the passenger door she used her hip to bump me out of the way.

"This never stops, man," Draco said to Bishop.

"I've noticed," Bishop replied calmly.

"Fine," I said with a huff, reaching for the back door handle. "I'll sit in the back."

Bishop smiled at me as he climbed in the other side.

"My legs are way longer than yours," Kara said, continuing the argument. "You're more comfortable back there."

"If we're going by height then Bishop should be in the front seat," I replied.

"I'm cool back here," Bishop interrupted.

I shushed him. "Let the adults talk."

Draco laughed.

"I'm sorry, Bishop," Kara said, turning to look at him. "You can have the front on the way back."

"I have seniority," I complained. "I should get the front."

"Stop bitchin' and sit still for once," Draco ordered as he drove the Jeep onto the road.

I sat quietly for a few minutes, but just as Kara reached out to turn on the radio, I leaned forward in my seat.

"Are we there yet?"

Chapter 6
BISHOP

"THIS PLACE IS discount paradise," Charlie informed me, winding her arm through mine as we walked through the parking lot of a strip mall. "We'll find you some boss ass sheets here. Maybe even a comforter."

"Sounds good," I replied, letting her lead me into the store. "They don't need to be anything fancy."

"Not fancy," she confirmed. "But nice. High thread count."

"Alright." I had no idea what she was fucking talking about.

"High thread count makes them soft," she said with a laugh. "And having nice sheets means you don't have to replace them all the time. They last."

I had a feeling that my interpretation of *nice* stuff was different than Charlie's. That's why I'd asked her to help in the first place—well, one of the reasons. If things went well, I wanted her comfortable in my bed… I'd also just wanted to hang with her and having her help me set up my room seemed like a logical excuse.

Both the women grabbed shopping carts while me and Draco naturally fell into place behind them.

"I blame you for this," Draco grumbled, his expression already slack with boredom.

"I just asked her to help me find bedding," I replied. "I didn't realize she'd drag you two along."

"Uh huh," he said knowingly.

"Your grandparents hooked me up," I said. "They just gave me an entire bedroom set."

"Wouldn't take no for an answer?"

"Pretty much."

"They like you," he said simply. "If they weren't usin' it, they were probably glad it was goin' to someone they knew."

"It's nice shit," I argued. "They coulda sold it."

"You offered to buy it, didn't you?" Draco asked in amusement.

"Well, yeah."

"Sure that went over like a fart in church."

"That's a pretty accurate analogy," I replied dryly.

"Little tip," he said as we followed the women into the home section of the store. "Someone gives you somethin' just say thank you."

"That's what Charlie said."

"For once, she's not wrong."

"You bite your tongue," Charlie said, turning her head to glare at Draco. "I'm never wrong."

"Let's start in the bedding," Kara said, oblivious or ignoring the argument brewing.

"What colors are you thinking?" Charlie asked me as we reached an entire aisle of nothing but sheets.

I looked at her blankly.

"Right," she said, trying and failing to hold back a smile. "Stick with me, kid. We'll figure it out."

"I'm older than you," I said, following her as she started down the aisle.

"Yet, you know so little about bed linen," she countered happily.

She crouched down in front of me to look at sheets on a low shelf, and the sight of the top of her head so close to my dick made me stumble back a step. Yeah, letting my mind wander that direction was not a good idea while we were in public and her nephew was standing two feet away.

"I'm thinking white," Charlie said, glancing up at me.

She must have seen the panicked look in my eye, because she smiled evilly and glanced at my crotch.

"White sheets are kind of a pain in the ass," Kara said from down the aisle. "But you can bleach them, which is a plus."

"What do you think, Bishop?" Charlie asked.

Was her voice breathier than it had been before?

"White's fine with me if that's what you want."

"They're for *your* bed," she countered.

"Just tell her you want white," Draco said with a laugh.

"White's good," I repeated automatically.

"I'll find you a gray set, too," she mumbled to herself as she went searching through the shelf again.

She pulled out at least ten sets of sheets and we all just kind of waited around while she compared them.

"We're going to the kitchen aisle," Draco finally announced, ushering Kara away. "Or we're gonna be here all night."

"Don't rush us," Kara warned as they left. "Or we'll take even longer."

"I think these two," Charlie said, putting a light gray set and a white set of sheets in the cart. She looked up and smiled at me. "They're really nice. You scored. Sometimes they only have funky colors here and you'd end up with like orange or lime green sheets."

"I'm just sleepin' on them," I replied with a shrug.

"But these will look nice," she said, pointing to the cart.

I followed her down the next aisle and almost ran her over when she stopped abruptly.

"Well this is disappointing," she said with a scowl.

The entire comforter selection had been pretty much wiped out.

"Come on," she said, moving again. "Maybe we'll be able to find a blanket or something.

I watched as she grew more and more irritated when she didn't find what she was looking for.

"This is bullshit," she muttered.

"You wanna go someplace else?" I asked, looking over her shoulder.

"No," she replied stubbornly, turning to face me. "This is the place. Anywhere else we go we're not going to find brand names."

"I don't need brand names—"

"This is the high-end stuff," she said, cutting me off. "Not like the difference between store brand and name brand. This is where we should've been able to find the nice stuff."

"You're overthinking it," I said quietly, reaching out to rest my hands on her shoulders. I rubbed my thumbs down the sides of her throat. "I don't need anything fancy."

"You asked for my help and I don't want to hook you up with crappy stuff."

"What's up?" I asked, searching her expression. She was too frustrated about something so inconsequential.

"You deserve nice things," she said, her chin jutting out a little. "Not some shitty comforter that's going to be all lumpy after the first time you wash it."

"Honey, if it keeps me warm I don't care. You should've seen some of the places I've slept."

"No," she replied fiercely, her eyes meeting mine. "Not good enough."

"Then why don't you just let me borrow the blanket I had last night," I said, stepping closer. "We can come back and look for something later."

"Fine," she said with a sigh. "But you still need pillows. Do you like the down ones that kind of flatten under your head or the really stuffed ones?"

"No idea," I said, dropping my arms.

"We'll get you one of each," she said determinedly.

Wrapping my arm around her shoulders I turned her toward the shopping cart. I kept my hand on the nape of her neck as we went searching for pillows. I still wasn't sure why she'd been so frustrated about a stupid comforter, but I could tell just by looking at her that the moment hadn't passed. She was practically vibrating with pent up energy with no outlet.

"Look," Kara said excitedly when we met them in the kitchen area. "Pink salt."

"Fancy," Charlie replied. She seemed to shrug off her mood as she and Kara started browsing the shelves, but there was a lot of low voiced conversation going on between the two of them that I couldn't hear.

"Everything good?" Draco asked me as we headed to check out.

"She's pissed she couldn't find me a comforter?" I replied, hoping he'd understand more than I did.

"Huh," he mused.

"They didn't have much," I said with a shrug. "But she was really worked up about it."

Draco nodded in understanding. "Thing you gotta understand about Charlie," he said, watching the women as they walked side by side ahead of us. "She's crazy protective of the people she considers hers."

"I've noticed," I said, watching as she put one foot on the bottom of the cart and used the other to push off so she could coast down the aisle.

"You ask her for help," he said, looking at me. "And she'll move heaven and earth to do it."

"And I asked her to help me choose some bedding," I said in understanding.

"She takes that shit seriously," he said, nodding. "Too serious sometimes, but hey. There are worse things. She probably just wanted to make sure you got the best, since you went to the trouble of asking for help."

"Hell," I said, rubbing the back of my neck. "It was mostly just an excuse to spend time with her."

Draco laughed. "Clearly."

We caught up to the women as they reached the check stands and pulled out our wallets to pay for the odds and ends they'd found throughout the store.

"You don't need to pay for my stuff," Charlie said, hopping a little to look over my shoulder as I moved to keep myself between her and the cashier. "Seriously. I can get it."

"Consider it payment for your help."

"Ew," she replied, trying to duck under my arm as I paid the cashier. "I don't want you to pay me."

"Fine, I'm not payin' you," I said, handing her the little glass bowl and tank top she'd picked out. "Just take the gift and say thank you."

Charlie glared at me, the items held against her chest. "Oh, how the tables have turned."

I smiled, grabbing my sheets and pillows from the counter.

The ride home was loud as fuck, with Charlie and Kara arguing in the back seat about where we should grab dinner and Draco turning up the radio to drown them out. I had a feeling it was a common occurrence because the thumping speakers didn't even slow them down. At least I had a little more room in the front seat and I could stretch out my legs a little. They decided on fast food and I ignored my disappointment. I'd planned on taking Charlie to dinner after shopping, but since the moment Draco and Kara had walked in the front door shit had definitely gone sideways. Making a decision, I relaxed into my seat and let it go. There would be plenty of time to hang with Charlie without them there, and if I was being honest, it was pretty fucking fun hanging out with the entire group.

"I'm going to throw your sheets in the washing machine," Charlie said as soon as we got home. "You don't want to sleep on them before you wash them. Ick."

"Oh, let me know when they're done, Charles," Kara said as she kicked off her shoes. "And throw down any towels from your bathroom. I'm going to wash a load of them."

"Cool," Charlie replied. "I will."

"I can do it," I said as Charlie pulled the sheets out of my hands.

"I'm not making a habit of doing your laundry," she replied dryly. She handed me her things from the store. "Will you put these on my bed real quick? I'll just throw these sheets in. You can put them in the dryer when it's time, okay?"

Draco and Kara went off to their room and I stood for a moment in the entryway after Charlie walked off to wash my new sheets. I'd lived in a lot of houses, but the vibe in this one was different than anywhere I'd ever been. The three of them just kind of meshed together and I figured Curtis fit right in with that when he was home. I knew already that there wouldn't be any weird shit like individual shelves for each person in the fridge or bitching that someone had used someone else's stuff.

Jogging up the stairs with my pillows and Charlie's stuff in my hands, I smiled as I heard Kara laughing somewhere downstairs. I could live anywhere, I'd made it work in everything from shitty studio apartments to trailers to prison, but I still couldn't help the little jolt of contentment that hit when I realized that I'd landed somewhere good this time. Talk about luck, landing in the same cell as Draco Harrison.

After putting Charlie's things on her bed, I went to my room and threw my bags on the bare mattress. I didn't have much anymore, but thankfully when I'd been put away an old friend had stored some of my shit in her garage and since then I'd added to it here and there. First things first, I pulled out a couple of picture frames from the top of my duffle bag and set them on top of the dresser.

In the first photo, me and Uncle Beau stood in front of a river, holding up a stringer of fish that I'd been obscenely proud of at the time. Uncle Beau was wearing his signature half smile, his eyes pointed down at me, and I was grinning so wide that it pretty much distorted the rest of my face. The second photo was just me and my mom. I guessed I was around two, maybe a little younger, and I was sitting on her lap. Her hair was hanging down and you couldn't see much of her face, but what you could see looked just like mine did now. The same cheekbones and chin. Same smile. It was wild to me that I was older now than she'd been in the photo.

I spent the next hour putting clothes away and trying to organize a bit. Eventually, I laid down on my back and stared at the ceiling while I listened to the old house creak and the rest of my housemates moving around the place. Charlie dropped her towels off the top of the stairs and yelled, "Heads up!" making me chuckle. It was kind of nice hearing other people doing their thing. The halfway house I'd just moved out of had been pretty quiet. No one had wanted to be there and most didn't want to make friends either, so there hadn't been a ton of interaction. I grimaced thinking of the only real time I'd hung out with my housemates—my first night out when another of the boarders had come into my room interested in one thing. It had been a while and she was attractive, so I'd been more than willing. But she hadn't talked to me the next day and honestly, I'd been kind of fine with it. I'd later realized that she never slept with the same person twice—she was only interested in the new boarders. I didn't fault her for it—but it wasn't really my thing. I'd steered clear of everyone after that.

Eventually I must have fallen asleep because I woke up later to Charlie standing over the bed, her hand on my shoulder.

"It's just me," she said, flexing her hand. That's when I'd realized that I had her wrist gripped tightly in my fist.

"Sorry," I replied hoarsely, letting go like her arm was on fire.

"No worries," she said, giving me a small smile. "I shouldn't have startled you."

"I hurt you?" I asked, sitting up in bed.

"Please," she scoffed. "I'm made of stronger stuff than that. I brought your sheets."

"Oh, thanks," I said, still a little fuzzy as I stood up.

"You stay on this side and I'll do the other side," she ordered, rounding the bed.

"I can do it," I replied as she swung the bottom sheet out over the bed.

"It's so much easier when there are two people," she responded with a grin, continuing with what she was doing. "I'll just help you real quick and then get out of your hair."

"I didn't mean it like that," I said, reaching for my side of the sheet. "You don't need to go anywhere. I like it when you're here. Thanks again for doing this."

"Sure," she replied. "I was happy to help. Oh—I have something else for you."

She straightened out her side of the top sheet and walked quickly out of the room. When she came back a minute later, she had a quilt in her hands.

"Help me put this on," she ordered, unfolding it.

The quilt had a geometric pattern done in all grays and blues. Some of the pieces were solid, some were striped, some had tiny flowers and some looked almost tie-dyed, but they all somehow fit perfectly into the design. In my experience most quilts looked like they belonged to little old ladies that had a bunch of cats, but this one didn't by any stretch. It was honestly one of the most masculine quilts I'd ever seen, even the flowers didn't look girly.

"There," Charlie said. She tossed a pillow at me so I could put a pillowcase on it and started on the other one.

"That isn't the blanket I used the other night," I said as I copied her movements.

"Nope," she replied. "This my friend, is a Rose Butler original."

"Cool," I said, nodding. "Who's Rose Butler?"

"My grandma," Charlie replied with a laugh. "Technically my great grandma, but whatever. She was a quilter and this is one of hers. Me and Kara saved the quilts before my parents' house burned down."

I was just about to drop the pillow onto the bed when I froze. "I can't use your great grandma's blanket."

"Well, she's not using it," Charlie said dryly. "She died before I was born."

"Where's that blanket from last night," I asked, glancing from her to the quilt and back again. "I'll just use that one."

"This is nicer," Charlie replied simply.

"Charlie," I argued as she sat down on the bed. "No. What if I fuck it up?"

"Planning on using power tools in bed?" she asked sarcastically.

"I could spill something on it," I replied, staring at the quilt.

"It'll wash."

"I could stain it."

"Then it'll have a little more character than it had before," she said, staring at me like I had two heads. "What is your deal?"

"This is a fucking—" I paused to find the right words. *"family heirloom."*

Charlie snorted. "Chill," she said, leaning toward me a little. "Seriously. We are not that fancy. The quilts were made to be used and this one looks great with your new stuff. I knew it would."

"They're made to be used by *your* family."

"Look," she said, patting the bed so I'd sit down. She stared at me until I gingerly dropped my ass to the bed. Were my jeans clean? I hadn't worked that day, but I had been moving furniture and shit and who knew what I'd picked up—

"My gram made tons of quilts, alright? And when we got them out of my parents' house they were split between the grandkids and great grandkids. I got three. One is on my bed, one is folded up in my closet, and this is one. It's mine and I say you can use it on this kick-ass bed."

"I appreciate it," I said quietly. "But if I fuck it up—"

Charlie cut me off, shoving my shoulder gently. "Then every time I take it out I'll remember that time I let Beauregard Augustus Bishop borrow it. These quilts were made to be used. Loved."

I sighed, knowing I was fighting a losing battle.

"They were made to make you feel at home," Charlie said, giving me a soft smile. "And I never met my gram, but from everything I've heard, I have a feeling she'd insist you use it."

"You're nicer than everyone thinks you are," I muttered, making her gasp dramatically and backhand my shoulder.

"Everyone loves me," she argued, laughing. She looked around the room. "It looks good in here. Hey, is that your mom?"

"Yeah," I replied as she climbed off the bed and picked up the photo.

"She looks just like you."

"I know."

"What was her name?"

"Jenny," I said, clearing my throat. It was weird, but I couldn't remember the last time I'd told someone my mom's name.

"Jenny and her sunshine boy," Charlie murmured softly. "Look how sweet you were."

"I grew out of it," I joked, trying to lighten the conversation.

"Nah," she glanced at me. "Still sweet as sugar." She set down the frame and picked up the other, giggling at the photo of me and Uncle

Beau.

"Look at you two in your straight-guy-holds-fish pose."

"Our what?" I asked with a confused laugh.

"Yeah, you know?" She posed, standing straight, her chest pressed forward and a big grin on her face, one hand held in a fist at shoulder height like she was showing off a fish.

"Shit," I said, understanding exactly what she meant.

"He looks like a guy you'd want to have a beer with," she said, accurately describing Uncle Beau. She looked up at me. "And he looks so proud of you."

"About thirty minutes before the picture was taken, he'd been swearing like a sailor and calling me a dumbass because I'd caught my hook in his t-shirt," I said dryly. "I almost gave him an unintentional nipple piercing. I think the pride came and went."

Charlie laughed. "Ooh, bad form. I don't think I've ever caught someone with a hook."

"You fish?" I asked in surprise. I honestly couldn't imagine Charlie sitting still long enough for her to go fishing.

"I have," she said. "With my uncles, mostly. You couldn't tell by looking at him, but my dad isn't really the fishing type. He grew up in Southern California and went to prep schools and all that."

I imagined Casper at a prep school and choked.

"Yeah," Charlie said, grinning as she set the photo back down. "He even went to Yale."

"No shit?"

"No shit. He's crazy smart, did it all on scholarship."

"How the fuck did he end up in the Aces?" I asked curiously.

"That's a story for a different day," Charlie said dryly. "And not mine to tell, anyway. You should ask him about it some time."

"Yeah, I doubt I'll be asking your dad about his backstory," I replied, making her snicker.

"You might want to get to know him a little better first," she agreed, wrinkling her nose. "Okay, well I think you're all set now, so I think I'm going to go straighten up my room and watch some TV."

"Thanks again, Charlie," I replied.

She ran her hand over the quilt absentmindedly, tracing her fingers over the stitching. After a moment, she looked at me, her eyes soft.

"Welcome home, Beauregard Augustus Bishop."

Chapter 7

CHARLIE

WE SETTLED INTO a new routine with Bishop in the house, and I liked it. His schedule was much more set in stone than mine was, and he didn't seem to go out much, so I always knew when he'd be home which secretly thrilled me. Evenings became my favorite time of day, and though our activities were pretty fucking tame for people our age, I wouldn't have had it any other way. We all ate dinner together during the week, had Reb over to play poker and board games, and watched TV shows that we all promised not to continue unless everyone was present. Bishop and I usually ended up in my room at the end of the night, hanging out after Kara and Draco had gone to bed. On the weekends when I wasn't working, Bishop would sometimes go for a run with me and Kara. When she left us in the dust because the girl couldn't do a leisurely run if there was a gun to her head, we would talk the entire time about everything and nothing.

Three weeks in, there was only one topic that we hadn't broached, and I flew right past that invisible barrier after a long ass day of working and a couple drinks.

"What were you in prison for?" I asked, lying sideways in my bed with my head propped up on my hands.

Bishop had been lounging on my couch, his feet crossed at the ankles and his arms folded behind his head—and he stayed that way—but I still could've sworn I saw his entire body freeze in place.

"I'm sorry," I choked out, instantly remorseful. I'd overstepped big time and I knew it. I'd grown up with men who'd been in and out of prison for a variety of reasons and I *knew* how shitty it was to ask them why they'd been there. If they wanted to offer up the information, it was their place to do it. If they didn't, you kept your curiosity to yourself because frankly it was none of your goddamn business.

"Weed," he answered quietly, his chest rising and falling on a big breath. "Anything else you wanna know?"

"It's none of my goddamn business," I said, covering my face while I shook my head.

"I'm sittin' in your room," he said easily. "Been in your room almost every night since I moved in. I'd say that makes it your business."

"No it doesn't," I argued sitting up. I felt weird having the conversation while laying down. "I knew you'd been in prison. If I had reservations about that, I could've said something before you moved in. Asking now is just—it's shitty. It doesn't matter."

"Charlie," he said chidingly. "I meant it—anythin' you wanna know, I'll tell ya."

"Full out of questions," I said quickly, shaking my head.

"Honey, if I thought you were bein' an asshole or would be an asshole about it, this would be an entirely different conversation."

"How did you go to prison for weed?" I blurted. "That doesn't make any sense."

"Between my record and the amount of green I had on me, they pretty much bent me over and fucked me," he said quietly.

"But it's legal now," I replied, still confused.

"Only legal up to a certain amount," he said.

"Was it worth it?"

"Fuck no," he said, giving me lopsided smile. "See if I ever buy in bulk again."

I let out a startled laugh.

"Don't ask me to go to Costco," he continued. "I'd have nightmares for weeks."

"You're a shit," I replied, throwing my pillow at him.

"Oh, now *I'm* a shit," he said insinuatingly as he stood up, my pillow in his hands. "I see how you turned the tables."

"That's not fair," I replied, scooting backward on the bed. "I apologized."

"I know. And you can't help it," he said, lurching toward me. I scrambled even further back. "You're naturally nosy."

"I'm not nosy!"

He put a knee to the bed and a very undignified squeak burst out of my mouth as I tried to escape. Unfortunately, I'd underestimated the size of my bed and I fell backward ass over elbows onto the floor beside it.

"Holy fuck," Bishop yelped, hurrying around the bed. He was struggling not to laugh. "Are you okay?"

"Yes," I wheezed, lying flat on my back with one foot still awkwardly clinging to hope on the bed.

He crouched down next to me and reached out.

"Don't move me," I said urgently. "I may have broken something."

The smile lingering on his lips instantly vanished as his eyes widened with worry.

"Fuck," he breathed, his gaze running over me. "What hurts?"

"Nothing," I replied easily, reaching out to jab him in the side with my thumb. "But that's what you get for laughing."

I rolled over and got to my knees in one smooth movement while he stared at me.

"I thought you were actually hurt," he said accusingly.

"Good," I replied, pointing at him. That was as far as I got before he lifted me from the floor and slung me over his shoulder.

"What the hell are you doing?" I yelled, kicking my legs and twisting to try and get away.

"You know," he said conversationally as we left my room. "You really should be more careful about who you pull shit with."

"It was just a joke," I choked out as his hand connected firmly with my ass. It wasn't a smack, but Jesus, it was a clear sign of something.

"Jokes are funnier when they're shared," he said, jogging down the stairs.

"It was shared," I argued, pinching his ass. "We shared it."

"But I didn't think it was funny."

"I never said I was a comedian," I spat, pinching him again. "You win some, you lose some."

"That is true," he said as he strode through the entryway and into the kitchen.

"What are you doing?" I asked, starting to get nervous as he just kept walking.

"What's happening out here?" Draco asked, coming out of his bedroom. Kara stood behind him in one of his t-shirts.

"What was that big thump upstairs?" Kara asked.

"Sometimes," Bishop said, ignoring both of them as he opened the back door. "The joke just isn't funny to the person it's gettin' played on."

With those words he set me on my feet, right on the soaking wet patio.

I stared, rain pouring over my head and instantly soaking through my clothes as he took a quick step back and closed the door between us. By the time I'd reached for the doorknob he'd already locked it and was watching me smugly through the window.

"It's fucking freezing!" I hissed, banging on the door.

"Sorry, I can't hear you," he said, shaking his head as he pointed to his ear.

"Yes you can!" I snapped, banging harder. "Don't leave me out here!"

He strode away, letting the curtain fall back into place and I stood there, struck completely dumb. What the everlasting fuck had just happened?

"What the hell is going on?" Kara asked as she threw open the door just seconds later.

"Where is he?" I growled. As soon as I'd said it, I knew. The pipes were old, and because of the way the plumbing was designed, everyone in the house knew when a shower was turned on.

"Do you want a towel?" Draco asked in amusement as I stomped past them.

"No, I don't want a towel," I barked as I gained speed. By the time I'd reached the top of the stairs I was freezing and stripping my wet clothes piece by piece. Bishop and I shared the Jack-and-Jill bathroom and up until that point we'd been overly courteous of each other in regard to it. Because of that courtesy, I had a feeling he would've forgotten to lock the door to my bedroom, and I was right.

"You're dead," I announced as I stomped inside.

He was already in the shower and he must not have heard me come in, because the minute I whipped the curtain back he jumped like he'd been electrocuted.

"Get the hell out of the way," I snapped, using his surprise to my advantage as I pushed past him into the hot water.

"Your skin is like ice," he yelped, shuffling back. "And you're naked."

"I usually don't take showers with my clothes on," I replied sarcastically, letting the hot water run over me. "And my skin is like ice because you left me out in the fucking rain."

Bishop's lips twitched with amusement. "Funny, right?"

"No."

"You win some, you lose some," he said dryly, repeating my words back to me.

I had never been what people liked to call *slow to anger*.

"You ass," I shouted. I went for him. I'm not sure what I thought I was going to do, we were both naked and slippery and he had a good seventy pounds on me, but I was determined to do it. Maybe I'd scratch his face off.

I barely made it a step before he caught my wrists and whipped them above my head. Using his hips he maneuvered me against the wall until I was stuck.

"You done?" he asked, breathing hard.

"You're naked," I replied, staring into his eyes.

I was the one who'd done it. I'd put us in that situation. And still, when the realization sunk in that his wet naked body was pressed against mine I was almost shocked.

"I usually don't take showers with my clothes on," he whispered back.

Bishop shuddered, then slowly and gently let go of my wrists and slid his hands down my upturned arms. He took half a step back until we weren't plastered together anymore. Then he just stood there.

"It was really fucking cold outside," I said, letting my arms fall.

"And I really thought you were fucking hurt," he replied.

"You thought it was funny," I argued.

"Until I thought you were actually hurt," he countered. "Then I was scared as hell."

"Oh."

"Yeah, oh," he said, shaking his head. He reached up and slicked his wet hair out of his face. "Not cool."

I nodded.

"This really wasn't how I imagined seein' you naked for the first time," he said in frustration.

"Ditto," I murmured, glancing down.

"Eyes up here, honey," he said in amusement.

"Well it's right there," I replied defensively.

Bishop laughed.

I glanced down again.

"Charlotte," he said, his voice gravelly. "Either stop lookin' or fuckin' touch me. I'm trying to be respectful of your stupid ass boundaries but I'm about to lose it."

"You're trying to be respectful of my boundaries?"

"Stupid ass boundaries," he clarified.

"Sweet as sugar," I murmured. It was the same thing I'd told him the day he'd moved in and it still held true.

Bishop shook his head. "Fuck it."

His hands went to my ass and I scrambled for purchase as he lifted me until I could wrap my legs around his waist. I held on for dear life as he leaned down to shut off the shower. Then we were on the move, he grabbed a couple towels off the rack and strode through the bathroom door and straight into his room.

"Drop," he ordered, letting go of me.

I landed on my feet with a thump and stood there as he wrapped a towel around me. My stomach churned with disappointment for only a moment before he'd dropped to my feet and began to dry my legs with the other towel.

"What are you doing?" I asked, my voice raspy as I stared at the top of his head.

"What's it look like I'm doin'?" he asked brusquely.

I jolted at his tone, suddenly wondering if I should just walk away. The entire vibe in the room had changed and I wasn't sure I wanted to stay until he ordered me out. Giving it a minute to see what he would do, I absentmindedly wrung out my hair with the edge of the towel wrapped around my shoulders. Every cell of my body was focused on the feel of the towel as he moved his way up my legs.

"Shit," he breathed, pausing. Then his head fell forward, his hair brushing against my bellybutton as his hands moved higher.

"Oh my god," I mumbled, when without a word, he pressed my legs apart.

Then he was drying me again. Higher and higher until the towel brushed between my legs.

I wasn't proud of the way my knees buckled, but hey, no one could really blame me for it. The man was chiseled to perfection and his hands were *everywhere*.

"Steady," he said quietly as he rose to his feet.

Instead of responding I reached out and wrapped my hand around his dick, not bothering with the whole towel thing—even though I had to admit it was erotic as fuck.

He groaned and dropped the towel he held, his hand wrapping around mine.

"We doin' this?" he asked, leaning down until our noses nearly touched.

It was the moment of truth. I was one week from graduation and in two days I'd sign a contract and empty my savings, betting on a business with zero experience. It wasn't the right time. Not at all. I couldn't afford to lose focus.

At my hesitation, his hand fell away.

"Do you have condoms?" I asked, tightening my grip.

"New box in the nightstand," he said, his eyes crinkling at the corners as he leaned toward me.

As his lips hit mine we became a tangle of limbs, sliding and pressing, learning all the little dips and valleys. Bishop paused long enough to pull the quilt to the bottom of the bed and I let out a breathless laugh.

"Wouldn't want to get it dirty," I teased as he pressed me onto the sheets.

"Stop givin' me shit," he murmured as his lips met the base of my throat. "I'm busy here."

"Carry on," I said, running my fingers through his hair while he moved south.

It had been a long time since I was any kind of self-conscious about my body. I was short because my parents were short and I was muscular because I'd always liked physical activity. I had an ass because, well, I wasn't sure about that one. I mean, I worked at it, but some of it was just a natural abundance.

I didn't think my appearance was any better or worse than other women or compare myself to them. But suddenly in that moment, I really *really* hoped that Bishop liked what he saw. That in his mind, I was the most beautiful and alluring woman he'd ever seen. That no one could compare.

He was braced above me, his lips dragging along my skin, closer and closer to first one nipple and then the other. I shivered as his wet hair dripped on my torso, the mixture of his hot mouth and the cold water making me gasp. Then, he was finally there, wrapping his lips around my nipple, his tongue brushing lightly and then harder, making me arch off the bed.

"Sensitive," he said to himself as he moved to the other nipple. "This one too."

"Whoa," I moaned, my fingertips digging into his shoulders. I shivered again and he stopped.

"What are you doing?" I asked, reaching for his head as he shifted. If he didn't put his mouth back I was going to murder him.

"You're cold," he replied, moving off of me.

I didn't even have a chance to reply before he was off the bed and jerking the top sheet out from under me. Then, he was back, and we were cocooned inside the sheets. With our combined body heat it didn't take long before I was warm and shivering for a completely different reason.

"I can't see you," I complained as he worked his way down my stomach, pulling the sheet up over his head so I'd still be covered.

"You can watch next time," he promised.

Then, without warning, his tongue was exactly where I needed it. He didn't fuck around and while I had no problem with directing him, I never had to. He brought me to the edge once, then twice, then finally when I was clawing and cursing him, he knocked me right over. He stayed where he was, his tongue thrumming in exactly the right way until I started to press at his shoulders because it was too much.

He moved back up my body and braced himself over me as he reached for the nightstand. While he grabbed a condom, I ran my hands over him. His shoulders were broad, and while he wasn't built like a bodybuilder, his muscles were evident and defined. From what I'd seen, beyond the occasional run, Bishop didn't work out. His strength came from daily hard work and it was sexy as hell. I traced the definition between his pectoral muscles with my fingertips and my fingernails lightly over his nipples, making him jerk. As he leaned back on his knees to tear open the condom, I had more room to explore and I did. His chest hair was soft against my palms and the skin of his stomach was smooth except for a narrow line of hair that started below his belly button. While he rolled the condom on, I distracted him by brushing my fingers over the pubic hair he'd trimmed short, reaching under his busy hands to cup his testicles in my hand.

"Fuck," he grunted, his hips jerking forward involuntarily.

"You're incredible," I murmured. I'd thought that Bishop was handsome with his clothes on, but without them he was almost otherworldly. I'd never seen anyone as perfectly put together as he was.

"I'm supposed to be sayin' that," he said, pulling my hands away as he leaned back down.

"Feel free to worship me," I joked just before his lips hit mine.

"Plannin' on it," he replied against my mouth.

There was no hesitation or awkward positioning as he wrapped his hand around the back of my knee and thrust inside.

I'd had a lot of sex. I liked it and I didn't really see the need to hide that fact. I'd never felt any sense of shame about my sex life. I was always careful, but there wasn't much that I wouldn't try at least once, just to see if I was into it. But in all the crazy, raunchy, athletic ways I'd gotten down, nothing had ever felt as good as Bishop's first thrust inside me.

I moaned so loud that Bishop let out a breathless laugh.

"Remember when I told you," he said, nipping my earlobe as he pulled out and thrust back inside. "You'd scream first?"

I laughed and groaned again, my nails scoring down his back making him hiss in surprise.

"We'll see," I whispered back.

I flattened one leg against the bed, changing the angle and making us both gasp, then braced the opposite foot on the bed and shoved, rolling us over before he knew what I was up to.

"You wanna be on top?" he asked, grinning up at me. He crossed his arms behind his head and I took him in, his upper body stretched out before me like a feast.

I rolled my hips, grinding against him with each pass and I swear his eyes rolled back in his head, but I could see his jaw flexing as he held back any sound. It was only a matter of time. I reached up and slowly licked the fingertips of both hands, then brought them to my nipples and pinched.

His sharp inhale was music to my ears until one of his arms unfolded and his hand went between us, the tips of his fingers pressed against my thigh as his thumb found my clit.

I shuddered, and slammed down, taking him deep.

"Fuck," he muttered as I did it again.

The competition between us completely lost my focus as my head fell back and my hands dropped to his chest.

"You're too quiet," he said, his voice gravelly.

I grunted a complaint as he lifted me off of him, but it only took a moment before my face was pressed into his damp pillow, my hips high in the air.

"Brace yourself," he ordered quietly, gripping my hips.

I barely had time to reach for the headboard before he was slamming inside me again, using his hands to jerk me back as his hips thrust forward.

I tried to push myself up onto my arms but a gentle hand held me down flat, my back arched to an angle just short of uncomfortable.

"Feel free to make as much noise as you want," he said, his other hand sliding and squeezing my ass cheeks as I got closer and closer to climax.

"You too," I huffed, clenching around him as tight as I could.

Bishop gasped, his hand on my ass tightening.

The hand on my back disappeared and I shot upward, my hands scrabbling on the headboard as I pulled my body up.

I could feel his fingers between us as he continued to thrust and I gripped the headboard tighter. Then, without any warning or hesitation, a gentle finger slid into my ass and I went off like a fucking bomb.

I had no idea if I screamed or moaned or made any noise at all. What little attention I could muster was focused completely on the climax that hit with the force of a grenade, every muscle in my body tightening as it throbbed and roared through me.

By the time I had come back into some kind of coherency, Bishop was no longer inside me. He was gently unpeeling my fingers from the headboard and carefully helping me straighten my body until I was prone on the bed, his hands sweeping gently over my skin as he kissed me, first the cheeks of my ass, then the backs of my thighs, the base of my spine and further up my back, until he finished, sweeping my hair to the side so he could press a lingering kiss to the back of my neck.

"Gonna go take care of this," he said softly, pulling the sheet and then the quilt over me before leaving the room.

If I'd had any doubts about how Bishop would completely upend my life, they were gone now. As he crawled back into bed beside me, laughing at the fact that I hadn't moved a single inch, I knew nothing would ever be the same.

Because I could not imagine wanting to ever have sex again with anyone but Beauregard Augustus Bishop. He'd ruined me.

Chapter 8
BISHOP

Long after Charlie had fallen asleep, I laid next to her, running my fingers through her long blonde hair. I'd known that we'd be good together—our chemistry was off the fucking charts and it had only been a matter of time before we ended up in bed—but I hadn't realized how phenomenal it would be. I'd had fantastic sex before, plenty of times. If you got the right two people together, who were into the same things and had that spark, it usually turned out pretty fucking well—but sex with Charlie had been different. Fun. Intense. Goddamn mind-blowing.

I wasn't sure if it was because of the fact that I genuinely liked her, or that we were both hell bent on making it good for each other, or the fact that I hadn't been with anyone in a while—hell, maybe it was a mixture of all three. Whatever the magic potion had been, it had worked in a big way.

Luckily for our housemates, neither of us had screamed, but it had been a close thing. When she'd come and her pussy had clamped down on my dick, there was a moment when I thought I was having a goddamn heart attack. I'd immediately followed her down the rabbit hole, stopping it had been impossible at that point.

"I feel like I've been ridden hard and put away wet," Charlie grumbled, rolling onto her back. "Oh, wait."

"That's pretty accurate," I said, leaning up on my elbow to look at her.

The temptation to touch her was too strong to ignore. Sliding my hand under the bedding I found her hip and lightly brushed my fingers over the skin there as she arched slightly.

"More?" I asked quietly, pressing my hand between her thighs as she turned her head to look at me.

"I'm wrung out," she replied hoarsely, even as she spread her legs.

"Poor thing," I murmured, kissing her shoulder as I slid my fingers over her, brushing against her clit as I moved downward. I slid first one, and then a second finger inside her easily, enjoying the way her eyes seemed to glaze over.

I brought her to orgasm lazily, enjoying the way her skin slickened and her body tightened ever so slightly every time I thrust my fingers inside her. When she finally came, it was with a small whimper, her eyes on mine.

Her nostrils flared as I cleaned off my fingers with my mouth.

"I don't think I could take another orgasm," she said ruefully. "But I'd be willing to try."

I laughed and kissed her, nipping her bottom lip as I pulled away.

"You warmed up now?" I asked jokingly.

"Understatement of the year," she replied with a snort. "I *hate* being cold."

"Yeah?" I said innocently. "Wouldn't have guessed it."

"You're lucky I didn't maim you earlier," she said, lifting her hand out of the bedding to point at me. "I was this close."

"Honey," I said, smiling. "You could've *tried*."

"Pfft," she replied. "You wouldn't have even seen it coming."

"At the time, I had a hard time seein' anythin' else," I muttered dryly. "The image of you stompin' into the shower bare assed naked is burned into my memory."

"Well," she said, pulling her arm back. "You're welcome."

"Where are my manners?" I asked, rolling so that I was half on top of her. "Thank you, Charlotte, for that magnificent display of skin."

"And thank you, Mr. Bishop," she said, grinning. "For the two orgasms."

"Three," I corrected.

"Whatever," she said, rolling her eyes. She leaned up and gave me a quick peck on the lips. "Three, then."

I fought the urge to stop her as she rolled away and climbed out of bed, wrapping a towel around herself.

"Where you goin'?"

"I'm sticky," she said with a laugh. "I'm going to clean up and then I'm going to crash."

"Goin' to your room?" I asked. I tried to be nonchalant but must have missed the mark because she looked at me for a long moment without speaking.

"Yeah," she said quietly. "See you in the morning?"

"I'll be gone before you wake up," I reminded her.

"After work, then," she said with a small smile. "Night, Bishop."

"Night, honey."

I didn't expect to fall asleep, but sometime after I heard her leave the bathroom and go into her room, I passed out. I slept so hard that I nearly missed my alarm going off. As it was, I didn't have time to shower and had to just throw some clothes on and rush out of the house to get to work on time.

When I got to the house we were working on, I nearly groaned.

Charlie's mom was doing her daily walk through a little early, and there was no way I could slip by her without notice.

"Hey Bishop," she said cheerfully. "I got coffee for the crew!"

"Cool," I replied. "Thanks."

"You don't have to do that, Farrah," Harry reminded her as he came from inside the house. "It's not gonna make us go any faster."

"I'm just being nice, Harry," she replied, putting a hand on her hip.

"I'm sure you guys are going as fast as you can." She smiled at me and raised her eyebrows like we were in on some private joke.

"Thank you for the coffee," he grumbled.

"My pleasure," she said forgivingly. "Now, what are you working on today?"

"Gus," Harry said, raising a hand to stop me as I tried to pass them. "I want you on drywall in the kitchen today. I know the work sucks, but you've got an eye for detail and I don't want those bozos fuckin' it up."

"Got it," I replied, hiding my irritation. Drywall was dirty ass work and by the time I got home I was going to be covered from head to toe in dust.

"Don't forget your coffee!" Farrah called.

"Thanks, I'll grab some in a bit," I said, moving quickly away from them as it dawned on me that I hadn't cleaned the scent of Charlie off my skin.

I hadn't even washed my face.

As soon as I was across the house, my lips began to twitch. At least that was one bright spot in what I was sure was going to be an exhausting and filthy day. If I inhaled hard, I could still smell her on my lips and chin.

Three days later, though, the smell of her was gone, even from my sheets, and I still hadn't seen her. I knew she'd been in the house, because I saw shit she'd used and moved, but I hadn't actually been in her presence. She was gone until after I'd crashed for the night and still sleeping when I left for work.

It wasn't until day four that I finally ran into her as she was leaving.

"Where's the fire?" I asked as she nearly ran me over.

"You're home," she said in surprise, jolting to a stop.

"Usually happens when I'm done with work," I replied cautiously.

I'd gotten off a half hour early because we were waiting on the cabinet guys to install everything, and as I watched her laugh a little too hard at a comment that wasn't even funny, I had a sinking feeling that she'd been trying to avoid me.

"It's like that, is it?" I said, opening the door wide so she could pass me.

"Like what?" she asked innocently, putting her backpack on her shoulder.

"Avoidin' me?"

"Of course not," she said instantly. She scoffed like she was offended, and I stiffened. "I told you I had a ton of shit going on before we—before."

"Right."

"I can't afford to—"

"Be distracted," I said flatly. "Yeah, I got it."

"Bishop," she replied in exasperation.

"Thought you were headed out?" I asked, glancing at the open doorway.

"Don't be like that," she said, crossing her arms over her chest.

"I'm not into playin' games," I replied. "You got places to be, go."

"I'm not playing games."

"You've been avoidin' my ass," I argued, kicking off my boots.

"I've been busy."

"You couldn't say, hey Gus, I got a ton of shit happenin' the next couple days. If I don't see you, thanks for the fuck?"

"Well, no," she said stubbornly. "Since I've never and will never call you Gus."

"Right, that's what you took from that sentence."

"I'm sorry you thought I was avoiding you," she said, shrugging. "I didn't realize you needed me to check in with you."

I stared at her. She was completely missing the point—on purpose—and I wasn't going to keep up the back-and-forth. Charlie was the shit and she had everything I'd ever wanted in a woman, including being the hands down best lay I'd ever had. If she was willing, I was pretty sure we'd make a successful go of it. But I had absolutely no interest in whatever high school bullshit she was pulling.

"You don't," I said finally. "See ya later."

I headed up the stairs to take a shower, ignoring the feeling of her eyes on me until I'd rounded the corner into the hallway. It wasn't like it was hard to find me if she came looking. Charlie knew I was into her—I wasn't going to fucking chase her.

Unfortunately, my stance backfired in a big way and it wasn't until a couple of weeks later that I saw her for more than a few minutes.

"Are we crashing at the club?" Kara asked, moving around me in the kitchen as I refilled my water bottle.

"Nah," Draco said from across the room. "Someone will be sober enough to drive us or we'll just call for a pickup. You comin' Lover Boy?"

"I'll be there," I said, turning to lean my hips against the sink. "Doubt I'll be drinkin' much. I can give you guys a ride back."

"Excellent," Kara said, doing a little dance.

"This one didn't use to party," Draco said with a laugh. "Now she's a lush."

"I am not," Kara replied, throwing a kitchen towel at him. "But we haven't all hung out together in a while and I'm excited."

"I never asked you how Charlie's graduation went," I said, curious. I had barely seen any of my housemates lately. Kara and Draco had been working on finals but they finally seemed to be coming up for air.

"It went great," Kara said, smiling. "You should've heard everyone cheering, I think we almost embarrassed her."

"Not possible," Draco argued, shaking his head. "You, on the other hand, are going to be mortified at graduation."

"I'll be so glad to be done, I won't even care," Kara replied with a laugh.

"How's that goin'?" I asked Draco. He'd discussed college with me when we were on the inside, but it hadn't been much but wishful thinking back then. I wondered how it measured up for real.

"Hard," Draco replied. "Good though. Nice workin' toward somethin,' you know?"

"Yeah, I get it," I said with a laugh. "I work toward *other* people havin' a nice new house."

Draco grinned. "You're a giver."

"Charlie said her parents' house is almost finished," Kara said. "And that it looks awesome."

"It's gonna be a nice place," I agreed. "Her mom's got an eye for how shit should be, and she's up our asses so much that it's all gonna be exactly how she wants it."

"Sounds like Farrah," Kara replied. "Okay, I'm going to go finish getting ready. Leave in fifteen?"

"I just gotta hop in the shower," I replied. "Shouldn't take longer than that."

We actually left the house closer to thirty minutes later—but that wasn't my fault. Kara had been the one who held us up. By the smug look on Draco's face, I had a feeling he'd sidetracked her for a while.

I'd been to the Aces clubhouse a handful of times for barbeques and parties. It was a long building with garage bays taking up most of the space on the left side and a smaller section on the right that had a common area with a bar and a hallway full of bedrooms. I hadn't actually been in any of the bedrooms, but I'd been in the hallway to use the bathroom and knew where they were.

The guys always made me feel welcome, but I couldn't really tell if it was because they liked me or because I'd watched Draco's back while we were in prison. Hopefully it was a little of both, but it was hard to tell. To say that they were a group that kept to themselves would be an understatement. The women contradicted that, though. They'd welcomed me in with open arms and tried to mother me. It was an odd experience.

"Good to see ya, Boyo," a raspy old voice greeted me from the bench of a picnic table.

"You too, Poet," I said, reaching out to shake his hand.

"Bah," he grumbled, pulling me toward him with surprising strength so he could kiss my temple, his other hand cupping the side of my head.

I felt my throat tighten and I cleared it as I rose back up. The man was older than the earth, and looked it, but his presence seemed to fill the entire yard we were standing in.

"How you been?" I asked, taking a seat beside him.

"Eh," he said with a shrug. "Woke up this mornin.' I consider that a good sign."

"Barely," his wife Amy said, making her way toward us. "I had to shake you for a good three minutes."

"Ignore her," he told me, lowering his voice. "Her mind's not what it used to be."

"Patrick," Amy scolded, smacking his arm as she set a plate of food on the table. "If anyone's losing their mind, it's you."

Poet looked up at her innocently.

"See if I get you seconds, you old goat," she said with a laugh, patting his shoulder. "It's nice to see you Bishop."

"You too," I said, smiling back at her.

"Don't listen to anything this man says," she ordered, pointing at me. "He'll get you into trouble."

"Look at her," Poet said, watching as Amy walked away. "That woman has still got it. Don't you think?"

I choked a little on my own spit and panicked. Did he expect a response? Should I say she was hot? I held back a shudder. Would he kill me if I said I didn't see it? Would he kill me if I said I did?

"I'm fuckin' with you," he said, after watching me squirm. "Too easy. These fuckers will eat you alive."

"I'll keep that in mind," I mumbled, standing up.

"Go find the young ones," Poet said with a laugh. "They'll protect you."

I walked toward the building, greeting people as I went. I'd been to some of the rowdier parties at the clubhouse and this one was tame in comparison. Kids ran around, stealing shit off of people's plates and generally causing chaos and the adults sat in clusters bullshitting and trying to ignore them. If it hadn't been for the sea of Harleys and the leather vests on nearly every male in attendance, it would've seemed like any middle-class family barbeque.

"Hi Bishop!" Rebel said as I rounded the side of the clubhouse.

"Hey Reb," I replied, stopping abruptly so I didn't run her over. "Whatcha doin?"

"I'm looking for little Mick," she said, peeking around me. "He put a piece of pie on Charlie's chair trying to get her to sit on it and ruin her dress so we're gonna get him."

"What'll you do when you find him?" I asked. I glanced around, but I wasn't sure I could even tell Tommy's kids apart.

"Bring him straight to Charlie," Reb replied. "They're in the back."

She left without another word and I made my way to the grassy area out back, where Charlie and Kara were talking with Charlie's mom and her aunt Callie.

"I was wondering where you were," Callie said as I reached them. "Draco said you all rode together but you disappeared."

"I was out front talking to Poet," I said, accepting the hug she gave me. "What are you guys doing back here?"

"We're gonna have a softball game," Charlie replied, smiling huge.

"I don't know how you're gonna get them all out here," Farrah said uncertainly.

"It's my fucking party," Charlie said, putting her hands on her hips.

I felt my lips twitch and I scratched my jaw to hide it. I'd seen her mom stand in the exact same pose when she was irritated.

"If you build it," I said dryly, letting the sentence hang in the air as I nodded toward the pile of baseball plates at her feet.

"Did you just quote a movie?" Charlie asked, staring at me.

"Did I?" I asked easily.

Kara laughed. "You get the field ready and we'll start rounding everyone up."

"I'll grab all the mitts you asked me to bring," Callie said. "You're lucky that I kept them. No one's used them in the last decade."

"We had about a million in the house," Farrah complained as the women walked away. "Stupid fucking forest fire."

"You gonna play in that?" I asked Charlie, looking at the short dress she was wearing. It wasn't super tight, but it was small, only covering her ass by a few inches.

"I came prepared," she said, bending over to grab the plates. As she started pacing out the bases, she flicked the back of her skirt up, showing off a tiny pair of spandex shorts.

"Not sure that's gonna cut it," I said as I straightened out the plate she'd left behind.

"Stop messing with my home plate," she called over her shoulder. "And I'll still kick your ass."

"You think I'm playing?" I asked in amusement.

"Everyone plays," she said stubbornly. "The only people who get a pass are Poet and Amy—because they're too old and I don't want them to break a hip."

"You better not let Poet hear you say that," I called to her as she set down second base and glanced toward me.

"Ha," she said, moving on. "It's Amy you have to watch out for.

Poet's a big softy."

I wasn't sure that I agreed with her assessment, but we didn't have a chance to continue with the conversation because people started making their way around the back of the building.

"Captain," Tommy yelled, raising his fists in the air. "I call captain."

"Sure," Charlie replied. "I didn't want you on my team anyway."

"You're going to be the other captain?" Tommy asked in mock confusion. "But you're a *girl*."

"It's going to be really fun making you cry like a baby," Charlie replied easily.

As more people came out back, lawn chairs were set up along the edges of the makeshift field. Kids tried to convince Charlie to pick them and the adults ranged from good natured grumbling to trash talking, even though the teams hadn't even been picked yet. By the time everything was organized, we stood around, waiting to be chosen. It reminded me of PE when I was a kid, hoping I wasn't the last person picked.

"Reb, obviously," Charlie said, choosing first.

"Hey," Kara yelled in outrage, throwing her arms in the air.

"I'm in it to win it," Charlie told her best friend, grinning.

"Will," Tommy picked.

"Kara," Charlie said, laughing when Kara grumbled.

"Tommy, if you don't pick your wife we're gonna have an issue," Hawk said, striding toward her husband without waiting for him to call her name.

"Draco," Charlie said, pointing.

"Molly," Tommy said.

"You know, if you don't pick some young ones this isn't going to be very fair," Charlie teased. Then she looked over the crowd. "Dad."

"Little Mick."

"I didn't mean that young," Charlie whispered loud enough that everyone started laughing. "Brody."

They went down the line and I got more and more irritated the longer Charlie didn't pick me for her team. She seemed to be making a point, but I wasn't sure what it was. About halfway through the process, Tommy acted like he'd forgotten my name and just pointed to me. "You."

I walked over to his side and stood next to Molly and Will. She leaned a little and bumped her shoulder into my arm.

"I know Charlie's really good," she said consolingly. "But don't discount Will and Tommy. They're surprisingly athletic for guys that sit on their asses all day."

"Hey," Will said, pinching Molly's ass. "I have a labor-intensive job."

"Sorry," she joked. "He stands around looking at cars all day."

"Motorcycles, too," Will said, wrapping his arm around her shoulders. "You weren't complainin' about how lazy I was last night when—"

His words cut off as she slapped her hand over his mouth.

As soon as the teams were picked Tommy and Charlie made a big show about flipping a coin. I couldn't tell who the winner was, but our team ended up batting first.

"I'm not playing in heels," Hawk said to me as we lined up. She wrapped her hand around my arm to keep her balance as she pulled off her shoes. We both looked down at her feet as she wiggled her toes in the grass. Her toenails were painted black.

"Good call," I said as she let me go.

"Can you run in those boots?" she asked. "Because this game might seem all friendly and fun, but the minute it starts they're all going to be out for blood."

"I'll do alright," I said with a laugh. I'd run in everything from work boots to flip flops—that's what came from being a juvenile delinquent and constantly having the cops on your ass.

"Hey," Will yelled as he took a couple practice swings. "Charlie can't pitch."

"Says who?" Charlie yelled back.

"At least give us an even playing field," Charlie's uncle Grease said with a laugh.

"Fine! You guys are a bunch of whiners," Charlie complained, waving Draco's grandma Brenna over from third base so they could switch places.

"That's my girl," Poet shouted, making everyone laugh. "Give 'em hell, lass!"

Will walked over to home plate and nodded at Brenna. The woman had a surprisingly good arm.

"Damn," I muttered.

"She's a drummer," Charlie's older sister Lily murmured from behind me. "Good muscle tone."

"No kidding," I said as Will got a hit and made it to first.

Tommy struck out even though he'd tried his best to get hit with the baseball so he could take a base.

"Cheater," Charlie yelled.

"Fuck off," Tommy yelled back, laughing.

Molly struck out.

Heather was right in front of me and she walked out to the base like she was going to the gallows, giving the bat a couple of halfhearted swings. Then, like a fucking boss, she hit the softball with a loud thwack, and half our team screamed with glee as she took off running.

Charlie's team was grumbling by the time they'd recovered the softball and got it back to the pitcher.

"Just one more out," Charlie called to Brenna.

I looked across the field and met her eyes. Then I pointed over her head, making her laugh.

"This kid's got balls," I heard someone joke behind me.

"Watch him strike out," someone else said, laughing.

Brenna was a passable pitcher for a pick-up game of softball and she'd been doing really well. But she was so focused on getting the softball into the glove of the catcher, that it wasn't anything fancy.

I didn't swing at the first pitch. I could've, but it was a little lower than I would've liked.

"Strike one!" Charlie's dad Casper yelled behind me. Then he lowered his voice. "You gotta swing it, kid."

"You won't have to catch this one," I murmured back.

After I'd hit the softball so far into left field that all the kids had to go searching for it, I took a second to grin at Charlie.

"Run, jackass," she yelled, laughing as she waved her arm at me, motioning for me to go.

I jogged around the bases, watching the field while the little kids argued about where the ball had gone and Draco ran out to help them find it.

"You didn't tell me you played baseball," Charlie accused as I reached her.

"You didn't ask," I said, touching the base deliberately with my foot. I laughed as she slapped my ass to get me moving again.

"We've got a motherfuckin' ringer," Tommy shouted as I came off the field.

"Yeah," I said, raising my eyebrows. "And I think it's your wife."

"Nah," he said, shaking his head. "I've watched her with my boys. I already knew she was good."

As the game continued, shirts were discarded, trash talk increased, and someone carried a huge cooler of beer and soda over to the field. I grinned like an idiot as I watched Charlie come up to bat. She sauntered. There wasn't any other word to describe it. Playing in a tiny sundress, no helmet, with her hair streaming down her back, she stepped up to home plate like she owned the damn field. When she met my gaze and pointed above my head, my smile grew.

"Bring the heat, Tommy!" Molly yelled.

"Woman," Tommy yelled back, turning his head to look at her. "I got one speed, alright?"

Molly lifted her hands in surrender as she laughed.

"Just try not to hit me," Charlie called out dryly.

She hit the first pitch, and just like she'd foreshadowed, the softball went flying over my head and into the field.

"Oh!" she yelled, dropping her bat and throwing her hands into the air. "That's right!"

She did a little dance to first base, then moonwalked halfway to second before spinning on her heel and marching like a tin soldier.

"My girl's always gotta be the center of attention," Farrah joked.

"Wonder where she got that," Callie said with a snicker.

I was watching the field and keeping my mouth shut, because they'd found the ball and were trying to get it back to me at third base. My lips started twitching as one of the younger kids threw it toward me, and Charlie must've noticed my distraction because suddenly, she was running hell bent for leather in my direction. Just as I stepped off the base to catch the ball, she came sliding in at my feet.

"Motherfucker," she gasped.

As I turned toward her, the ball hit the ground behind me.

"Oh, shit," I muttered, crouching down.

We were playing in the grass, and it was all pretty soft, but somehow she'd found the one spot on our makeshift diamond that must have had a rock or branch, because she'd tore the hell out of one leg from knee to hip.

"I'm okay," she said, climbing to her feet. "I'm good. Get the ball."

"Fuck that," I muttered, watching as blood started to drip down her leg.

"No pain, no gain, baby," she said, grinning at me.

"You're fuckin' nuts," I replied, reaching for her.

"If you think I'm quitting before I get a run, you're nuts."

"Fine," I said, clenching my jaw as even more blood ran down her leg. I waved her forward. "Go."

"What's goin' on?" Casper yelled.

"All good, father dear," Charlie called back as she started jog-limping toward home plate.

"Aw, shit," someone said from the sidelines. I wasn't sure who it was and I didn't even bother turning to look. I was too busy following on Charlie's heels as she made her awkward run home.

"Boom," she said as she touched her foot to the base. "Nailed it. Home run."

"Molly," I yelled as I literally swept Charlie off her feet. I gingerly held her legs, trying not to hurt her. "She's gonna need some first aid."

"It's just a scratch," Charlie said, wrapping her arms around my neck.

"At the very least, you need to clean it out," Farrah said as she reached us. "That looks nasty."

"Thanks, mom."

"Game's over," Casper yelled. "We won."

"The hell you did," Tommy argued, throwing his glove at us. "Charlie's run was a fuckin' pity run!"

"Tommy's gonna kill you," Charlie sang in my ear.

"Just ran over to tell you, sorry," Molly said, out of breath. "I can't help you, I'm off the clock."

I looked at her in surprise.

"She's joking," Charlie said, squeezing my shoulder. "She always says that."

"Better take her inside," Molly ordered, smiling. "We need to clean that out and see what we're working with."

"I can walk," Charlie said as I strode toward the back door of the clubhouse. "You're overreacting."

"I can feel blood running down the back of my hand," I replied, glancing down at her.

"My legs aren't broken. It's just a scratch."

"Good man," Kara's dad Mack said with a nod, holding the door open for us.

"Oh, good grief," Charlie said with a huff. "You've been in way worse shape and people let you walk on your own two feet!"

Mack glanced down at himself as we passed him.

"Who you think's gonna be able to carry *me*?" he asked with a laugh.

I followed Farrah and Molly into a room and sat Charlie on the bed.

"Roll onto your side," Farrah ordered. "You're getting blood on my quilt."

"See," Charlie said, grinning up at me. "The quilts are meant to be used."

"Oh," Molly said, grimacing. "That might need stitches."

"Fuck that," Charlie replied as she laid down on her side and rested her head on her arm. "Get some of those butterfly bandages and hook me up."

"We better clean it first. Do you want to take off those shorts? I can cut them off—"

"I can take them off," Charlie replied, hopping to her feet. She reached under her dress and peeled the shorts off, gingerly pulling them away from her thigh.

I glanced at Farrah and then looked at the floor as Charlie crawled back onto the bed, her whole ass on display around a purple thong.

"He's seen it all before," Charlie said to the women, making Molly snicker.

"I figured," Farrah said dryly. "When he stopped making eye contact." She elbowed me in the side.

"Holy crap," Kara yelped as she came in the door behind me. "That looks gnarly."

"Looks worse than it feels," Charlie said. She hissed as Molly laid a wet washcloth on the scrape. "Okay, that smarts a little, but not terrible."

"I found the branch you scratched it on," Kara said, holding it up in the air.

"Sweet," Charlie said, reaching for it. "I'm putting that thing up on my wall."

She grimaced again as Molly started scrubbing gently at the wound and I grit my teeth so hard my jaw ached. She was acting like it was no big deal, and it didn't hurt, but I could see the tightness around her eyes and the way she kept freezing in place any time Molly hit a particularly tender spot. It was making me crazy.

"Maybe you should go out, doll," Farrah said to me quietly. "Think it's bothering you more than it's bothering her."

"I'm good," I replied, stuffing my hands into my pockets. I could feel the dried blood on my hand scraping against the denim and pulled them back out.

"It's really no big deal," Charlie said to me, shooting me a small smile. "I've had worse. I bet you have, too."

I crouched down near her head. "You've seen the scar on the back of my calf?" I asked.

She nodded, inhaling sharply as Molly did something to her leg.

"Wiped out on an old rake at my Uncle Beau's when I was thirteen," I said, reaching out to smooth her hair away from her face. "So, on top of fifteen stitches, I also had to get a damn tetanus shot that made my arm sore for days."

"You gotta keep an eye out for rusty rakes," she said sympathetically.

"That sounds like the title of a romance novel," Farrah said with a chuckle. Then more quietly to Molly, "I'll get some tweezers."

"Make sure they're clean," Molly replied. "Just wash them off with soap real quick."

"Got it," Farrah said.

"How's it going in here," Casper asked, peeking his head in the door.

"I'll live," Charlie said, looking up at him. "But my ass is hanging out, so you might want to—"

"I'm gone," he replied quickly, disappearing into the hallway.

"I'm gonna go out and check on Reb," Kara whispered to Charlie. "You need anything before I go?"

"I'm good," she replied. "Go."

After Kara was gone, Charlie sighed and looked at me. "This was not how I thought my grad party would end."

"Who said it's ending?" I asked. "We'll get you patched up and back out there."

"Just no more softball today," Farrah said with a huff as she came back into the room.

"Right," I agreed.

"Only you would slide in a damn dress," Farrah said, watching Molly work.

"I was wearing shorts," Charlie pointed out.

"Are those shorts?" Molly joked. "I thought they were an extra pair of underwear."

Charlie pointed at her mom. "I've seen you in shorts smaller than that."

"Well, I was probably dancing on a table, not sliding into third." She paused. "At least until you were no longer present."

"Oh, ew!" Charlie snapped. I felt the back of my neck heating in embarrassment, but I couldn't stop my laugh and tried to cough to cover it up.

"It's not funny," Charlie said to me. "It's gross."

"How the hell do you think you got here?" Farrah asked mildly. "Immaculate conception?"

I laughed outright at the look on Charlie's face.

"Can we please change the subject?" she spat.

"You really need stitches," Molly said, sitting back on her knees. "It's still bleeding a bit and it's deeper than I'd like."

"Just the little bandages," Charlie replied stubbornly.

"It's going to leave a scar if—"

"Bring it on," Charlie said shortly, cutting her off. "Seriously, I'm not going to the hospital."

"Charlotte," Farrah said in admonishment.

"Sorry, Mol," she said with a sigh. "Please just bandage me up."

"I swear to God," Molly said, shaking her head. "Sometimes I think you're just like your mother."

Farrah smiled.

"And then shit like this happens and I see you're just like Casper," Molly continued. "I'm going to go over it one more time and make sure there aren't any slivers I've missed before I close it up."

"Thank you," Charlie said, closing her eyes. "I could really go for a drink."

"What's your poison?" I asked, trying to distract her as Molly did her thing. "Beer?"

"Hell no," Charlie said, the hand by her face clenching into a fist. "Something harder."

"That's what she said," Farrah said distractedly.

"Vodka," Charlie said, ignoring her mom. "No, Jaeger. No… tequila. Shots, no mixer."

"Oh, so we're gettin' fucked up, then."

"Oh, yeah," Charlie breathed. "Absolutely hammered."

"I'll watch," I said, running my thumb along her cheek. "I'm designated driver tonight."

Charlie's eyes popped open. "Make Draco do it."

"I'm bettin' he's already past the point of drivin' home," I said with a smile.

"Damn," Charlie said jokingly, wiggling her eyebrows at me. "I was hoping to have drunk sex."

"Sorry, honey," I said, lowering my voice. "With me, you're gonna wanna be sober so you can replay it later."

"Ahem," Farrah said loudly, making me choke on my own spit. "I'm still standing here."

"Shh, mom," Charlie said, grinning at me. "It was just getting good."

"Let's keep it PG, guys," Molly said with a chuckle. "Okay, we're good. I'll close it and wrap it and then we're done."

Charlie let out a relieved sigh.

"You're tough," I said, letting out my own relieved breath.

Charlie laughed. "Like I was going to freak out with you here."

"What?" I asked, jerking in surprise.

"Honey," she said softly, throwing the word back at me with the force of an axe. "You were already about to lose it, I wasn't going to make it worse."

"I wasn't gonna lose it."

"You carried me in here."

"You were bleeding."

"It's a scratch. I didn't even need stitches."

"You do need stitches," I argued. "You're just too stubborn to go get them."

"You carried me in here," Charlie said again, her lips twitching.

"Like a damsel in distress."

I opened my mouth to reply and then shut it again.

"It's okay, kid," Farrah said, slapping me on the back. "So, you're a bit overprotective? You're in good company with this bunch."

"Yep," Molly said. "Almost done. Then I'll have you stand up while I wrap it. You're going to be black and blue, Charlie."

"Eh, no worries," Charlie said, leaning up to look at her leg. "No one can see it through the window."

"How's that going?" Molly asked, gesturing for Charlie to stand.

I got to my feet and moved out of the way so she could get up.

"It's good," Charlie said, nodding. "I had to let a couple people go because they weren't pulling their weight, so I've been covering their shifts."

"She's always working," Farrah said. "Downside to being the boss."

"There are no downsides," Charlie countered, grinning as she braced her hand on Molly's shoulder. "Being the boss is sweet."

I stood there quietly, listening. Since me and Charlie hadn't been hanging out, I hadn't heard anything about how the coffee shop was doing. I knew the sale had gone through and it was hers, but beyond that it was kind of a mystery.

"We barely see her anymore," Farrah complained. "I swear, if I didn't know any better I'd think she was avoiding us."

I met Charlie's gaze and my stomach sank when she shrugged.

She hadn't been avoiding me. Well, shit.

Chapter 9
CHARLIE

My leg hurt like hell, but I wasn't about to let it show as I limped gingerly out of my parents' room. I hadn't been exaggerating. I'd been elbowed in the face during my short stint as a basketball player when I was a preteen. We'd thought my nose was broken—it hadn't been—and I remembered that hurting much worse. This scratch or cut or whatever didn't even come close to that, but it still smarted a bit and the bandages and tape pulled a bit every time I took a step.

I wasn't going to let a little softball accident ruin my night, though. I had booze to drink—wait, maybe no booze—and songs to dance to and shit to talk. The coffee cart had been sucking up every waking minute and I was so overdue for a little fun that it was ridiculous. I'd set the schedule so that I had the entire next day off and I was going to make the most of my graduation party.

"What the hell did you do to yourself, little sister?" Cam asked, the moment I stepped into the main room. He came striding toward me, his eyebrows raised.

"Slid into third like a fucking boss," I replied as he pulled me in for a hug. I loved Cam's hugs. His arms were like tree trunks. When he wrapped those things around you they blocked out the entire world. "Where the hell have you been?"

"Had some shit to do today," he replied, vague as always. "Looks like I missed the fun."

"Fun's just getting started," Heather said gleefully as she danced by us.

"Shit," Cam mumbled, laughing. "She'll be pregnant by the end of the night."

"I heard that," Heather called, flipping him off over her shoulder.

"If she's pregnant by the end of the night, we're gonna have problems," Tommy joked, grabbing his junk.

"Ew," I yelled. "Stop fondling yourself!" Everyone knew Tommy had a vasectomy because he hadn't shut up about his precious balls for weeks afterward. We really didn't need the visual.

"Where's Trix?" I asked, tipping my head back to look at my brother.

"Kissin' the ring," he joked.

I snickered and scanned the room for Poet. Sure enough, Trix was there, crouched down by her grandfather, saying something that made him laugh.

"Come on," Cam ordered. "I'll buy you a drink."

"You know, that joke is never funny when the drinks are free," I replied, letting him tow me to the bar. "It's a dad joke."

"I am a dad."

"Yes, I believe I saw your son somewhere around here. But where could Curt be?" I rolled my eyes. "He'd never miss my graduation party."

"Don't start," Cam warned.

"It's bullshit that none of us know where he is," I complained. "He could've at least come to graduation."

"No he couldn't," Cam said calmly. "Stop acting like a baby."

"Easy for you to say – you know where he is!"

"Stop hasslin' your brother," my dad ordered, setting his hand on my shoulder as he came up behind us at the bar. "You know he's not gonna tell you shit."

I clenched my jaw and didn't respond. I'd been doing okay having Curt gone. I missed him, we all missed him, but we'd gotten into a rhythm and I was dealing. But in the back of my mind, I'd kind of thought that he'd show up and surprise me at my graduation. I'd even set aside a ticket for him, just in case.

"How's the leg?" my dad asked, giving my shoulder a squeeze.

"It's fine," I replied, scooting over slightly so his hand slipped off my shoulder. "I want Jager and Redbull," I told the prospect behind the bar. I could have just one, right? "On ice, please."

"It's gonna be that kind of night, huh?" Cam asked dryly.

"Don't talk to me," I snapped, crossing my arms over my chest.

"You're too old to be actin' like a toddler," he replied, his tone even.

"Fuck off."

"Farrah," my dad yelled, making me jump. "Come take care of your daughter."

"Which one?" my mom asked.

"Guess," dad said sarcastically as he walked away.

"You ever think that it's better you don't know where he is? That it's for *your* protection?" Cam said quietly, leaning down so our faces were close. "Grow up, Charlie. The world doesn't revolve around you."

I kept my mouth shut as my eyes burned. Fuck him for making me feel small just because I wanted to know where the hell Curtis was.

"Hey," my mom said, pushing Cam a little as she reached us. "What's going on?"

"Charlie's makin' everythin' about her, as usual."

"Don't be an ass, Cameron," my mom snapped.

Cam lifted his hands in surrender and walked away.

"I hope you weren't the ass here, since I just stuck up for you," my mom said, wrapping her arms around my waist as she rested her shoulder on my chin.

"I just want to know where Curt is," I said quietly, smiling at the prospect, Justin? Jake? Joey? Something with a J. "He's been gone a long ass time."

"Yeah, I know the feeling," my mom grumbled. "But you know what I've learned after a lifetime surrounded by these guys?" She tightened her arms. "There's a reason for everything they do. If they're not telling us where he is or when he'll be back? They've got a damn good reason."

"Sometimes I hate this fucking place."

Mom laughed. "Baby, you're preaching to the choir. But the good outweighs the bad, always."

"Did you ever wish for a less complicated life?" I asked, leaning back against her.

"I go where your father goes," she whispered, kissing my shoulder. "I wouldn't ever wish for anything but that."

"You could've been married to a businessman," I pointed out. "A rich, Yale educated one."

"I wouldn't know what to do with a man like that," my mom said with a chuckle. "So boring. I'd probably be fucking the pool boy and popping pills like gummy bears."

I snorted and then coughed, making my mom shake with laughter.

"He'll be home soon, honey," she said with one last squeeze. "Asking questions is just going to piss you *and* your dad off."

"I still think it's bullshit," I said, turning toward her.

"Hell, I think a lot of stuff is bullshit," she said with a shrug. "I don't go picking fights about it though." She looked at me closely. "I think there's more going on here. You were fine a few minutes ago."

"I was distracted a few minutes ago," I said, gesturing to my leg. "I wasn't even mad when I asked Cam about Curt. I didn't get mad until he acted like a condescending ass. And then dad chimed in with his two cents."

"Don't let this ruin your party," mom said with a smile. "You've been waiting weeks for this thing and running yourself ragged in the meantime. Let loose a little, kid. Find Kara—or better yet, Bishop."

"Bishop's been pissed at me for almost a month."

"He didn't look pissed when he carried you inside," she said with a smile.

"Who would've guessed he'd be so disturbed by a little blood," I said casually.

"I don't think it was the blood," my mom said sarcastically. "And neither do you. The two of you are like magnets. It's ridiculous to watch."

"I've got my hands full right now, mom," I reminded her. She and my dad were the only people who knew what I'd been dealing with since I'd finished school. I was too embarrassed and confused to tell anyone else.

"Your hands aren't full tonight, Charlie Bear. Go get him."

I shook my head as she walked away. "You're not like any other mom I know!"

"That's because I'm a cool mom," she said, waving her hand at me.

I sighed and looked around the room. Kara, Draco and Bishop were standing by the pool tables talking to Will and Molly. My mom was right, me and Bishop were like magnets. Or maybe it was just him. He was the magnet and I couldn't help but be drawn toward him. He didn't seem to have a problem staying away from me.

How many times had I gotten home late and stopped outside his bedroom door, chickening out at the last second? How many times had I made excuses to myself about why I didn't just knock on his bedroom door? How many times had I paused outside his open doorway when he wasn't home? Too many to count, if I was being honest. I'd spent so much time staring at his bed, that I'd noticed the small teeth marks I'd left on his headboard when he'd fucked me to oblivion.

The stress of trying to make my new business successful had completely drained me. It felt like I was unable to make decisions about anything else—even Beauregard Augustus Bishop.

I finished my drink and set it down on the bar.

"You just going to stare at him all night or are you going to go over there?" my sister-in-law Trix asked with a grin as she scooted in beside me.

"Probably just stare," I replied honestly, making her laugh.

"Life's too short for that nonsense," she said, reaching out to pat my back. "He's a good boy."

"He's all man," I muttered, making her wrinkle her nose in amused disgust.

"Don't wanna know," she replied. "You could do a lot worse, though."

"I know," I said with a sigh as Jacob—no, that wasn't right—put another drink down in front of me. Jesse! "I've just got a lot going on at the moment. Hey Jesse, could I just get a water instead?"

"If you wait until you don't have anything going on, you might miss your chance," Trix said, running her hand over my hair. "And his name is Jake."

"Fuck," I muttered. "Sorry Jake!" I turned to Trix. "You're kind of a downer today."

"I'm a ray of fucking sunshine," she said, pointing at me. "I just tell it like I see it. Someone is going to snatch him up. He looks like a damn Adonis statue."

"It's nuts, right?" I asked, shaking my head as I grabbed my water glass from the prospect with an apologetic smile. "How is anyone that good looking?"

Trix laughed. "Looked in a mirror lately?" she asked dryly.

I snorted.

"He's kind," she said quietly. "And respectful. Helpful. Funny. He loves Draco almost as much as Curtis does. All of that goes a lot further than the way he looks."

"I'm aware," I said, just as quietly.

Trix shrugged. "Maybe he's shit in bed and it amounts to nothing. But you never know until you—" she paused when she saw the look on my face. "Okay, well, maybe something else will turn you off. Who knows. You're young. Just don't be afraid to try, kiddo."

"Did my mother send you over here?" I asked suspiciously.

"Nope," she said as the prospect switched out her empty beer bottle for a full one. "It was Cecilia."

I looked around the room until I found my sister, staring at me smugly. I flipped her off.

"I'm going," I snapped to Trix. "Tell my sister to mind her own beeswax."

I made my way through the room, running my fingers over my Aunt Callie's back as I passed her, elbowing Kara's brother Brody in the side, and high fiving my nephew Grey as I went. I loved being surrounded by family—it was one of my favorite things—even when I was pissed at the men and honestly, the whole damn club they belonged to.

"Where's Reb?" I asked nonchalantly as I reached the group by the pool tables.

"Bathroom?" Will said.

"I think she went outside," Kara countered. "She got a phone call."

"Probably the boyfriend," Will said flatly.

"We like him," Molly said, smacking Will lightly on the chest.

"Yeah, he's alright."

"He's a sweetheart," Kara said happily. "And he thinks Reb walks on water."

"How's your leg feelin'?" Bishop asked, his eyes on me.

"Just sore," I replied. "The Jaeger helped."

"Ibuprofen would be better," Molly said in exasperation.

"I'm good," I replied with a smile.

"Who slides on a makeshift field?" Draco asked with a huff.

"Winners," I replied, toasting him with my glass. "That's who."

"Charlie's a bit competitive," Kara told Bishop.

"I noticed," he replied, the corners of his mouth curving up.

Holy crap. With two words he'd instantly brought back memories that weren't at all appropriate for a family barbeque.

"Uh, I'm gonna go find Reb," I said. "Outside?"

"She went out the front," Kara replied.

"I'll go with you," Bishop said, taking a step toward me.

I was acutely aware of him as he followed me back through the room and out the front door.

"She's not good with blood," I said as I searched the yard for Reb. "Or any injuries, really. They freak her out."

"Understandable," he said easily.

"That's why she stood outside my parents' door while I was getting patched up," I continued explaining. "She wanted to make sure I was okay, but she didn't want to actually see anything—if that makes sense."

"Yep," he said, nodding his head. "Lots of people are like that."

I found Reb sitting under a tree across the yard talking on the phone and I headed toward her.

"You look good," Bishop said as we walked side by side.

"Thanks," I muttered, distracted. Reb seemed upset.

"So," Bishop continued. "You weren't actually avoiding me."

A startled laugh burst out of my mouth and I turned to look at him. "Well, yeah, I kind of was," I confessed. "But you're not the only one. I've been avoiding everyone."

"Why?"

"I'm up to here," I said, holding my hand over my head. "In coffee shit. I dream about it. Drink recipes and to-do lists and stock and profit margins. I have zero room for anything else."

"Sounds unpleasant," he said, reaching up to scratch his jaw.

"It's just a lot," I said with a sigh. "I'm not trying to be an asshole, here. I'm just working really hard toward a goal and I get tunnel vision."

"I can understand that."

"I'm really glad you're here, though," I said with a smile, reaching out to give his bicep a squeeze. "On my one night off."

Whoops. I probably should've kept my hands to myself, because the moment my fingers touched his skin, both of us froze.

Bishop glanced at my hand, still wrapped halfway around his bicep.

Without thought my gaze dropped.

"Charlie," Bishop said, a smile in his voice. "You want another round, all you gotta do is say so."

I averted my eyes so fast I almost made myself dizzy.

"What's with you staring at my dick?" he asked with a laugh. "My eyes are up here, honey."

"I can't help it," I snapped, dropping my hand. "I know what you can do with that thing."

"If I can keep it PG while you're flashing your bare ass around, you can keep it PG when I'm fully dressed," he joked.

"It wasn't bare," I countered. "I'm wearing underwear."

"That's not underwear, honey."

"Yes it is."

"Isn't underwear supposed to cover your ass?"

"A G-string isn't supposed to."

"G-strings are a misguided attempt to cover the promised land and nothin' else," he said, laughing. "What's the point?"

"I didn't want underwear lines!"

"Then fully commit and don't wear any," he argued.

"I wasn't going commando to my family's barbecue!"

"Because a G-string is better?" he asked.

"Yes!"

"You're nuts."

"I am not."

"It would take two seconds for me to reach under that dress and snap the string of those *underwear* in half," he said with a laugh. "Who you think you're foolin'?"

My skin flushed in an instant and for just a moment I almost forgot we were standing right in front of the clubhouse. I almost dared him to do it.

"Charlie, are you okay?" Reb asked, calling to us and snapping me out of the trance I seemed to be in.

I swallowed hard and turned to face her.

"I could ask you the same thing," I said, striding toward her. "You looked upset."

"I was just telling Wesley about your accident," she said, getting to her feet as I reached her.

"No big deal, toots," I said, lifting up my skirt a little so she could see the bandage. "Your mom fixed me right up."

"That scared me," she said, reaching out to touch the top of the bandage with her fingertips.

"It looked worse than it was," I assured her. "I didn't even need stitches or anything. Just a scratch."

"You were bleeding."

"Well, yeah," I said, pushing on her shoulder. "Scratches bleed."

"Mom cleaned it?" she asked, looking up from my leg. "If you don't clean it, it'll get infected. You have to get the germs out."

"She cleaned it really well," I assured her. "Your mom knows what's up."

"Yeah," Rebel replied. She looked at Bishop. "My mom's a nurse."

"I heard that," Bishop replied easily. "She seems like a good one."

"A really good one," Rebel agreed. "She should be a doctor but she had me and I took up too much time."

"Please," I said with a laugh. "If your mom wanted to be a doctor, she'd be one by now."

Reb looked at me in surprise.

"She knows the nurses run everything," I said with a smile. "Why would she want to be a damn doctor?"

"I bet you were an easy kid," Bishop said to Reb. "Not like me, I was a menace."

"My mom said that I was so perfect that she and my dad decided they didn't want me to overshadow any other kids they had," Rebel said with a shrug. "But I heard them talking once and I think they tried to have more but they couldn't."

I stood there for a second, stunned. I hadn't known that Rebel had even thought about siblings.

"Sometimes that happens," Bishop said, nodding. "I'm an only child, too."

"Did your mom want more kids?" Rebel asked curiously.

"You know," Bishop paused, thinking it over. "I'm not sure. She died when I was pretty young so I don't think we ever talked about it."

"That's really sad," Rebel replied, her voice hoarse.

"It was," Bishop agreed. "But I think she was happy with the kid she got, even though I was probably a pain in the ass."

Rebel smiled. "I bet my mom would love you, too, even if you're a pain in the ass."

"Yeah," Bishop said with a chuckle. "She seems like the type."

"And Charlie's mom can be your new mom when you get married. She likes pain in the ass kids."

"Rebel," I sputtered, my eyes wide.

"I'll keep that in mind," Bishop said seriously.

"Oh my god, Reb," I said, gaping like a fish. "We're not getting married!"

"Not yet," she said easily.

"We're not even dating," I argued.

"Why not?" Rebel asked Bishop.

"She's too busy for me," Bishop replied.

"Stay out of this," I ordered.

"She asked me a question."

"You should just be her boyfriend," Rebel said simply. "Then she won't be too busy for you."

"You're saying I need to commit?" Bishop asked, all serious, nodding his head.

"Probably," Rebel replied. "Yes."

"Jesus Christ," I spat, throwing my hands in the air. "I'm going inside. You two can talk this out yourselves."

"She's mad," Rebel told Bishop. "But don't worry, Charlie never stays mad for very long."

"I don't stay mad at *you*," I clarified as I stomped away. "I can hold a grudge against anyone else *forever*."

Chapter 10
BISHOP

"I SHOULD PROBABLY follow her, huh?" I asked Rebel as we watched Charlie stomp away.

"I'm going to call Wesley back and tell him she's okay," Rebel replied. "He was really worried."

I nodded as she pulled out her phone and then headed for Charlie. For once, the forecourt was pretty deserted and I caught up with her before she'd even reached the picnic tables by the front door.

"Quit pouting," I said as I came up beside her.

"I'm not marrying you."

"Don't remember asking."

"I'm not dating you either!"

"Don't remember asking," I repeated.

Charlie came to an abrupt stop and turned toward me. "I don't have time," she said, crossing her arms over her chest. "I'm not fucking with you, I literally have no time in the day to deal with any kind of relationship."

"You feel like I've been pressurin' you for one?" I asked in confusion.

"No," she spat, throwing her hands in the air. "You don't ask for anything!"

"Not sure what the problem is."

"Everyone else is all, *he's so dreamy* and *go get him, tiger!*"

"Take it up with them," I said with a laugh. Honestly, it was kind of flattering. "You asked for space and I gave it."

"I know," she said through gritted teeth.

"Charlie," I said, smiling at her frustration. "You wanna hang out, I'm down. You wanna crawl in bed with me, I'm down. You want a relationship, hell, I'd be down with that too. What do you want?"

"I want to have sex with you," she muttered. "Pretty much all the time."

I laughed. I couldn't help it. She said it so reluctantly. Like she was embarrassed or something. I'd never seen her embarrassed before.

"Cool," I said, reaching out to run my fingers through her hair. "Should we leave now, or—?"

"I can't leave my own party," she said with a short laugh.

"Tonight then."

"Yeah?"

"Start drinkin' soda, and then *yeah*."

"You're saying I can't drink at my own graduation party?"

"Drink all you want," I replied. "I'm sayin' if you want me to fuck you tonight, you'll be sober when I take you home."

"You're a real bummer, you know that?"

"Not into sloppy drunk sex," I replied easily.

"Who said I'm sloppy when I drink?"

"I bet you're a hell of a good time when you drink," I countered. "But I don't fuck anyone who's not sober."

"Hmmm," she said, her hands on her hips. "Seems like there's a story there."

"No story," I replied. "Got more respect for my partners than doing shit to them when they might not be fully aware of what's happenin.' Simple as that."

"Wait, you're saying we'll never ever have drunk sex?" she asked curiously.

I thought about it for a moment. "You and I are together a while, really together, and you want to party and fuck me afterward—maybe."

"So, like at our engagement party," she said dryly.

"Yeah," I said with a chuckle. "That sounds good."

"I should be thankful you're such a gentleman," Charlie said as we started walking toward the clubhouse. "But it's a little irritating."

"It'll grow on ya," I promised.

We made our way back inside and hung out with Kara and Draco for a while, but eventually we got separated. I didn't mind. I liked hanging out at the clubhouse. The party was relaxed and everyone was having a good time, and it was interesting to see the different dynamics between the people. Everyone deferred to Poet and Dragon, which made sense since they were the retired VP and president. Most people deferred to Grease, too, since he was the current VP—but a few of the guys didn't, including Charlie's dad... and her mom for that matter. Farrah was a wild card. She wasn't mean to anyone, and she was pretty much the life of the party, but she also didn't take any shit. You knew just by the way she held herself that there wasn't anyone in the world that she answered to. Casper seemed to like her that way, though.

I understood the feeling. Watching Charlie go head-to-head in arguments didn't bother me either, it just made me kind of proud. I watched her from across the room as she seemed to be lecturing her sister's husband Leo, her hands flying around as she tried to make her point. Leo didn't show any emotion, but as soon as Charlie stopped speaking he gave a little nod and said something back to her, making her laugh. She replied, and I could tell by the look on her face that it was something sarcastic. Leo laughed loud enough that even I could hear him over the thirty other conversations in the room.

"She gives him so much shit," Charlie's sister Lily said as she came up beside me. "But he loves it. It gives him a reason to argue."

"She gives everyone shit," I replied, glancing down at the pretty brunette.

Lily didn't look anything like her sisters. While Charlie and Cecilia had both inherited their mom's blond hair and fairer skin, Lily looked more like their dad with dark brown hair and olive complexion. If you didn't know they were sisters, you'd never guess it... until they smiled. All of them had the exact same smile.

"She gets that from our mom," Lily said with a snicker. "They're always willing and ready for an argument. I'm more like my dad—we like to wait and let the other person prove they're an idiot without our help."

I laughed.

"She's crazy loyal though," Lily said, taking a sip of her drink. "We're all kind of protective of her, because she never gives up on someone once they've got her trust, you know?"

"I can see that," I replied. It didn't take a genius to know where the conversation was headed.

"From what Draco says, you're the same way."

I just looked at her.

"That you're loyal."

I wasn't sure how to reply. Yeah, I was loyal to Draco. The guy had saved my ass more times than I wanted to remember when we were locked up. Having a friend his size on the outside was a bonus, having a friend his size on the inside saved your fucking life. He'd argue that we both looked out for each other, and that was true. But I knew that the scale wasn't balanced. How could it be? He'd been the kid of an Aces MC member and built like a tank, I'd been a nobody who was so pretty, people sometimes did a double take when they saw me.

It wasn't vanity that made me aware of how I looked—it was survival. I'd learned young that the way you looked, even if it was pretty—especially if it was pretty—made people treat you differently and sometimes that wasn't a good thing. Sometimes it was very bad.

"He's a good friend," I replied finally.

"He says the same about you," Lily said, smiling at me. That's when I realized their smiles weren't exactly the same. Lily had a dimple and it was fucking adorable.

"Lily," Rose called as she walked toward us. "The boys think they can beat us at beer pong."

"Who gave our boys beer?" Lily asked in surprise. "They're not old enough for fucking beer."

"They're going to play with soda," Rose replied, waving away Lily's concern. "Come on, they've already pulled the table outside."

"How the hell do they know how to play beer pong?" Lily asked stubbornly.

"Who cares," Rose replied easily. "I'm going to make them drink until they puke."

"I'll see you later, Bishop," Lily said to me, with a sigh. "I've gotta go collect my mother-of-the-year trophy."

Not long after that, I found myself standing next to Charlie as we watched Rose and Lily annihilate their sons at beer pong. Almost everyone at the party was crowded around the table, watching as Kara's little brother Jamison turned paler and paler as he downed his cups of soda.

"Call uncle," Rose said, laughing at the look on his face.

"Never," Jamison croaked.

"Jamo's gonna puke, Grey," Lily said sympathetically. "Want to call it?"

"Hell no. He'll rally," Grey said, not looking any better than his teammate. "We could still beat you."

"Poor deluded boy," Charlie said under her breath, leaning against me. "He's up against over thirty years of friendship. They'll never win."

"It's kinda cool how you guys have these built-in friendships," I said, putting my arm around her shoulders.

"So many cousins," Charlie said, taking a sip from her glass. She looked up at me. "It's water."

"Stickin' to water, huh?" I asked with a smile.

"So you'll stick it to me later," she replied, smiling back.

Luckily, my laugh was lost in the chatter of the crowd around us.

"If someone pukes, we're callin' it," Kara's dad Mack announced.

"You coddle him," Rose accused jokingly, looking across the table at her man. "He threw down the gauntlet, baby."

"And you picked that shit right up," Mack said, grinning.

"You didn't expect anything less." She blew him a kiss.

The game continued, and thankfully no one threw up, but Lily and Rose won so easily that the boys accused them of cheating. After that, the crowd started thinning out.

I stood with Charlie, Draco, and Kara out front as everyone stopped to congratulate Charlie on her graduation and say their goodbyes. Every single adult, old and young, handed her something as they left. Some were clearly greeting cards and others just plain white envelopes, but every time she got one, Charlie's eyes widened in surprise.

When mostly everyone had left, we headed toward my truck.

"Holy shit," Charlie said, stopping in the middle of the forecourt.

"What?" Kara asked, spinning toward her.

"Money."

"What?"

"They're full of fucking *cash*," Charlie choked out. Her eyes were wide with shock.

"Did you expect checks?" Kara joked. "Half of them don't have fucking bank accounts."

"Damn government," Draco mimicked.

"I didn't know they were giving me money," Charlie said in disbelief.

"Graduation gifts," Kara said with a shrug.

"You gonna stand out here and count it?" Draco joked. "Or can we go home?"

"I think I need a safe," Charlie said, walking toward us as she glanced between us and the envelopes. "This is a lot of fucking money."

"You should probably send out thank you cards," Kara said as she reached us. "That would be the nice thing to do."

"Of course you're thinking about thank you cards when I'm holding this much cash," Charlie joked, shaking her head.

As we reached the truck, I realized something.

"There's only three seats," I said dumbly, pausing with my hand on the door. "Fuck."

"You're just realizing this now?" Charlie asked.

"We can double up!" Kara said, smiling happily.

She'd said it so easily, like it was no big deal. But for me—it was. I was on parole. I couldn't be driving around with too many people in my truck. It wasn't legal and there wasn't any way to hide it.

"I brought my car," Charlie said to me quietly. When I looked at her, she winked. "And I'm sober as a judge. I can drive home."

"I'm riding with Charlie!" Kara announced.

"Looks like it's just you and me," Draco said as the girls walked toward Charlie's car. "And I don't care how nicely you ask, I'm not riding bitch."

We were quiet as we followed the girls home. Draco and I could spend hours talking about anything and everything, but we were just as easy sitting in silence—which I appreciated. After spending the day surrounded by people and thirty different conversations happening at once, I was thankful for the quiet. I was also anxious as fuck to get home. I hadn't touched Charlie in so long, I was dying to get my hands on her.

"You and Charles seem to be gettin' along again," Draco said nonchalantly, taking me by surprise.

"We weren't ever not gettin' along," I replied, glancing at him.

"I don't know man," he said, chuckling a little. "The two of you have been tiptoein' around the house for the last month."

"She's been busy," I said flatly. "Hell, so have I. Casper and Farrah want their house done yesterday."

"Whatever you say," Draco replied as we parked along the sidewalk in front of the house.

"It's all good, man," I assured him as we got out and started toward the house.

"That was a fun party," Kara said, stumbling out of Charlie's car. "We should do that again."

"We can party whenever you want," Draco told her, grinning as she leaned heavily against him. "Unless it's a school night."

"When did you get to be such a stick-in-the-mud?" Kara teased.

She howled with laughter as Draco threw her over his shoulder and carried her toward the front door.

"You know," Charlie said to me as she rounded the car. "Drunk people aren't as fun when you're sober."

"Truth," I replied, waiting for her to reach me before I started walking to the house.

"I can see why you'd want a sober person in your bed," she said grinning. "Kara's bound to pass out as soon as her head hits the mattress."

"Yeah," I said, following her inside. "That would put a damper on my plans."

"Ooh," she replied, looking over her shoulder at me. "You have plans?"

"At least a hundred," I said, making her smile. "Maybe a thousand."

"You think we'll get to all of them tonight?"

I looked down at her leg. She'd stopped favoring it, but I knew it must still be sore. By the time she woke up in the morning, I had a feeling her entire thigh would be black and blue bruises. "I think we'll make it through about half," I replied jokingly. "If you're still up for it."

"Definitely," she said, hurrying up the stairs.

I closed the door behind me and flipped the lock before following her. About halfway up the stairs, I glanced up to see Charlie mooning me from the top of them, her dress pulled up around her waist.

"Get a move on," she ordered, shaking her ass from side to side.

I went to my room first, but she wasn't there, so I continued down the hallway. Her dress was in a pile in the doorway of her room, and as I stepped inside I saw her standing next to the bed, stripped down to nothing but her G-string and the bandages covering her leg.

"So, I thought this would be a lot sexier," she said jokingly, gesturing to her lower half. "And then I looked down and well—"

"Looks pretty fuckin' sexy to me," I replied, closing the door behind me.

"I'd take off the bandages, but—"

"Better to keep them on," I said, cutting her off. "That way we're more careful of 'em."

She looked down and her leg and picked at the piece of tape at the top of her thigh.

"Leave it," I ordered, leaning down to unlace my boots. "You know what wouldn't be sexy? You start bleedin' all over because your scratch opens back up while we're busy."

"Blood bothers you, does it?" she asked insinuatingly.

I laughed and pulled off my boots and socks. "You askin' if I'm into blood play or are you askin' if I care if a woman's on her period?"

"Uh, both?" she replied, grimacing.

"Not into blood play—honestly don't understand that shit—but to each their own," I said as I continued stripping, dropping my clothes into a pile. "I don't care if a woman's on her period as long as she's comfortable with it. If she's self-conscious or whatever, it's not fun for either of us, know what I'm sayin'?"

"Perfectly," She replied, licking her lips. "It's never really bothered me if a woman's on her period, but if it bothers her, it's a no-go, obviously. But I know it's different for everyone, I think guys are probably just generally more squeamish about it than women."

I paused with my thumbs in the waistband of my underwear.

"Yeah, I've been with women," she said, laughing at the look on my face. "I love women."

"I knew that," I said, coming out of my stupor. "I'd somehow just forgotten for a second."

She stood there, staring at my face as I dropped my boxer briefs to the ground.

"What?" I asked curiously. I was standing there naked and she hadn't even glanced down my body—it was very un-Charlie.

"I was waiting for you to say something about how hot it is that I've had sex with women," she said dryly. "Or ask for a threesome."

"Oh." I was a little dumbstruck. "Well, yeah I guess the idea is kind of hot—you with another woman," I said finally. "But, no, I'm not lookin' for a threesome. I wouldn't want to see you with someone else."

"Really?" she asked dubiously.

"I want you to myself," I replied simply. "Call me selfish, but when you're in bed with me I want your focus to be on me. Just like I'm not gonna be thinkin' about anyone but you."

Chapter 11

CHARLIE

Be still my heart.

I stood there looking at Bishop, the way his hair fell forward on his forehead, and the brackets around his mouth when he smiled, and the broad expanse of his shoulders and I was a goner. No one had ever looked at me the way he looked at me. No one had ever treated me the way he treated me.

I'd been in other relationships. Good ones even. But not one person in my entire life had made the butterflies in my stomach go crazy the way Bishop did.

I hadn't really expected him to say something disgusting about the fact that I was bisexual, but I guess I was always prepared for a conversation to move in that direction. Women usually had strong feelings about it, either they didn't understand my attraction to men or fully supported it, but they rarely asked for some novelty sexual experience. It was always the men who asked. Who insinuated and implied how much they'd like to see me with another woman or assumed that I would be interested in a threesome because I found women attractive. It didn't matter if I was in a relationship with the man or I was just getting to know him—the conversation almost always veered in that direction.

Bishop was the first to accept it without strings or jealousy. I wasn't a novelty to him.

"I've had threesomes," I blurted out. I don't know why I said it. Maybe to test him? To make sure he wasn't too good to be true? To see if I could turn him off?

"Cool," he said, bracing his hands on his hips. "I haven't."

"Just so you know," I mumbled awkwardly.

"Honey," he said, his brows creased in confusion. "Are you *askin'* for a threesome?"

"No!"

"Then I'm not sure where this conversation is goin'," he said with a short laugh. "I'm more than happy—hell, grateful even—to have you in my bed. Don't need anythin' beyond you and me."

"Okay," I said, nodding. "Okay, cool. I'm always careful and stuff, just to clarify."

"Good to know. So am I." He just stood there, his hands on his hips, waiting for me to figure out what the fuck I was doing.

Letting out a long breath, I pushed my hair away from my face. Then, I couldn't help but laugh at myself. I was being so weird. Sex was easy. It was fun. I was good at it and I already knew that Bishop and I were good together. Why the hell was I being such a dork?

"Still gonna wear a condom, though," Bishop said after a few moments.

"Uh, *yeah*, you are," I replied, making him grin.

"Come here, honey," he said, his lips still turned up at the corners. "I've been waitin' all day for this."

Because I clearly hadn't gotten the weirdness out of my system, I did a dorky skip-step over to him, making him laugh. I was slightly mortified as he gripped my bare hips and smiled down at me.

"I might need you to do that again," he said in mock seriousness. "Because your tits were bouncing all over the place and it was fuckin' fantastic."

"Shut up," I replied, laughing.

"You're beautiful, you know that?"

"I'm gorgeous," I joked, wrapping my arms around his neck. "But

I've got nothing on you."

"Honey, the scales aren't anywhere close to even," he replied, sliding his hands around until he was gripping my ass. I could feel the scratchy edges of the condom tucked between his fingers. "You've got me beat by a mile."

He leaned down to kiss me, and it was like every molecule in my body danced. *There he is.*

We made our way slowly to the bed, a single step backward, then two, both of us sliding our hands over anything we could reach. His fingers traced the base of my spine and the crack of my ass, mine trailed along his ribcage and the muscles of his abdomen. He kissed my neck. I bit down gently on his nipple, freezing him in place until I'd let go.

When the back of my knees hit the side of the mattress, Bishop pulled away.

"Careful now," he murmured, helping me onto the bed.

"It's just a scratch," I said quietly, pulling him toward me. "You'll probably have worse on your back by the time we're done."

"Charlie," he said, fitting his hips between my thighs. "You draw blood with your fingernails, we're gonna have a problem."

"I was joking," I said, fighting a smile.

"So was I," he whispered, leaning down until our noses were almost touching. "Doubt I'd even notice. The roof could fuckin' cave in and I'd still be oblivious."

He was careful this time around. The last time we'd had sex, things had been so frantic. A game. Built up frustration that had finally exploded. This time, things went slowly. A touch here, a kiss there, his fingers entwined with mine.

When he finally slid inside me, I gasped. The puzzle pieces analogy was so damn cheesy, but so true in that moment. We fit together so perfectly. There was no struggle. No discomfort.

Missionary had never been so damn good before.

"Fuck," he muttered, closing his eyes for a moment as he tipped his head toward the ceiling.

I knew exactly how he felt.

My skin tingled. Every inch of my felt overly sensitized. Then he began to move, and I was the one cursing under my breath.

I watched him through hazy eyes as he braced himself on one hand above me, his other hand wrapped around my thigh. He shifted, searching my face. Then he shifted again and I yelped.

"Perfect," he breathed, pulling back and then sliding forward to hit the same spot, again and again.

I was barely aware of gripping his arms, sliding my hands over his chest, running the tips of my fingers down his back and over the globes of his ass to the backs of his thighs. All of my focus was on that single spot inside me that thrummed, pulling tighter and tighter until it felt like I was going to lose my mind.

"Do it," he said quietly as my hand slipped between us.

The minute my fingers reached my clit, I came so hard that I was shaking with pleasure and relief.

"You feel so fuckin' good," he murmured, his lips on mine. Only seconds later he followed me down the rabbit hole.

As he rolled to the side I took a huge breath and reached for my thighs. They were still shaking like I'd run a marathon.

"All good?" he asked, reaching out to put his hand over one of mine.

"It was worth staying sober at my own graduation party," I said with a shrug, making him chuckle.

"Jesus," he said, tucking his bent arm under his head. "I'm halfway surprised I didn't black out."

"We do good work together," I replied, smiling.

"Understatement."

We lay there for a while in the quiet as the sun set outside my windows, the room growing darker.

"The pictures look nice," he said, jerking his chin toward the wall. "Haven't seen those before."

"Thanks," I murmured, looking up at the collage I'd put together. I'd found a huge set of picture frames of all sizes at a garage sale and I'd been slowly finding the perfect photos for each one. I thought they looked pretty fucking cool now that they were all hung up.

"Is that your parents in the bottom corner?" Bishop asked.

I didn't even have to look to know which one he was talking about. It was a photo of my parents when they were young, canoodling in a chair and completely unaware that anyone was taking their picture. Mom was dressed like she'd just stepped off a train from the 1940s and because my dad was just wearing a white t-shirt and jeans, he didn't break that illusion. I'd printed it black and white, and unless you looked closely, you'd think the photo was much older than it was.

"Yeah, it's them," I said, rolling to the side so we were face to face. "I didn't pick any photos where they're actually looking at the camera. I didn't want them watching me in my bedroom."

Bishop laughed. "That's honest to God something I woulda never thought of. I better put that photo of Uncle Beau and I away the next time you're in my room."

I shrugged one of my shoulders and scooted closer to him. "I don't care if other people are looking at the camera—it only creeps me out if my parents are looking."

Bishop yawned, quickly putting his fist over his mouth. "Damn, sorry about that. I'm beat. It was a long ass week."

I smiled at him as he wiped at his eyes. "I'm going to sleep in tomorrow," I said, rolling away from him so I could climb off the bed. "And it's going to be fucking glorious."

"No work tomorrow, huh?" he asked, getting off the bed on the opposite side. He stood with his back to me for a moment and when he turned toward me, he'd concealed the condom in his hand. It was kind of sweet, the way he did it. Like he was shielding my innocent eyes.

"No work tomorrow," I confirmed. "Back at it the day after."

"How's that going?" he asked as he went into the bathroom. He left the door open as he got rid of the condom, and I laughed silently as I heard him peeing. He hid the used condom but peed with the door open? Like I'd find one gross but not the other?

"It's going well," I called out as I grabbed a tank top and pulled it over my head. "Hard, but good."

I'd been telling everyone that. Things were hard but everything was fine. The shop was doing well. It was everything I'd hoped and I was just working overtime to keep it that way. Only my parents knew the truth.

I heard the faucet running as I threw on a pair of underwear and by the time I was done, Bishop was out of the bathroom.

"Aw, ya got dressed," he said in disappointment.

"Just pajamas," I countered with a smile. "You done in there?"

He gestured for me to go into the bathroom and then lightly swatted my ass as I passed him. When I closed the door between us—I was not going to pee with the door open—I wondered if he'd still be there when I got back.

I wanted him to stay the night. I wanted to catch up on things and I always slept so good when he was there but I didn't feel like I had a right to ask. Things hadn't changed for me. I was still neck deep and drowning in my new business and I knew I didn't have any extra time to spend cultivating something with Bishop. In a perfect world, hell yes, I'd have my cake and eat it too, but the world we were living in was far from perfect.

Bishop was sitting on the side of my bed in his boxers when I came back into the room.

"Wasn't sure if you wanted me to leave or not," he said easily, his eyes on mine. "Up to you."

"Stay?" I asked quietly. "It's still early."

"Can't promise I won't pass out," he warned. "Your bed's comfortable and I'm tired."

"Fine with me," I told him, moving forward to give him a kiss.

"How's the leg?" he asked, laying his hand gently over the bandage.

"Totally fine," I assured him. "Sore but no big deal."

"Wasn't sure if we'd pulled on it while we were distracted," he said, standing up so I could pull the bedding back.

I laughed. "You pretty much held it immobile the whole time," I assured him, climbing into bed.

As soon as we were cocooned inside the bedding Bishop pulled me against his chest.

"Your parents' place is gonna be so nice," he said, running his fingers through my hair. "Your mom's got an eye for makin' shit look good."

"You have no idea," I joked. "Are you guys getting close to being finished?"

"Not too much longer," he replied. "But don't tell your parents. I think Harry's givin' them worst case scenarios on the timin' so he can be the conquerin' hero when we finish early."

"Probably trying to impress Farrah," I said with a smile.

"Oh, for sure. Your ma's got everyone on the job wrapped around her finger," he murmured.

"Even you?" I asked, kissing his chest.

"Even me," he confirmed. "She's so nice—but it's not that fake-nice bullshit. I can spot that a mile away. Just genuinely nice…but with an attitude. Don't fuck with her, but also, would you like a sandwich because she made extras."

I burst out laughing. "That's Farrah to a T," I said through my giggles. "She doesn't give a shit what anyone thinks of her, but she's not an asshole about it. She wants you to feel good but she's not going to take your shit."

"You're like her," he said.

"Yeah, I am," I agreed. "Mostly. I was never as wild as she is—that was Cecilia."

"Oh yeah?"

"Christ," I said, shaking my head a little. "Yeah. She was a nightmare."

"She's always seemed cool when I'm around her."

"She figured her shit out," I replied with a sigh. "I didn't really know her when she was an asshole. Partying and lying, treating people like shit and worrying the hell out of my parents. She left when I was little and by the time she moved back home she was a different person."

"You never worried your parents?" he asked, his voice growing husky as he relaxed toward sleep.

"Not really," I said, closing my eyes. "We got into normal scrapes and did the regular stupid kid stuff, but I always had the twins and Kara to pull me back from doing anything epically stupid."

"Or shielding you from shit so you didn't," Bishop said knowingly.

He'd been at our apartment when we'd found out just how bad Kara had been bullied back in high school. It had stunned me, to say the least. After Kara realized that we'd unearthed all her secrets, she'd kicked me out of the apartment. Ironically, that was the night me and Bishop had become friends.

"Too bad we couldn't have shielded Draco," I said quietly.

"There was no shieldin' him from that shit," Bishop said, pulling me closer and dropping a kiss on the top of my head. "No matter how good you are at keepin' secrets, he always woulda found out, and probably woulda done the same thing again."

"You're just saying that to make me feel better," I mumbled.

"I'm probably sayin' it to make me feel better," he said with a chuckle, his chest shaking under my cheek. "I don't know what I woulda done if he hadn't been inside with me. Even after he'd left that umbrella of protection still stood. I got super fuckin' lucky."

I lay there thinking about what he'd said after his breathing evened out and I knew he was asleep. If Kara hadn't had half naked pictures taken of her at prom and then sent to the entire school, if Draco hadn't beat the shit out of the douchebag who'd taken them, if Draco hadn't been sent to prison… none of us would know Bishop. We'd never have met him. It was funny how you could find a tiny silver lining even in the worst circumstances.

I fell asleep to the sound of Bishop's heartbeat but woke up later to curses flying out of his mouth.

"What?" I said in confusion, pushing myself up onto my hands and knees. I looked around blearily. "What?"

"You do sleep like a fuckin' octopus," he wheezed. "Arms and legs fuckin' everywhere."

"What did I do?" I asked, my eyes widening as I became aware of how he'd curled up like a potato bug.

"Kneed me in the stomach," he said, his voice a little less raspy. "Perilously close to my dick."

"Oh, no," I said, leaning back on my knees. I couldn't help the small laugh that burst out of my mouth. "I'm sorry! It's not funny."

He glared at me as I tried to stop smiling.

"Honey, you are beautiful," he said, reaching out to touch my cheek. "And I fuckin' dig you in a big way."

"Okay," I said, a little confused at the change of subject.

"But I'm gonna go sleep in my own bed before I'm seriously injured."

My mouth dropped open in surprise as he started to smile.

"Fine," I said, pulling the pillow out from under his head. "Go then." I smacked him with it.

"You're a goddess," he said, sliding out of bed. "So fuckin' gorgeous."

"Yeah, yeah," I replied. We were both laughing by that point.

"You're just a terrible person to sleep with," he said, backing up with his hands in the air. "Not sure how I forgot that."

"You weren't complaining the other times," I said, throwing the pillow at him.

"I think the other times we ended up spoonin' and I could keep ya somewhat contained," he said apologetically, still chuckling. He tossed the pillow back to me.

"See you in the morning?" I asked, hiding my disappointment quite well, I thought.

"You want me to stay?" he asked, pausing at the doorway. "We can figure somethin' out so—"

"It's fine," I said, waving him off. "Really. I'm going to crash for like twelve more hours and catch up on all the sleep I've been missing. I can see you tomorrow."

He leaned down and grabbed his clothes and shoes before striding back to the bed. "I had a good time tonight," he said, leaning forward to kiss me softly. "Until the sleep Mortal Kombat, that is."

"Me too," I replied, pushing him away. "Go. Let me get my beauty rest."

"Night, Honey," he said as he opened my bedroom door.

"Goodnight, Beauregard Augustus Bishop."

He was shaking his head as he closed the door behind him.

For all the assurances I'd given about how I was going to fall right back asleep, you'd think that I would've been able to actually go back to sleep. I didn't. By the time Bishop had left my room I was wide awake. My body must've gotten used to just a few hours of sleep at night after the last few weeks of non-stop work.

I curled back up under the covers and stared at the ceiling, the calm of earlier completely lost. I was in some serious trouble with my business and I had no fucking clue how to dig myself out of it.

At first, I'd thought that it was a fluke that we weren't bringing in as much revenue as we had before. I told myself that it was the weather, the full moon, the fact that the shop had switched owners and people were unsure if we would be the same little coffee shop they'd come to know and love.

Me and my dad had gone over the statements Mal had given us again and again, looking for any discrepancies. I'd never believed it, but dad had suspected that she'd fudged some numbers so she could increase the sale price of the cart. It turned out she hadn't though, not unless she had someone cooking the books that was better at it than my genius father which was unlikely.

I'd let two baristas go while I tried to find the leak in the boat. Kara was able to cover some of their shifts and I took the bulk of them. It was partly because they were lazy and never showed up to work on time and I just didn't like them in general, but it also meant that I didn't have to pay them. If I was paying myself for only forty hours of work while actually working closer to seventy—well, that wasn't anyone's business. I knew it wasn't sustainable, but for now, it was my only option.

Fewer and fewer people were coming to the cart. It was so confusing. We'd had a solid customer base when I'd taken over. Lately, I hadn't even seen some of the regulars that knew us all by name.

I couldn't figure out what was going on. I spent hours of my day posting shit on social media, making sure all of our signs were visible from the road, hell, I'd even added Christmas lights to the cart so we'd attract more attention—and still I hadn't been able to make a cent.

I felt like I was swimming against the current but I refused to give up. I'd put all my savings into the fucking coffee cart. I'd been so sure that I could make it more successful than it had been before.

I really hated that I seemed to be tanking the entire business.

I also really hated that my fantastic night with Bishop was over and I was back to stressing about what the hell I was going to do about the business. I rolled over to my stomach and yelled quietly into my pillow. Then, I remembered what was in my purse.

I scrambled out of bed and turned the light on, grabbing my purse from the top of my entertainment stand. Dropping back onto the bed, I reached inside and pulled out the stack of envelopes that people had handed me as they left my graduation party.

It had sucked that we'd had to wait so long after graduation to actually have a party, but I was thankful that my parents had understood. It had taken me weeks to make a schedule where I could take two days off in a row, and I couldn't describe the relief I felt about the break. The party had been exactly what I wanted—just family and friends, hanging out and having fun. Nothing fancy. Just time together, a little booze, and an epic game of softball.

There were all kinds of envelopes in the pile and I made myself go through them slowly, one by one. Some of the envelopes were plain white, like something you'd send a letter in and on the outside were short messages.

Congratulations!
Way to go, kid!
Congrats!
To the college graduate!

None of those envelopes were signed and none of them had anything inside except cash. I was pretty sure I knew who they were from, though. The bachelors. Our family made up the bulk of the Eugene branch of the Aces MC, but not all of it. There were other men, most of them single, who me and Kara had started calling *The Bachelors* when we were in high school. They were gruff. Quiet unless they'd been drinking. They didn't call attention to themselves often, but when they did they were usually hilarious. And I would've bet all the cash in those envelopes that they hadn't signed them because they didn't want me to thank them. They were more comfortable in the background and didn't want me to make a big deal out of it.

Which was incredible, considering the amount of money they'd given me.

There were cards from my aunts and uncles that my aunts had clearly bought and signed. Cards from my cousins and siblings. My parents. One from Poet and Amy that they'd both signed, with five crisp one-hundred-dollar bills inside.

Everyone had given me money. Not a single card was empty. Not one. Some of them were smaller amounts, but many of them had at least a few hundred dollars inside. I couldn't believe it.

I could take my damn car through the car wash. I could buy a reading lamp for my bed. I could—God, the possibilities were endless.

I looked at the cash spread out on my lap. I could also put it all toward the business.

I was running my hands over the bills, letting the paper flutter between my fingertips, when there was a knock on my bedroom door.

Bishop poked his head inside and his mouth dropped open a little in surprise. "Can't say I was expectin' to find you covered in money."

"I wasn't expecting you at all," I said with a laugh, gathering up the money. "I thought you were headed to bed?"

"About that," he replied sheepishly. He came inside and shut the door. "Turns out bailin' on you in the middle of the night means I can't fall back asleep."

"That's cute," I said, my lips twitching. "You know I wasn't mad, right?"

"Yeah, I know," he said, walking toward the bed. "Guess I got used to havin' you next to me. Now my bed is too cold."

"You sound like a country song," I replied as I stuffed the cards and cash back into my purse. "But I'm not complaining."

"You're not?" he asked, dropping my purse onto the floor.

"Who will I knee in the balls if you're not in bed with me?" I asked jokingly, falling back on the bed as he leaned down to kiss me.

"I must be a fuckin' masochist," he muttered against my mouth. "Scoot over."

I moved over to make space for him and let him pull the blankets over us.

"I'm wide awake," I said with a sigh as he maneuvered us onto our sides, his knees tucked in behind mine.

"You want me to tire you out?" he asked, kissing the back of my neck.

"That's okay," I replied, lacing my fingers with his. "I *am* tired. Just wide awake. I can't turn my mind off."

"Downside of bein' the boss," he said sympathetically. "You still lovin' the cart now that you're in charge of it all?"

I thought about it for a moment. "Yeah," I said softly. "I really do. I like seeing the customers and making them something that starts their day off good. I like mixing new drinks and trying new roasters to find the right fit. Making sure the cart looks organized and welcoming and homey. Not a huge fan of the paperwork—" that was an understatement lately. "But even that isn't all bad."

"That's good," he replied. "And it's rare, honey. Most people search their whole lives to find the thing they love to do."

"Do you think construction is what you'll do forever?" I asked. "Wait, hold that thought."

I climbed out of bed and hurried to the light switch, blanketing us in darkness again. As soon as I got back, he pulled me right back into the curve of his body.

"Back to your question," he said in amusement. "Yeah, I think I'll stick with it. I like designing shit, but I'm not going back to school to be able to do that."

"You could," I replied.

"I could," he agreed. "But I've got no interest. I like workin' with my hands. I like the sense of accomplishment when somethin' is done right. When the finished product exceeds expectation. I like that no two days are exactly the same."

"Maybe one day you'll be the big boss," I said, smiling into the darkness.

"That's a possibility," he agreed. "Start my own company. Hell, I think I'd be a damn good foreman if nothin' else. Gotta pay my dues first."

"It's funny you say that," I said, his words triggering an unpleasant memory. "One of the women I fired from the cart said I hadn't paid my dues. She was pissed that I bought the cart because she'd been working there longer than I had. I think she's a year older than me."

"She offer to buy it?"

"Nope."

"She have the money to buy it?"

"Nope."

"Was it surprisin' that your old boss was sold it?"

"Nope."

"Then she was talkin' out her ass," he said flatly, making me chuckle. "Sounds like sour grapes to me."

"I really didn't feel bad when I fired her," I replied with a huff. "She talked shit about everyone—customers, coworkers, her family, strangers. She disliked everyone. The other woman I fired wasn't much better. She was never on time for her shift and I swear to God she called in sick at least once a week. She was a nightmare."

"That doesn't sound like a recipe for success when you're dealin' with the public all day long."

"Right?" I asked in exasperation. "I have no idea why Mal kept them on, but I wasn't about to deal with their shit when I was running the place."

"It sounds like you've got it all handled," Bishop said confidently, making my stomach twist. He sounded so sure of me.

For just a moment, I considered unloading it all on him. The fact that the cart was like a ghost town now, that I was working so much because I couldn't afford to pay someone else, that I felt in over my head. Instead, I just nodded. I was too embarrassed and frustrated to tell him how it was really going. I just wanted our night to be simple, uncomplicated and fun, easy. Because when I woke up in the morning, it would all be over. I'd be racing around trying to finish laundry and grocery shopping and a thousand other little errands that I hadn't been able to get to.

"Tell me about life," I said. "Anything exciting happen lately?"

"Not really," he said with a small huff of laughter. "I work on your parents' place, come home and shower, eat somethin', laundry, and pass out. Oh, and I swamp out the truck about once a week—you wanna hear about that?"

"Swamp it out?" I asked, grinning.

"Clean it," he said, brushing my hair away from my neck so he could tuck his face against it. "I don't pay attention when I'm workin', so there's usually coffee cups and fast-food wrappers, that kind of shit. By the end of the week, it's pretty nasty."

"I bet it smells fantastic, too," I joked.

"Oh, yeah. The last few bites of a hamburger give off a nice aroma after a day or two in a hot truck."

"That's filthy."

"It really is." He laughed silently. "That's why I make a point to clean it once a week."

"My car is always a little messy," I confessed. "My dad always forced me to keep it clean or he would take the keys in high school, but once I was out of the house, I kind of let it go. It never stinks or anything, I just never remember to bring everything inside when I get home."

"Makes sense since you're always movin' about a mile a minute," he replied. He reached down and gently readjusted my leg, running his fingers over the bandage there.

"It doesn't even hurt," I told him.

"The word *motherfucker* has never made me nearly shit my pants before," he said ruefully, making me smile. "But I knew you were hurt by the way you said it."

"It stung!"

"I bet it fuckin' did. When you stood up and I could see the blood runnin' down your leg I wasn't sure whether to start yellin' at you or baby you."

"You clearly went with the babying."

"You're tough as hell, you know that?"

"I just have a high pain tolerance," I countered. "I'm really a big softy."

"Well, yeah, I've noticed that much," he said teasingly. "I could not fuckin' believe you insisted on walkin' to home plate."

"I wasn't about to let Tommy win," I replied honestly. "I would've crawled to that fucking base."

"I'm glad it wasn't worse than it was," he said, tightening his arm around me.

"Me too," I confessed. "I've slid a million times wearing shorts. We all wore shorts when I was playing and it wasn't a huge deal. I didn't even think about it when I saw that you were going to tag me out."

"Not exactly the same as a manicured softball diamond," he said dryly.

"It was grass," I defended. "How was I supposed to know there was a stick hiding in there?"

"Common sense?"

"Ha," I replied flatly.

"You're gonna have a big ass bruise when you wake up," he said, kissing my shoulder. "And it's gonna be sore."

"Yeah, I'll deal," I replied, shifting a little. All the talk about my leg had made me super aware of it and the soreness that was already setting in. I wasn't about to admit it though.

"It's gonna be hell standin' on it all day."

"I'll be okay," I said, lifting our hands so I could kiss the back of his. "I have a stool inside the shop that I can rest on. It's sweet of you to worry, though."

"You get a lot of time to rest when you're workin'?"

Well, wasn't that just a minefield of a question?

"No, not a lot," I hedged. "We have a lot of regulars that come through in the morning, but there's usually a lull later in the day."

"That's good."

"Speaking of regulars," I said, anxious to change the subject. "So, do you remember how that cop was practically stalking Kara around the time Draco got out?"

"I think I remember hearin' a little about it," he replied. "Wasn't he fired or somethin'?"

"Yeah, he was," I replied. "He works as a security guard now. Anyway, he comes by the cart at least once a day. Isn't that weird?"

"Say what?" Bishop replied, his voice losing the relaxed tone.

"Yeah, he comes at least once, sometimes twice a day."

"What the fuck?"

"He's an asshole, but he's a paying customer," I replied, shrugging my shoulder. "And I don't think he stops if Kara is working—she would've said something."

"But he stops once or twice when you are?"

"Yep."

"Charlie," he said. It was practically a growl.

"What?" I turned my head to look at him.

"Have you told anyone?"

"There's nothing to tell," I replied defensively. "He stops for coffee and then goes on his way, usually with a couple of asshole comments thrown in. No big deal. I've been tempted to accidentally spill his hot coffee when I'm handing it over, but I'm not turning down the sale."

"He needs to stay the fuck away from you," Bishop said firmly.

"I own a coffee shop that's centrally located. The chances of running into him are pretty high. Why are you getting all riled up about it?"

"If he's not stoppin' when Kara works there then he must know when she's not workin' and when *you* are."

"Well, yeah," I replied. "He probably knows what cars we drive."

"And you're not seein' why this is a problem?"

"No." I shrugged. "I mean he's annoying and an asshole, but it's not like he's done anything to me. I hate the guy for the shit he put Kara through, but he stays in his car and orders his coffee and pays for it. There's no reason not to serve him."

"You see any other customers twice a day?"

"Well," I said, drawing out the word. "No. But like I said, it's a sale."

"That's because it's fuckin' weird that he's comin' through more than once. People grab a cup on their way to work, or on their way into town for whatever reason. They don't keep comin' back all day."

"It's not unheard of," I hedged.

"Just keep an eye out," Bishop said, his tone dark. "Men like that, the bullies, they always escalate. You don't give him the attention he wants, he's gonna take it anyway he can."

"He can fucking try me," I replied, unconcerned. "I'll put that little douche in his place."

Bishop burst out laughing.

"What?" I snapped.

"Honey, you're adorable—"

"I don't think I like where this is going," I cut in.

"—but you're tiny," he continued. "You goin' up against a full-grown man ain't gonna go well for you."

"I grew up in an outlaw motorcycle club," I replied slowly. "I know how to even the odds."

"I bet you do," he said, reaching out to cup my cheek. "But you need to keep your eyes open anyway, Charlie. All it takes is one time catchin' you off guard and you're in a world of trouble."

"I know."

"Alright, then."

"Okay."

"You gonna keep sayin' somethin' so you get the last word?"

"Yep."

"Alright."

"Cool."

I flipped back around and lay my head down on the pillow, letting him pull me in close against his chest.

While I was irritated that he'd pointed out how much of a disadvantage I'd be in if Officer Asshole decided to do anything physical—it also made me pause. I'd never given the douche much thought because he hadn't done anything aggressive. Once he'd stopped fucking with Kara and Draco, I'd kind of just put him in the annoying category and went on my way. Yes, I saw him more than anyone else, and no, it wasn't the best part of my day—but it wasn't as if he made me nervous. If anything, he just pissed me off most of the time. He was a creep—but I'd dealt with a lot of creeps.

"I know you can take care of yourself, honey," Bishop said, on the edge of sleep. "Just keep your eyes open, yeah?"

"I will," I replied quietly.

I closed my eyes and listened to the sound of his breathing, letting it lull me, finally, back to sleep.

Chapter 12

BISHOP

Monday morning was a shit show. I woke up late for work, didn't have time to stop for coffee and see Charlie at work, and realized that I'd put my t-shirt on backwards after I'd already gotten to the job site.

I hadn't seen Charlie again since Sunday morning when I'd left her bed. When she'd given me a kiss good morning and told me she had shit to do, I'd taken her at her word. I wasn't going to get all bent out of shape again, thinking she was avoiding me or putting me off. From the comments I'd heard at her party and the amount of time she'd spent away from the house—I knew she actually was just really fucking busy.

I hadn't had a chance to talk to her again in the light of day about the cop that had been showing up at the coffee cart, which bothered me. She'd seemed pretty unconcerned with the whole thing, which made the back of my neck tingle. Something was off, even if she wasn't seeing it.

I fucking hated that there wasn't anything I could do for her. I knew that if the guy pulled something, there wouldn't be a punishment in the world that would stop me from going after him—but he hadn't done anything. Yet. And that meant that there wasn't a whole hell of a lot I could do. Keeping my nose clean in all respects was fucking important. I was still meeting with my parole officer every week, proving that I was doing just that.

Having my hands tied drove me out of my goddamn mind. That

was the only excuse I had when I waved Casper down when I saw him out on the gravel driveway to the house.

"Hey man, you got a minute?" I asked, jogging over to him.

"Sure, kid," he said, swinging his leg off his bike. "What's goin' on?"

"I was talkin' to Charlie this weekend—"

"Any sentence starts that way makes me automatically brace," he joked.

"She said somethin' about that guy—the cop that was hasslin' Kara—showin' up at her work a couple times a day."

"What?" Casper replied, his entire body shifting from the relaxed way he'd been leaning on his bike.

"She said he comes by every day, sometimes twice a day."

"The fuck?" Casper said quietly.

"I don't know," I said, lifting my hands in a don't-shoot-the-messenger gesture. "She seemed pretty unconcerned, but it fucked with me. Don't know why he'd be showing up all the time when she clearly wants nothin' to do with him."

"Because he's lookin' to change her mind," Casper spat. "Or is willin' to look past it."

"Just thought I'd give you a heads up," I said. "I'm here all day so there's not much I can do."

"And you're still answerin' to a parole officer," Casper replied knowingly.

"That, too."

"I'll take care of it," Casper said firmly, then he shot me a small smile. "You keep your ass on the outside if you can."

"I'm tryin'," I replied with a sigh. "I pretty much go to work and go home."

"Finish out your time," he said, nodding. "Sucks, man. I get it. But your pretty ass doesn't wanna be inside without someone at your back, and we don't have any men in county at the moment." He paused for a moment. "I'll take care of this. You just worry about gettin' those kitchen counters my woman wants installed."

"I don't work with granite," I said with a laugh. "But I'll keep an eye out and make sure they do shit right."

"Good man," Casper replied.

As I walked away, I felt a little better about the Charlie situation. At least now her pop knew what was going on and I was sure within minutes the rest of the club would, too. It wasn't ideal—I wanted to take care of it—but it was the best I could do under the circumstances.

The day went by quickly because there were always a thousand tasks to get done, and by the time I said goodbye to Harry and the guys, I was dragging ass. Farrah hadn't ever shown up to chat and look through the place, so we'd actually gotten a lot done. I wondered if she realized how much she slowed things down when she made her unexpected visits and then decided that she probably just didn't care. She wanted to be involved in every step—which was a new experience for most of us. I'd spent a lot of time building new places in developments that hadn't even been sold yet. You get a set of plans, the shit you need is ordered, and you get to work building a few cookie cutter houses on each block. It's easy and pretty routine—which wasn't the case with Casper and Farrah's place. They continually thought of new shit they wanted or made changes and it slowed everything way down.

I couldn't really complain though. I was pretty sure that Casper was the one who'd convinced Harry to hire me. Construction jobs weren't hard to get, but my felony record made things a bit tricky. I was grateful for the opportunity, and Harry was a good guy. I liked working for him. He didn't put up with any bullshit, but he was decent and he spelled out exactly what he expected from you so there weren't any misunderstandings. I appreciated that.

When I got home Kara and Draco were in the kitchen, a pile of books and random papers spread out all over the table.

"Hey, Bishop," Kara said happily. "I'm glad you're home."

I stopped on my way to the fridge. "Why's that?"

"Because she's been wantin' to take a break for an hour," Draco said dryly, stretching his arms above his head.

"School's goin' well, huh?" I joked.

"It's fine," Kara said, pushing her fingers through her hair. "I'm just tired. I have to get all this done because I have to work early tomorrow before class."

"You workin' with Charlie in the mornin'?" I asked, finishing my walk to the fridge.

"I'm always working with Charlie," Kara said, rolling her eyes. "Everyone's always working with Charlie. She's always there. I can't believe she took the weekend off."

"She surprised me," Draco said. "I figured she'd be checkin' in all weekend, but I didn't notice her doin' it."

"Tough bein' the boss," I said, taking a drink of my soda.

"It's beyond that," Kara replied, leaning forward like she was grateful someone else had brought the subject up. "She's always there. She's always working. It's like she never takes a break or lets anyone else take the shifts."

"She always been like that?" I asked curiously. "She takes shit pretty serious when she's focused—"

"She's never been like that," Draco said with a huff. "Yeah, she takes shit seriously when she gets her mind set on somethin'." He shook his head. "But she's about the last person I'd expect to work nonstop. The girl used to finish her homework in class so she wouldn't have it at home and she could fuck around whenever she wanted."

"Work to live, Kara," Kara mimicked. "Don't live to work."

"It probably hits different when you're in charge," I said. It almost felt like I was defending her—which was stupid since Draco and Kara were a couple of her best friends in the entire world. I felt protective but mixed in with that was a little concern. Charlie seemed to be burning the candle at both ends.

We all startled when the front door slammed.

"Beauregard Augustus Bishop!" Charlie yelled. "Where the fuck are you?"

"Oh, shit," Draco muttered, getting to his feet. "You wanna run out the back, we'll tell her we never saw you."

"Why the fuck would I do that?" I asked, staring at him.

"Bishop," Charlie yelled again. We could hear her stomping toward us.

She stepped into the kitchen and I knew exactly why Draco had given me the option to run. Charlie was furious. Her hair was a tangled mess, her jaw was tight, and her hands were hanging in fists at her sides. She looked ready to deck me.

"What's up, Charles?" Kara asked easily, still sitting at the table.

"Did you go to my dad today?" Charlie yelled, pointing at me. "Are you out of your fucking mind?"

"I—"

"You know what," she said, still yelling. "Don't answer that. I already know you did, you little rat fink."

"Did she just call him a rat fink?" Draco asked Kara, trying to hold back a laugh.

"I'm at work all day—"

"Apparently, spilling your guts to my dad," Charlie said, cutting me off. "Did you also tell him about the sex we had while you two were braiding each other's hair?"

"Ooh, burn," Kara said quietly, grimacing.

"Someone needed to know about it," I replied, glancing at Draco, who all of a sudden seemed very interested in the conversation.

"I told you that in *bed*," Charlie snapped. "In confidence—or at least I thought it was. How dare you go to my dad."

"I didn't know it was a damn secret," I replied. Suddenly, I wasn't feeling confused or defensive. I was starting to get angry too. Who just came in yelling at someone without asking about the situation? I didn't deserve that shit.

"What the hell is she talkin' about?" Draco asked.

Charlie stared at me, daring me to reply.

"That cop who was messin' with Kara is going to the coffee cart a couple times a day, every day."

"The fuck he is," Draco spat.

"Not every day," Kara said, turning to look at us. "He doesn't go when I'm there."

"He knows better," Charlie replied.

"But he doesn't know better than to stay away from you," I pointed out through my teeth.

"And you thought you needed to clarify that?" Charlie asked, letting out a derisive laugh. "Who the fuck do you think you are?"

"A friend," I replied, instantly. "Your friend."

"You're a fucking narc," she said, shaking her head. "That's what you are. I *told* you I could handle it."

"You weren't handling it," I countered. "You were just accepting it."

"He hasn't done anything wrong!"

"Why the fuck is that asshole goin' to the coffee cart at all?" Draco asked furiously. "I know he was told to stay the fuck away."

I looked Charlie over as she tried to formulate a reply to Draco's question, and I was suddenly furious.

She was wearing a tank top with a pair of cutoff jean shorts that were so short and frayed that the pockets hung out the bottom. On any other day I would've taken a moment to appreciate the beauty of those shorts, but I couldn't see past the massive bruise that took up her entire thigh.

"Why the fuck don't you have a bandage on your leg?" I asked, my voice level.

Charlie's head turned slowly in my direction and I knew it was the wrong thing to say.

"Because I had to take a motherfucking shower and Molly said that letting the wound get some air was totally fine," she said, talking slowly like I wouldn't be able to understand her otherwise. "Not that it's any of your goddamn business."

"Damn, Charles," Draco said with a hiss. "That looks painful."

"You know what's painful?" Charlie asked through clenched teeth. "Having your father pull up on his Harley and sit outside your work, watching. All fucking day. Not visiting or getting coffee or making himself useful—*watching*."

"Bet that asshole didn't show up, did he?" I asked.

"No," Charlie snapped. "He didn't. Which was two sales less than I had yesterday and it doesn't even fucking *matter* because my dad can't sit outside the shop every goddamn day!"

"Why didn't you say something?" Kara asked, watching Charlie with her arms crossed over her chest. "You know what a menace that guy is. You should have told someone."

"I told Bishop!"

"And now you're bitching him out because he told someone else," Kara pointed out. "When we all should have known to begin with."

"That's rich, coming from you," Charlie replied shortly.

"Careful," Draco warned her. "You're not even mad at Kara."

"You're right," Charlie replied. She looked at Kara. "I'm not mad at you."

"Well, I'm mad at you, you idiot," Kara shot back. "You should have said something. That asshole lost his job. You know he isn't going to take that lying down."

"He hasn't acted like it affected him at all," Charlie replied.

"Just because he hasn't done anything yet, doesn't mean he won't," Kara said. "You know that. You remember when my parents were kidnapped. You know shit doesn't always happen right away. Sometimes it festers first."

"He's not going to fucking kidnap me," Charlie said, throwing her hands in the air. "He's annoying and a blowhard and he asks me out constantly—he's never once done anything that freaked me out."

"Stalking me wasn't enough?" Kara asked.

"I'm not you," Charlie replied stubbornly.

"What does that mean?" Kara said quietly.

"You're soft, Kara," Charlie replied, not unkindly. "You're quiet and kind and—"

"An easy target," Kara said flatly. "Is that where you're going with this? Because I don't tell the world to fuck off constantly, I'm an easy target for assholes."

"Kara," Charlie breathed, her voice apologetic.

"You're my best friend, Charles," Kara said flatly. "And when he couldn't get to me anymore it sounds like he went to the next best thing."

"Ouch," Charlie replied.

"Don't act offended," Kara snapped. "You know what I mean. What better way to continue fucking with us than to start bothering you?"

"He's not bothering me," Charlie replied. "That's what I'm saying! He's just coming through for coffee and then he leaves."

"He doesn't come when Kara's there," Draco said, his voice low. "He come when anyone else is working?"

Charlie paused. "Well, no," she replied. "But—"

"You're not stupid, Charlie," Draco barked. "Don't act like you are."

"Fuck off."

"Jesus," Kara said quietly. "I thought we were done with this asshole."

"It's never done with guys like that," Draco muttered. "They just get quiet for a while before popping up again like herpes."

Charlie opened her mouth and Draco lifted a hand to stop her from speaking. "No, I don't have herpes and you're not funny."

"I don't even know why we're having this conversation," Charlie said, looking over at me. "I came home to rip Bishop a new one."

"Why aren't you at work?" Kara asked.

"I closed up for the day because I didn't have any customers."

"What? None?" Kara asked. "Not even the after-school crowd?"

I saw something flicker over Charlie's expression, but it was gone in an instant.

"No one was coming in with my dad glaring at every car that passed by," she said, without missing a beat. She looked at me again. "I have you to thank for that."

"If you're expectin' me to apologize, it's not gonna happen."

"Of course it isn't," she said, shaking her head. "Because you're a man and it doesn't even occur to you that I didn't fucking ask for your help and you ignored the fact that I told you it wasn't a problem."

"Have you not heard a word I fuckin' said?" Draco asked in admonishment.

"Have you not heard a word I said?" Charlie countered. "You're overreacting to *nothing*."

"Charlie, he's a bad guy," Kara said, clearly frustrated with her best friend.

"I don't ask for references when I'm serving fucking coffee," Charlie replied. She shook her head tiredly. "I'm going to bed. I'm tired as fuck and I'm opening with you in the morning."

She left the room a lot quieter than she'd entered, and we all just stood there, wondering what the fuck had just happened.

"I'm gonna call my pop," Draco finally said, kissing Kara before striding out of the room.

"On a scale of one to ten," I asked Kara.

"Fourteen," she answered before I'd finished the sentence. "If you're going to try and talk to her now, wear a cup."

She turned back to her schoolwork and picked up a pen so I figured I should probably leave her to it. I went upstairs slowly, taking my time to make sure that I didn't cross paths with Charlie again, at least not until I figured out what I was going to say.

Honesty was generally the best policy, but I wasn't sure I wanted to get into it all when she was still so pissed. I understood why she'd been frustrated. She hadn't asked me to go to her dad and I'd probably crossed a line there—but had she really expected me to do nothing?

I stripped off my shirt as I walked into my room, closing the door softly behind me. I was covered in grime from working, but I wasn't about to shower in the bathroom I shared with Charlie…even though it had worked out pretty well for me the last time she was angry. A change of clothes was going to have to be enough until I could shower before bed. I'd just changed my underwear when my door swung open and Charlie stepped inside.

"Look," she said, brushing her hair out of her face in frustration. "I think we need to take a step back from whatever this is."

"A step back," I replied dryly. "Did we ever take a step forward?"

"I was so clear," she said, shaking her head. "I told you I didn't have time for this. You know I don't."

I just stood there. It had become such a common refrain that I wasn't even surprised. She was busy as fuck. I got it. We all got it. We fucking *saw* it.

"The drama is too much, alright," she said tiredly.

"Drama?"

"Going to my dad, Bishop?" she said with a scoff. "Really?"

"Someone needed to know what was going on."

"I have it handled," Charlie replied through her teeth. "I told you that and you ignored it and now I'm going to have the entire club on my ass, just adding on to the shit I was already dealing with."

"What shit?" I asked, frustrated. "If buyin' a fuckin' coffee cart makes you this overwhelmed then maybe you need to think of another life plan."

She looked like I'd just slapped her and I was immediately sorry.

"I'm just—"

"No, I know," Charlie said with a sad laugh. "The thing is, it shouldn't be. The numbers were good. Everything was good when I bought the place, and now it's tanking. No one is coming through. We barely have any customers and I can't figure out what the fuck is going on."

To say I was shocked was an understatement. Yeah, I'd known that she was stressed—but by the look on her face it was so much more than that. Charlie looked defeated.

"If I can't turn it around—I'm toast," she said calmly. "All those savings, gone for nothing."

"Holy shit, Charlie," I mumbled, unsure of what to say.

"I'd appreciate it if you kept *this* conversation to yourself," she said tiredly. "My parents already know."

"Hasn't Kara noticed?" I asked in confusion.

"I only put Kara on the morning shifts," Charlie replied with a rueful smile. "We still get a steady stream of cars then. It's just not enough to sustain the business without the afternoon traffic."

"What are you going to do?" I asked, dropping my ass to the bed.

"I don't know," she said softly. "But I'll figure it out."

"Let me know if there's anything I can help with."

"That's sweet," she replied with a laugh. "I'll expect you shirtless and waving a sign in front of the shop tomorrow."

I glanced down at myself, sitting in my damn underwear.

"I'm joking," Charlie said. "Mostly."

"If I didn't have to work," I replied with a shrug.

"This was good," Charlie said, gesturing between us. "It could be really good. End of the line, white picket fence kind of good. I just don't have it in me right now."

"Alright," I said.

"I'm sorry," she said hoarsely. She tapped on my doorframe. "I'll see you later, okay?"

She left the room and I got a sinking feeling in my stomach. When I'd thought she was dodging me before, I'd been pissed. This wasn't that. Charlie wasn't playing games—she was being honest. She was into me. She knew we'd be good together. She just didn't have the time or inclination to start something real with me.

She had time to fuck me when it fit into her schedule, but beyond that, she was out.

I was actually kind of stunned by it. I don't think I'd ever been in that position before—I'd never been the person wanting more than the other was willing to give.

Which really fucking sucked because I was pretty sure I was in love with her.

Chapter 13
CHARLIE

"Maybe you should move the cart," my dad said seriously, looking over the paperwork I'd brought over. "I know you talked about opening a new shop on Tommy's property, but maybe the better move would be to move the existing cart."

"It would make things pretty awkward at club barbecues when I have to default on rent," I said sarcastically.

"Could be, you wouldn't be defaulting on anything," my dad said. "New customer base."

"But then I'd be losing all the regulars we have now," I replied, playing devil's advocate. "They're all we have left at this point."

I got to my feet and started pacing my parents' little camp trailer. I felt like I was going to come out of my skin, I had so much nervous energy. It had been three weeks since I'd put a pause on anything between Bishop and I—and I was feeling it. He was polite when we crossed paths. He was *friendly*. And I was dying. He didn't look at me the way he used to. The affection was still there, the kindness, but the fire was gone. In the past I would have flirted, made a comment that I knew would bring it back—but I knew that was unfair. He was giving me the space I'd asked for and pulling him back in when literally nothing had been resolved would be a shitty thing to do. No matter how much I regretted the decision, I still knew it was the right thing.

My mom had always told us kids that with the right one, things would work themselves out. It might take time and it might really suck, but in the end, it would all set itself right. I'd seen the truth of that. Poet and Amy had been separated for most of their adult lives. When my aunt gave birth to Will, my uncle had been in jail. Hell, even Draco and Kara had been apart for years while he was in prison and they'd still figured it out. I was counting on the fact that for better or worse, I'd figure out the work stuff soon and I could go back to Bishop with my proverbial hat in hand and beg him to be with me.

I mean, maybe I wouldn't beg. Maybe I'd just strip down and climb in the shower with him again and tell him that I was all in. He'd probably like that better than begging anyway. Though, if I was on my knees—

"Charlotte," my dad snapped. "Focus."

"What did you say?" I asked, coming to a stop by their little table.

"I said that I think it's the best move," my dad said, leaning back in his seat. "You'll be closer to the club and get that traffic. Plus, the traffic is thicker on that corner than the one you're currently on. Baby girl, I think that you need to make a big move. If you don't—"

"I'm toast," I said, dropping down across from him.

"You're gonna be in real trouble," he confirmed.

"I just can't figure it out," I said, throwing my hands in the air. "There was plenty of traffic before. How the fuck did things change so fast? I haven't made any changes from when Mal owned the place beyond some new cups and one new drink on the menu!"

"I don't know, kid," my dad said, shaking his head. "Your mom says you're postin' on social media and getting' the word out. To be honest with ya—it's not makin' much sense."

"It probably didn't help that you guys keep parking and watching me all damn day," I muttered.

My dad shot me a look. "We stopped last week," he replied. "You get a sudden surge in sales?"

"No," I muttered.

"That's what I thought," he replied. "He been back?"

"Nope."

"Good," he said. "Looks like he can take a hint. Which surprises the fuck outta me."

"He probably will," I said honestly. "Just as he realizes you won't be back."

"He stops by the shop, you—"

"Call you," I said, cutting him off. "I know."

"You ever see me overreact?" my dad asked seriously.

"You're one of the most logical people I know," I replied with a sigh.

"Probably true," he said. "So, you see me overreact?"

"No," I replied. "Except if mom's shaking her ass on top of a pool table."

Dad laughed. "Even that's not an overreaction," he said, shuffling the papers on the table in front of him. "Only reason she climbs up there is so I'll come get her."

I made vomiting noises, dramatically bending at the waist and heaving.

"We were young once, you know," he said with a grin.

"I prefer not to think about it," I replied.

"Here's the thing, Charlie," my dad said, his tone growing more serious. "You need to cut down on what you're buyin' and streamline the menu options. Cut costs there, first. Keep the prices the same, 'cause you don't have the cash for a new sign. And you gotta get some more traffic comin' through the shop. You don't have that, none of the rest of it is gonna help you."

"Okay," I said.

God, I was so tired. When I wasn't working, I was thinking about work. When I was asleep, I dreamed about it—waking up in the middle of the night so I could go over numbers again. I couldn't believe that my big plan, the one I'd thought through for months, was failing.

I didn't fucking fail.

"You head over and talk to Tommy right now," my dad ordered. "He's at the garage and I told him you'd be stoppin' by."

"He's gonna give me shit," I complained, getting to my feet.

"Probably," my dad said, handing me the folder of papers. "But he'd give you the fuckin' moon if you asked for it and you both know it, so take the shit and say thank you when he eventually tells you yes."

"Yes, father," I said, leaning down to kiss his forehead.

"Your ma might be there," he said as he followed me out of the trailer. "Tell her I'll be there soon."

"Why is she at the clubhouse?"

"Bringin' me lunch," he said with a chuckle. "She didn't know I was meetin' you today."

"It wasn't a secret," I replied as he walked me to my car.

"I know, I just didn't want her here," he said, shooting me a grin. "They're deliverin' that claw foot tub today that she saw at the vintage place up north a couple months ago."

"The one she kept talking about?" I asked, my jaw dropping. "I thought you told her it wouldn't work."

"I lied," he said easily. "It's a surprise, so keep it to yourself."

"I will," I promised. "She's going to shit!"

I couldn't keep the smile off my face as I headed for the Aces compound. I wanted a relationship like my parents,' even though they grossed me out on a regular basis. They were so good to each other.

When I was growing up, it had been weird as one of the kids of the town's notorious motorcycle club. There'd been talk—I was pretty sure all of us had dealt with it in one way or another. Parents didn't want their kids playing at our houses. They called us worldly—as if that was a bad thing. Looked down their noses at us when they saw us at school events. But by the time I was a teenager, I realized that it was all bullshit. I'd had the most stable life out of any of my friends. Their parents cheated, split up, lost their jobs and houses. While mine, well, they just kept on loving each other and us kids. Outside forces may have made our lives harder in some ways, but our family unit was unshakeable. Most kids didn't have that.

You really can't judge a book by its cover.

My dad must have called him, because Tommy was waiting outside for me when I got to the club.

"Your pop said you needed to talk to me," he called out from his seat on one of the picnic tables. "You've got as long as it takes for me to finish this." He held up a smoldering joint and waved it from side to side.

"I better hurry, then," I said dryly. I started talking as I walked toward him, and by the time I'd reached him, I'd lined out exactly what I wanted and how much I was willing to pay him. I was hoping that by laying it all out quickly, he wouldn't have the opportunity to argue with every single word I said… maybe just the big points.

"Sounds good," he said easily.

I jerked in surprise.

"You'll have to go fully organic and make sure you have vegan options," he continued, making my jaw drop open.

"I—what?"

"Or just organic options," he said, waving his joint around. "And vegan ones. Vegans are no animal products, right? You can do that. Coffee comes from beans."

"Back up," I said, struggling not to laugh.

"The main building is gonna be one of those hippie dippie health food stores," he replied.

"It's tiny."

"I'm guessin' they don't have much variety," he said dryly. "The price was right."

I stood there staring at him, this man I'd known my whole life, that I'd seen eat four fast-food cheeseburgers in less than ten minutes, who treated his body like anything but a temple.

"Heather's putting you up to this, isn't she?" I asked finally.

"Woman's about to bankrupt me," he said, shaking his head. "Whole house is filled with organic shit. I'm hopin' they'll give us a discount."

I couldn't hold back the laughter any longer.

"Just sayin,' that off brand cereal she buys tastes nothin' like the real stuff," he said with a scoff. "It tastes like ass, Charlie."

I kept laughing. I couldn't help it.

"She's sayin' she might stop dyin' her hair because of the chemicals."

I snorted.

"I don't even know what her real hair color *is*," he continued.

"Wait it out," I said finally, gasping for air. "She won't be able to maintain it."

"I fuckin' hope not," he replied, dropping the last bit of his joint on the ground and pressing the toe of his boot on it. "Send me the paperwork and we'll get you all set up. There was a cart there a few years back, so you should be golden."

"Thank you," I said, throwing my arms around him.

"You're welcome," he said grudgingly, hugging me back. "I'll expect free coffee."

"I'll expect free rent," I countered.

"I'll pay for the coffee."

"I thought you would," I said, letting him go.

He went back into the garage and I skipped over to the clubhouse door, swinging it open with a huge grin on my face.

I mean, sure, going partially organic was going to cut into profit when I couldn't really handle it—but if there was a new health food store going in where I thought was going to be a mini-mart—my prospects were looking a whole lot better. People were going to want coffee while they shopped and there was going to be way more traffic than I'd thought. I could totally make it work.

"What are you so happy about?" my aunt Callie asked, grinning back at me from a table near the door.

"Your son is going to rent me space for the cart," I said excitedly, sitting down across from her and my uncle Grease.

"Was that ever really in question?" Uncle Grease asked with a laugh.

"I thought dealing with him would be a lot harder than it was," I replied dryly, making them both chuckle. "Have you seen my mom?"

"I told her that her bathroom looked nasty, so she's in there cleaning it," Aunt Callie said easily, waving her hand in the direction of my parents' club room.

"Dad told you about the tub," I said quietly.

"When she saw he wasn't here, she was going to go home and find out what the holdup was," she said, rolling her eyes. "I had to stop her somehow."

"Sneaky," I replied.

"It was that, or let this one start an argument," she said, pointing at my uncle. "and I didn't want to listen to them." Aunt Callie shrugged. "Go tell her your news, I'm sure she's almost done."

I found my mom scouring the sink wearing rubber gloves that went up to her elbows.

"Whatcha doing?" I asked, making her shriek in surprise.

"Cleaning this damn sink," she replied. "I swear, I'm going to talk to the cleaning lady. We pay her really well to do this shit for us."

"Be nice," I replied. "Sue is awesome."

"She is awesome," my mom confirmed. "That's why I don't know why this sink looks so fucking nasty." She sighed. "What are you doing here in the middle of the day?"

"I had to come talk to Tommy," I replied.

"Your dad told you about his idea to move the cart?"

"It's a good idea," I said, leaning my hips against the counter. "I should've thought of it."

"Hard to come up with good ideas when you're drowning," my mom said sympathetically. "What did Tommy say?"

"He said I have to go organic," I replied with a huff of laughter. "I guess they're putting in a health food store."

"Heather," my mom said, getting it right on the first guess.

"Yep. But he agreed to the rental terms and told me to get him the paperwork."

"That's good," my mom said happily. "How do you feel about it?"

"Excited," I said, cautiously. "Optimistic for the first time in over a month."

"Good," she said, peeling off the gloves. "You should be."

"I don't know what the fuck is going on, mom," I replied quietly. "Why can't I make this place work? I'm doing everything right."

"I don't know, kid," she said, throwing her arm over my shoulder. "But don't panic yet. We'll figure it out. Moving is just going to be the first step—your new space is going to be so rad, you won't know what to do with all those customers."

I spent almost an hour with my mom, thinking up new drinks and ways to stand out in the new spot, and by the time my dad got there for lunch we'd agreed to paint the outside of the cart and were still debating on changing the name to something a little more my style.

"You talk to Tommy?" my dad said, stepping into the room.

"Did you know he was putting in a health food store?" I asked.

"He'd mentioned it," he replied, going over to give my mom a kiss hello. "Should be even better for you."

"Than a mini-mart?" I asked with a smile. "Uh, yeah. You know the people around here love a good granola bar. We'll have way more traffic."

"You bring lunch?" my dad said, still looking at my mom.

"Subs," she replied, smiling up at him. "I threw them in the mini-fridge."

"Good, I'm starvin.'"

By the way he'd said the last few words, I knew that I needed to bail. Quickly.

Gross.

I said my goodbyes and left them smiling at each other like a couple of newlyweds. Since I'd already worked that morning, I had the rest of the day to get shit done—namely cleaning out my car and stopping by the pharmacy for a new bottle of lotion that Molly had recommended. I ran my hand down the new scar on my thigh as I drove back toward town.

Bishop had been right to be concerned about the stupid thing. Less than a week after my graduation party, I'd woken up with it hot to the touch and red as a cherry. Thank God I hadn't tried to get Molly to stitch it up, because they'd had to debride the nasty thing to clean it out. A heavy duty dose of antibiotics had kicked the infection, but by the time it started healing, I had a pretty gnarly scar to remember it—much worse than the original scratch. The lotion Molly had recommended was supposed to help the scar fade, but I wasn't super worried about it. I just hoped it would help with the way it itched as the skin healed.

After stopping at the pharmacy and the grocery store for a few things, I ran to the car wash and was in the middle of vacuuming out the back seat when my phone rang.

"What's up?" I asked, out of breath and still bent into a pretzel trying to reach the back floorboard.

"Are you coming home soon?" Kara asked ominously.

"I was just finishing up the car, why?" I asked, sitting up.

"I'm at the school. I'll be home in twenty. Meet you there?"

"Is everything okay?" I asked, getting worried.

"I'm fine. Draco's fine," she replied.

"You're freaking me out."

"Don't be," she said, sounding angry. "Meet me at home."

"Okay," I said, surprised when she hung up abruptly.

I didn't bother finishing the car. If she would be home in twenty, I wanted to be there when she got there. I couldn't think of any reason she'd be so fired up to meet me back at the house, and it drove me crazy. Did it have something to do with Bishop? I'd caught a glimpse of him when I'd gotten to my parents' house that morning, and he'd seemed fine.

Fine as hell, actually, wearing that fucking tool belt.

I beat Kara home by ten minutes.

"Charlie, where are you?" she yelled as she stormed in the front door.

"I'm on this fancy ass couch you bought," I replied, looking over the back of it. "What the hell is going on?"

"I was in my last class and we were talking about our favorite coffee places, and I said yours of course—"

"Obviously," I replied.

"And they started talking about how I shouldn't go there because you had all of these health code violations."

"What?" I yelled.

"Yeah," she said, throwing her bag down. "I was like, I work there and we've never had a single violation."

"What the fuck?"

"They said that someone at this other coffee shop is telling everyone about it and that it's all over the community pages that when Mal sold to you it all started going downhill—"

"That's bullshit!"

"I know that," she yelled back. "I told them that! They were talking about rats and bugs and mold and—I was so pissed I wanted to scream. There's all this bullshit going around and we had no fucking clue."

"What the fuck?" I whispered in confusion.

"I don't know," Kara said. "I don't know who would say that shit. Why would people even believe them?"

"Because people are sheep," I replied, pulling out my phone. "Jesus Christ, this explains it."

"Explains what?" she asked, dropping down beside me.

"That sales are so bad," I replied, trying to remember my sign in for the community pages. I'd deleted the app after one too many *stop letting your dog shit in my yard* posts, and I hadn't even thought of it since. No one I knew even used it, because we didn't give a shit. If we wanted to talk to our neighbors we talked to them. If we wanted to know when a business was open, we fucking Googled it.

"Sales are bad?" Kara asked in confusion, taking the phone out of my hand. "What are you talking about?"

"Sales have been shit," I said with a sigh, falling back on the couch. "Like so bad, we might've had to close if I didn't figure it out."

"What the hell?" she asked. "Why wouldn't you tell me that? I've been asking for more hours! I feel like an asshole."

I laughed. "Why? I have to pay someone to work, might as well be you."

"You still should have told me! What the hell is it with you and keeping secrets? We tell each other everything, you jerk."

"It's different now," I said easily. "You and Draco are a unit."

"You're still my best friend."

"I know that," I replied, taking my phone back. "I just wanted to fix it before I told you how bad it was. Like, hey guess what happened, but don't worry, I figured it out."

"If I didn't want to know who the hell is spreading this shit so bad, we'd be having a much longer conversation," she said angrily as I tried to get into the community page again.

I shook my head. "I thought I'd gotten it all figured out," I said, glancing at her. "I talked to Tommy today and he's going to rent me the spot on that store property near the club."

"That's awesome!"

"Yeah, he's putting in a health food store and it would've been a great place—but not if everyone thinks my shop is a fucking health hazard," I said, my stomach sinking. "I thought it was just a traffic issue because I couldn't figure out why the sales were so bad. You know all those hippies are on the community app—it doesn't matter if my drinks are organic and vegan if they think we—"

"We'll fix it," she said, gesturing to my phone. "Hurry up and sign in."

It took me two more tries before I finally figured out my password, and when I put Coffee Now—yeah, Mal wasn't real original—into the search bar, more than ten posts popped up.

"Has anyone been to Coffee Now lately?" I read out loud. "I went to another place today and one of the girls who used to work there said it's really bad. Like, disgusting, since it was sold to the new owner." I looked at Kara. "One of the girls that used to work there?"

"Mary fucking Jones," Kara hissed, leaning closer to my phone.

"Or Tabitha," I replied, rage boiling just under the surface. I set my phone down on the couch and walked completely away from it. I couldn't afford to buy a new one if I threw it across the room.

"Because you *fired* them?" Kara asked in disbelief. "These people must know its sour grapes!"

"Clearly not," I replied, pulling my fingers through my hair. "Did you see how many comments there are on those posts? Jesus Christ."

Kara picked up my phone and started scrolling. "The girl says she quit because her conscience wouldn't let her serve people anymore. Oh, that *cunt.*"

"Not that I fired her because she was never on fucking time," I yelled at the ceiling. "I wonder which one it is."

"I bet it's Mary," Kara said, scrolling through the posts.

"I'd be surprised if Tabitha isn't the one doing the heavy lifting," I muttered. "She's the one who never has anything nice to say about anyone."

"Yeah," Kara said, her eyes still on the phone. "But she does it behind people's backs. This is just blatant out in the open *lying*. This says you switched the cups because rats had eaten through all the old ones and they were unusable."

"We ran out of the old cups and the new ones were cheaper and biodegradable!"

"Well, *I* know that!"

"This is un-fucking-believable," I said, laughing darkly. "I mean, it makes so much sense now—but holy shit. I cannot *believe* this."

"It's pretty fucking brave," Kara said angrily. "Does she think we'll just let her keep—"

"They've been doing this for months," I said, cutting her off. "And we had no fucking clue. Whoever it is probably thought I was too chickenshit to do anything about it."

"Well, what are you going to do now?" Kara asked. "You should comment on every single one of these posts."

"No," I replied, taking the phone back. "Don't say anything."

"Well, you have to tell people that none of this is true!"

"I'm not getting into a pissing match on the internet," I replied, shaking my head. "Then I look as bad or worse than they do. How unprofessional. I can't play into it."

"You have to do something," Kara argued. "Someone just posted about you again, yesterday."

"I know," I replied, tossing my phone onto the couch. "I'm just not sure what."

"This is libel," Kara said stubbornly. "You should sue."

"Neither of them have any money," I replied, laughing. God, what a nightmare. "What coffee shop did your friends say they heard someone talking about us?"

"That little place off the highway by the gas station," Kara replied. "I don't remember what it's called."

"Morning, Joe?" I asked, trying to picture the place.

"Yeah, actually," Kara replied. "How the hell did you remember that?"

"Mal knew all the owners of the shops around town. I think I have that guy's number."

"Oh, man," Kara said gleefully. "Call him."

"I think I will," I replied. I jogged upstairs to my room and pulled out the small notebook that Mal had given me when she turned over the business. Inside were names and numbers that she'd thought I might need. Everyone from other small business owners to suppliers and two different garbage companies, just so I'd have options.

I went back downstairs before dialing the owner of Morning, Joe.

"This is Rick," he answered after the first ring.

"Hey, Rick," I said, glancing at Kara who was grinning maliciously. "This is Charlie Butler, I own—"

"Coffee Now, right?" he asked. "Mal told me she'd given you my number in case you needed anything. How's she doing? Enjoying that retirement?"

"I think so," I said, relaxing a little. The guy seemed really nice and I was crossing my fingers he'd be willing to help me. "Listen, Rick, I *am* calling to ask you for help."

"What can I do for you?"

"Well," I said, pausing for a moment. "Do you have anyone named Mary Jones or Tabitha Gates working for you?"

"Both of them, actually," Rick replied, his tone a bit more cautious.

"Well, I've heard from—" Kara held up five fingers. "Numerous people that one or both of them have been telling customers at Morning, Joe that Coffee Now has a bunch of health code violations. We don't. We have an A rating and always have."

"Well, now," he mumbled. "I haven't heard—"

"People are posting about it on the community app," I said, not letting him hem and haw. "If you sign on and search our name, you'll see them."

"I can't control what an employee does on their off time," Rick said with a sigh.

"I know," I replied. "I'm just asking that you tell them to stop telling customers that when they're working. I mean, I understand that there is a bit of competition—"

"Let me stop you right there," Rick said kindly. "I don't consider you competition at all, darlin.' There's room enough for all of us as far as I'm concerned and I'd never tell an employee it was okay to bad-mouth another business."

"Thanks, Rick," I replied.

"I'll make sure it's known that any further talk about your shop—or any other for that matter—won't be tolerated, how's that?"

"That's all I'm asking," I confirmed.

"I'm real sorry about this," Rick said with a sigh. "What a mess."

When I hung up the phone, Kara was looking at me expectantly. "Well?"

"He says they both work for him now," I said, pacing.

"Then it could be either of them," Kara replied in exasperation.

"Or both."

"Probably both," she grumbled. "So, what do we do now?"

"Drive over there and put the fear of God into them?" I asked jokingly.

"Seriously tempting," she replied. "We need to think of a way to get the word out that the cart isn't a fucking health hazard."

"I don't even know how to do that without looking like we're on the defensive," I said, defeat making my shoulders slump.

I dropped down on the couch and pulled my knees to my chest. I'd been wracking my brain trying to figure out where all of my customers had gone, making tweaks here and there to try and save my business, working unending hours to save money—and I finally knew. Someone was sabotaging us and there wasn't much I could do about it.

"I'm going to get a snack, you want anything?" Kara asked, getting to her feet.

"No, thanks," I replied, laying my head on the back of the couch. Even the idea of food made me want to hurl. My guts were churning with anxiety.

I wanted to confront them. I wanted to tell them they were horrible and disgusting and mean—but I knew that wouldn't change anything. Mary and Tabitha were adults. They already knew what they were doing was shady as fuck—they just didn't care. They resented that I'd bought the business from Mal and they hated me for firing them—even though they didn't do their fucking jobs and deserved it.

What had Tabitha said to me when I'd fired her? Something about how I hadn't paid my dues yet—that I had no idea what running a shop actually entailed. I guess when I'd actually done okay, she'd needed to make sure that it didn't last.

It was too much. Finding out that my old employees were badmouthing me and I'd been too stupid to see it, that I'd been posting on social media non-stop but hadn't even thought of using the community app—it was the shit cherry on top of the diarrhea sundae.

"Kara," I called as I slowly got to my feet. "I'm gonna go lay down."

"What?" Kara asked in confusion, coming out of the kitchen with a bowl of ice cream. "No, stay, so we can figure this out."

"I'm exhausted, dude," I replied, waving her off. "Let's make a game plan tonight, okay?"

"Okay," she said slowly, unconvinced. I could feel her eyes on me until I'd rounded the stairs.

The cart would be open for a couple more hours, and I'd normally make sure that I was available in case something came up—but I didn't have it in me. I silenced my phone and set it on my nightstand before crawling into my bed fully clothed. For the first time in a long time, I fell asleep almost instantly.

Chapter 14

BISHOP

"Shhh," Kara hissed as I closed the front door behind me.

"Sorry," I replied, raising my hands in surrender. I was usually a little more careful about not letting it slam behind me, but I hadn't been paying attention.

"Charlie's sleeping," Kara said, walking toward me.

"She sick?" I asked, taking off my boots.

"No, just tired," Kara replied. Something in her expression seemed off, but I had no idea what it was and I didn't really have time to figure it out.

"Alright," I said, nodding. "I'll be quiet."

"Why are you in such a rush?" Kara asked, laughing as I hurried toward the stairs.

"Runnin' late," I called back over my shoulder.

"Hot date?" she joked.

"Somethin' like that."

I ignored the shocked look on her face as I continued up the stairs. I knew what she was thinking. And yeah, I still had a thing for her best friend. Who wouldn't? But Charlie had made it perfectly clear that she didn't want to start anything with me—and that was fine. It was her call and she'd made it.

But I was tired of sitting at home alone all the damn time. It was different when I'd been hanging out with everyone, and we'd had this whole sitcom roommates thing going. It wasn't like that anymore.

Charlie was always busy and Draco and Kara had their own shit going on and were usually studying or hanging out in their room.

It wasn't wrong for me to have a life. It wasn't wrong for me to make other friends. It wasn't wrong for me to date.

So, I'd been branching out. I'd started going out for a beer with a couple of guys I worked with and their girlfriends. I liked them. It wasn't as easy as hanging out with Draco and the girls, but it was better than nothing and I was fucking bored at home. A week before one of the girlfriends had brought along a friend.

One thing had led to another and this would be the second date in a week—I glanced at my watch—which I was going to be late for if I didn't haul ass.

Ignoring the way my stomach flipped as I glanced at Charlie's closed bedroom door, I grabbed some clothes and made my way quietly into the bathroom to shower.

Charlie and I had come to a happy medium, I thought. We didn't see each other much, but we didn't avoid each other either. We'd parted on good terms and I still considered her a friend. I wasn't mad, by any means. I knew she was overwhelmed by the shit she was dealing with, and even if I didn't understand why she thought that hooking up with me would make things harder for her, I was at least sympathetic to it.

I refused to feel guilty about seeing someone else.

If I kept telling myself that, eventually it would be true.

Fifteen minutes later I quietly shut the front door behind me and headed back out to my truck. I hated being late. I think it was probably something I'd picked up from Uncle Beau. *Gus, bein' late is the quickest way to show disrespect for the person waitin' on you.*

God, I missed that old fucker. Part of me was glad that he hadn't been around when I'd gotten sent up—that he hadn't had to see me like that. He would've been so pissed that my life had gone off the rails. I was pretty sure that he'd be happy with where I was at now, though.

Working with my hands, good friends, nice place. Hell, the downstairs of the house I was living in was bigger than our entire trailer. He would've gotten a kick out of that, even if I was living with three roommates.

At some point, I was really going to make him proud though. Make good money, have a place of my own, a sweet woman, maybe a couple of kids. Yeah, definitely a couple of kids.

I parked outside Tally's house and watched as she hurried out the door toward me.

Tally's kids?

I immediately dismissed the prospect. She was sweet and sometimes funny, but I couldn't see anything long term with her. Something just wasn't right. We didn't really fit.

"Hey," she said, climbing into the passenger side. "I almost called to see if you were still coming."

"Sorry about that," I murmured, leaning over for a kiss. "Got hung up at work."

"Construction, right?" she asked, pulling on her seatbelt as I backed out of her driveway.

"Yep," I said, glancing over at her.

She was pretty. Short brown hair that curled wildly around her face, big brown eyes, and when she smiled she was a stunner. I looked back at the road.

"That's the nice thing about my job," she said with a small laugh. "I start so early that I get off pretty early."

I nodded.

"But it sucks if I want to stay out late," she continued. "Do you want to still get dinner before the movie?"

I looked at the clock on my dash. "We probably have time to run through somewhere?"

"Works for me," she said, getting comfortable. "I'm starving."

We ran through a fast-food joint and ate in the parking lot of the movie theater. It wasn't exactly the date I'd had planned, but she seemed unbothered by the whole thing, which was nice. We didn't really know each other at all and spent the whole time talking a little about everything. She had an older brother. Her parents were still together. She'd lived in the same house her whole life, but she was planning on renting an apartment with a friend soon.

It was easy and natural.

And I was bored as hell, which I really hoped didn't show on my face.

By the time we got to our seats in the theater, I was ready to be distracted. Where was the spark I'd felt on that first date? Was it gone because this was the first time we were actually alone? The first time we'd gone out with my friend from work and his girl, too, and the conversation had seemed so much easier.

Halfway through the movie, I just wanted to go home and sleep. It had to be the most boring thing I'd ever seen.

"This sucks," Tally whispered to me, grimacing. "Do you want to just go?"

"Fuck, yes," I replied, making her laugh.

We hurried out of the theater, trying to duck so we wouldn't get in the way, but people still bitched anyway.

"The previews were so good," she said as we walked toward the truck. "Talk about false advertising."

"I was tryin' really hard not to fall asleep," I confessed, making her giggle.

"I don't blame you," she said, wrapping her arm around mine. "It was pretty snoozeworthy."

"Jesus," I said, shaking my head. "First I show up late and then the movie sucked. What a date."

"Well, it's not all your fault," she replied, smiling up at me. "I agreed on the movie."

It was the smile. Here I'd been ready to leave the whole fucking date, and then she smiled and I was, well, thinking that maybe I didn't want it to end quite yet.

"You want me to take you home?" I asked, stopping by the side of my truck. She leaned against it, her eyes on mine. "Or we could hang at my place for a while."

"Your place," she said instantly.

"You sure?"

"Definitely."

"Alright." I opened the door for her and stopped myself from leaning in for a kiss. I wasn't about to make out in a parking lot like I was sixteen years old and had nowhere to go.

"I just can't stay out too late," Tally said apologetically as we drove toward my place. "I have to be up early."

"No worries," I replied as she slid her fingers between mine. "I can drive you home whenever."

"You have roommates, right?" she asked as we drove.

"Yep." I nodded. Anxiety pooled in my gut and I tried really hard to ignore it. It wasn't a big deal that I was bringing her back to the house. Hadn't Charlie told me in the very beginning that she expected me to bring women home—or something along those lines? It was my place, too. I glanced at Tally. "But we can hang in my room."

"Hey, it's better than my house," she said with a laugh. "My parents are probably sitting in front of the TV watching some show way too loud."

I chuckled, but it was kind of weird to think she still lived with her parents. I knew she was close to my age, not a kid or anything, I just couldn't imagine living with parents. I'd been on my own for so long, I could barely remember what that was like.

"Nice place," she said as I parked in the driveway behind Kara's car.

"Yeah," I replied. "I got lucky."

"Lucky for sure," she said as she followed me out of the car. "I swear, we haven't even been able to find a two-bedroom apartment in our price range."

"Our landlord is my roommate's cousin," I explained as I walked her to the door.

"That explains it," she replied ruefully. "I'll try not to be too jealous when I see the inside."

"Remember, I've got three roommates, not one," I said, putting my hand on the small of her back as I led her inside. "Cuts costs quite a bit."

I could hear everyone in the kitchen, and I debated just ushering Tally upstairs and avoiding all of them, but I didn't want to seem like I was trying to hide her.

"Come on," I said, making a decision. "I'll introduce you."

I led her forward, and as we got closer to the kitchen Tally seemed to stiffen.

"They're cool," I said reassuringly in her ear as we crossed the threshold.

It was only as I lifted my head that I realized all conversation in the room had stopped.

Draco was sitting at the table, his arms crossed over his chest and Kara sat on the counter, eyes wide.

But it was Charlie who made me freeze in place.

She was standing in front of the sink in her rattiest pajamas, her hands hanging at her sides, and the look of complete betrayal written across her face.

Oh, fuck that.

"Guys," I said, clearing my throat. "This is—"

"Tabitha," Kara said flatly. "Yeah, we know."

"Hey, Kara," Tally said quietly.

"You've got a lot of fucking nerve, showing up here," Kara said, her voice still level as she hopped off the counter.

"You know each other?" I asked, glancing between Kara and Tally, then back over at Charlie, who hadn't moved.

"We used to work together," Kara said, tilting her head to the side. "Right, Tabitha? Until Charlie fired your ass."

In a split second, I knew shit was only going to get worse and I needed to get Tally out of there before it did. Obviously there was some bad blood between them, but she didn't deserve to be ambushed.

"Give me a break," Tally replied, her tone surprising the hell out of me. The woman I was getting to know was sweet as hell and—

"I've got to hand it to you," Kara said, clapping. "You've got balls."

"I didn't know you lived here," Tally replied.

"Well, now you do," Kara spat. "Get the fuck out of our house."

"I live here, too," I said, irritated. Whatever they had going on between them had nothing to do with me.

"Then pack your shit," Kara shot back. "And *you* can get the fuck out."

"Baby," Draco said, his voice quiet. "Calm down."

"I'm going to count to five," Kara said, ignoring Draco as she straightened her shoulders. "If you're not out, I'll personally throw your ass out."

"Is she kidding?" Tally asked me, stepping closer to my side.

"She's not," Charlie said, finally speaking up. Her face was completely devoid of color as she stared at us. "Get out."

I looked at Draco. "What the fuck, man?"

"Take her home," Draco said seriously.

"Let's just go," Tally said, pulling on my arm.

We turned to leave, and I was furious. I wasn't asking them to welcome her with open arms if they didn't like her, but they could've at least respected me enough to be fucking polite.

"Oh, and Tabitha," Charlie called, making Tally turn. "I've already talked to your boss."

Tally jerked in surprise.

"The next time you say shit about me or my business, you'll be out of a job and living with mommy and daddy forever," Charlie continued. "It's funny how fast word travels when you start telling tales. You might never find another job around here, at least not as a barista."

Tally sped back up and we left the house in a rush.

"I'm so sorry," I said as she climbed into my truck. "I don't know what the fuck—"

"Just drive me home, please," Tally said quietly, closing the door in my face.

We were silent until I'd parked in front of her house.

"That was fun," she said sarcastically, shaking her head. "I'm sorry, this isn't going to work."

"I'll talk to them," I replied. "I don't know what the fuck that was."

"It's fine," she said with a short laugh. "Call me if you ever move out."

She hopped out of the truck and I watched her as she jogged toward her front door. When I'd picked Tally up earlier, I'd been on the fence about whether or not spending time with her was going to be a thing, but now that someone else had blown any chance of that I was livid.

I drove home white knuckled and practically shaking with anger. What a fucked up thing to do to someone. She'd come home with me expecting a fun time and she'd been embarrassed and talked to like trash. Plus, the whole situation made me look like a complete asshole, which really pissed me off.

I took a few deep breaths before walking in the front door, but I shouldn't have even bothered, because the group in the kitchen had disbanded. Kara and Draco were curled up on the couch watching a movie and Charlie was nowhere to be seen.

"Not tonight," Draco ordered as I turned in their direction. "We can hash it out tomorrow, yeah?"

I huffed in disbelief, but I knew from the way he was looking at me that if I pushed it, things were going to be much worse than they already were.

I jogged up the stairs and into my room, closing the door behind me, like a teenager that had just been grounded. I grew more furious as I shed my boots and took off the flannel I'd worn out.

Fuck it. I wasn't the one who'd done something wrong. I wasn't going to hide in my goddamn room. Still fuming, I didn't notice the water running in the bathroom and threw the door open.

Charlie was standing at the sink washing her hands. She didn't bother to look up or acknowledge my presence.

"So, you're ignoring me now?" I asked, as she dried her hands and then reached down to rub her hip.

"Hello, Bishop," she said, emotionless. She turned to walk out her side of the bathroom.

"No apology?" I asked, bracing my hands on the door frame. "Seriously?"

"What exactly am I supposed to apologize for?"

I stared at her in disbelief. "You think it's okay to just treat people like shit?" I asked, leaning forward a little.

"You have no idea what you're talking about," she said flatly.

"I bring a date home and you're so fuckin' petty that you chase her out of the house?"

"Get over yourself," she replied evenly.

"You didn't want to be with me, remember?" I asked, taking a step forward. "You're too busy tryin' to save your sinkin' ship. Remember that conversation?"

Charlie made a noise, her entire body jerking. It was a huff of sound, a sob or a laugh, I couldn't tell.

"You're right. You fuck whoever you want," she replied. She cleared her throat. "While I save my sinking ship."

"What you did tonight was super fucked up," I replied, unwilling to end the conversation. How the hell was she acting like the victim here? She hadn't wanted to be with me. She'd said it over and over and when I fucking believed her and moved on, she sabotaged my fucking date and made me look like a jerk.

"You know, Bishop," she said with a sigh. "I'm really fucking tired. You wanna argue, you can do it with yourself."

"Oh, you're tired," I said, laughing under my breath. "Must be exhaustin' bein' a bitch to someone after you bought the business they worked at for years and then fired 'em." I knew it was a shitty thing to say, but I couldn't seem to help myself.

"That's enough," Kara snapped from behind me.

I turned to look at her, and in that moment Charlie closed the bathroom door and locked it from her side.

"What the fuck is wrong with you two?" I asked in disbelief.

"You're being a douche," Kara said, her voice rising. "Draco asked you to drop it for tonight."

"I live here, too," I replied, pointing to myself. "I pay fuckin' rent. So why the fuck do you and Charlie think it's your place to tell me who I can have over?"

"You want to get into this now, I see," Kara said. The sound of footsteps echoed up the stairs. "Alright, I'll lay it out for you."

"Dyin' to hear it," I muttered as Draco came and stood in my bedroom doorway.

"Your little girlfriend," Kara said, dragging the last word out. "Is a piece of shit."

Draco shook his head, but his lips were twitching. He'd clearly come upstairs to stop the argument, but after hearing his girlfriend's tone, had decided to watch the show instead.

"Yeah, Charlie fired her. Because she talks shit about literally everyone. Doesn't matter if it's true or a blatant lie, she does it."

I tried to imagine Tally being malicious or mean, and I couldn't, but I remembered Charlie talking about the employee she'd fired.

"She also never showed up to work on time and called in all the fucking time for no reason," Kara continued. "And yeah, whatever, that's all water under the bridge."

Kara stopped, her face red with anger. She was so mad, that her hands were in fists at her sides.

"But considering the fact that she's been badmouthing Charlie's business to anyone that would listen, telling people that the cart is infested with mold and rats and God knows what else," she said, getting quieter and quieter. "If you bring her in this house again I'll scratch her goddamn face off with my bare hands. Have fun fucking a woman with no face."

"What?" I asked stupidly. It was taking me a minute to catch up.

"She's been tellin' everyone that Coffee Now has all these health code violations," Draco said flatly, pulling Kara back against his chest. "It's why Charlie's been strugglin' to keep the place goin' and gettin' no customers."

I stared at him in confusion. "Why would you think it's her?"

"We *know* it was her," Kara said sharply. "Probably Mary, too."

"You got proof?" I asked, still skeptical.

"She didn't deny it," Charlie said from the bathroom.

She was standing there, still in her ratty pajamas, a look of complete dejection on her face that I'd been too angry to notice before.

"Of course she didn't deny it," Kara said. "She knew that we knew. That twatwaffle."

"You can still fuck her if you want," Charlie said with a humorless laugh. "We'd just prefer if you did it elsewhere."

"Charlie," I said, something landing hard in the middle of my chest.

The fact that she still thought I'd have anything to do with Tally, even after the stuff they were saying she'd done—

"I was going to tell you we figured it out," she said, her hand absently rubbing that same spot on her hip. "I mean, I have some damage control to do but pretty soon everything will be normal. No more long hours."

Fuck. Fuck. Fuck.

"I didn't—"

"No big deal," she said, cutting me off. "You didn't know she was a snake. Now you do."

"I wouldn't have brought her here if I'd known."

"No," she said, shaking her head. "No, I know that. It's all good, yeah? Sorry if we embarrassed you."

Kara made a sound of incredulity behind me, but I couldn't take my eyes off Charlie.

"I really am, tired," she said, smiling halfheartedly at me. "I'm gonna go to bed. Night."

She walked back out of the bathroom and closed the door softly behind her.

"You're a fucking moron," Kara said as Draco pulled at her arm. "You know that? That *bitch* as you put it—" she pointed toward Charlie's room. "Wouldn't let me call Tabitha and Mary out because she said it was unprofessional. She didn't want to stoop to their level."

"Come on, baby," Draco said, wrapping his arm around her shoulder. "Leave it."

"And then you brought her to our house?" Kara spat as Draco pulled her away. "We were nice to you. We invited you to live with us to get you out of the cabbage house and this is how you repay us?"

The only reason she didn't keep going was because Draco slung her over his shoulder and carried her down the stairs.

I stood there like an idiot for a long time trying to figure out what exactly had just happened. The woman I'd taken out a couple times was one of the people Charlie had fired? She'd been badmouthing the coffee cart and that's why Charlie was losing the business? Out of all the women I could've been introduced to—what were the odds?

I dropped heavily onto the bed, thinking of the way Charlie had looked at me when I'd walked into the kitchen that night, and it finally hit me.

She'd looked small.

Charlie wasn't big, she was shorter than anyone else I knew and petite—but she'd never seemed small to me.

I closed my eyes and pictured her near the kitchen sink, her hair pulled back in a messy bun, her big t-shirt almost hiding the old running shorts she wore. She hadn't been wearing makeup.

Charlie, who felt naked without at least a little makeup, had been standing barefaced in her own damn kitchen, when I'd brought in the person who'd been trying to put her out of business.

She'd been the one who was ambushed.

I *was* an asshole. I'd been so sure that Charlie was being a bitch because she was jealous that I'd treated her like shit. That was on me.

I got to my feet and strode out of my bedroom, not even pausing as I tried her bedroom door. For some reason it felt less like an intrusion because I hadn't gone through the connecting bathroom—but it was.

She was standing in front of the mirror against the wall, her shorts pulled down to her thighs and her shirt bunched up under her chin as she looked at a big red spot on her hip. As her head jerked up to look at me, my stomach sank.

"I do that?" I asked hoarsely. I don't know why I knew it, but I did. The red mark was at just the right height for a doorknob. I'd hit her when I'd burst into the bathroom and I hadn't even noticed.

"It was an accident," Charlie replied with a shrug, dropping her shirt as she pulled her shorts back up.

"Jesus," I said, stepping into the room. "I'm sorry, honey."

"We really need to start locking those bathroom doors when we're using it," she replied with a halfhearted smile.

"I was a dick," I said quietly, walking toward her. "Swear to God, I had no idea you guys even knew Tally."

"No, I know," she replied, waving her hand in dismissal. "It was just a shock, seeing her there all of a sudden."

She laughed, but the sound was husky and broken. "I mean, I didn't even know you were dating."

"Only a couple times," I replied, rubbing the back of my neck.

"None of my business," she said quickly. "I was pretty clear I didn't have time, right? It's not like I expected you to wait or anything."

There was no accusation in her tone, but with those words I knew—we both knew—that she *had* expected me to wait.

I wasn't sure what to do with that.

Defensiveness rose in my chest. I hadn't done anything wrong, not really. She hadn't wanted to be together even casually and I'd respected that. Had she expected me to just be alone because she chose to be?

The feeling was gone almost as soon as it arrived, because in that moment, looking at Charlie's expression, I knew she was holding on to her composure by a thread. If we were never anything else—she was still one of the best friends I'd ever had.

"Come here," I said, striding forward. She let me pull her against my chest, and she wrapped her arms around my waist with a shudder. Her forehead hit my sternum with a thud.

Seconds later, though, she was pulling away.

"You smell like her perfume," she said hoarsely, avoiding my eyes.

Chapter 15
CHARLIE

I KNEW IT wasn't fair, but for the first time since I'd met him, Bishop disgusted me. I reached up to wipe off my face, but I could still smell the fruity perfume that Tabitha wore. I hadn't liked it when she'd come to work and make the entire cart stink, but now it made my stomach churn with nausea.

"She was in my truck," Bishop said, lifting his t-shirt to sniff it.

"You're making the entire room stink," I replied, wiping at my face again. Had it rubbed off on me?

"Sorry," he said, taking a couple steps back. His brows were drawn together in confusion, like he couldn't figure out why I was being a jerk.

I honestly wasn't sure why, either. I just knew that I wanted him out. It wasn't fair—but who the hell said life was fair? While I'd been hustling trying to get my life back on track, not exploring what Bishop I had, he had been dating the woman who was the whole reason my life had gone to shit in the first place.

What a cosmic fuck up.

"Can you just go?" I said, hysteria bubbling up in my chest. I wasn't sure how much longer I could manage to keep my emotions in check.

"You want me to leave?" he asked calmly. I knew he was trying to diffuse whatever was happening, but there was no stopping it. My skin started to tingle and itch as I got another whiff of that fucking fruit perfume.

"Please," I said, waving him off. "Please, you stink."

He huffed in disbelief but he didn't move. He just stared at me like he was trying to figure me out. Finally, when I reached up and covered my nose with my hand, he turned on his heel and strode out the door.

The smell was everywhere. No matter how I waved my arms around and opened all the windows, it still seemed to linger. Finally, I decided that the perfume must have gotten on me somehow.

I hopped in the shower and scrubbed, tears of frustration rolling down my face. God, how stupid I'd been.

Knowing that someone was badmouthing me was bad enough. I'd been a jittery mess all night while Draco, Kara and I had tried to figure out the best way to fix the situation. By the time Bishop had shown up with Tabitha, I'd already spent half the night in tears.

The sense of betrayal was so strong that I had no idea how I'd get past it. I knew that he'd had no idea. I knew that he'd done nothing wrong. But logic had absolutely no sway when it came to emotion.

I wanted to hit him. I wanted to hurt him. I wanted him to feel the way I was feeling. To hurt as bad as I hurt. I wanted to scream at him. To make him feel as small and embarrassed as I did.

It scared me, this overwhelming urge to get revenge.

Tabitha and Mary and Bishop had gotten all tangled up together in my fury and I couldn't figure out how to untangle them.

I got out of the shower and toweled off quickly, throwing my hair up as I hurried back into my room. I couldn't stay in the same house with him. I needed to get out of there before I did something stupid. I got dressed, and without bothering to pack a bag, I left.

I cried the entire way to my parents' house. I wasn't sure if it was anger or frustration or hurt that had me practically sobbing, but I guessed it didn't really matter.

"The hell?" my dad asked, swinging the trailer door open after the third time I'd knocked. "Charlotte?"

"Can I stay here?" I asked.

"Stupid question," he grumbled, stepping out of the doorway.

I made my way inside, running my hands along the walls as I climbed the stairs in the dark.

"What's going on, baby?" my mom called from bed. I could hear her rustling around, and less than a minute later, she was there, wrapped in a hastily donned robe, her arms around me.

"It's been a shitty night," I replied, my voice wobbling.

"Who do I need to kill?" she replied, rubbing my back. "Don't worry, your dad won't let me get caught."

"You're too pretty for jail, Ladybug," my dad joked as he scooted around us.

"Figured out why the business is tanking," I said, my face still buried against my mom's shoulder.

"You did?" she asked in surprise, pulling far enough away to see my face.

"The girls I fired have been badmouthing the cart," I replied, the news no longer seeming as important as it had that afternoon.

"That can't be all it is," my dad said, coming back from their little bedroom area in a pair of jeans. I took a second to be thankful that he'd at least been wearing boxers when he'd let me in.

"I think it is," I said tiredly, letting my mom sit me down at the table. "They're working at another shop now and they've been telling customers that they left because Coffee Now is a health hazard."

"Huh," Dad said, sitting down across from me. "I don't know, baby girl. Seems like customers would take it with a grain of salt."

"They probably did," I mumbled as mom got us each a beer. "But then people started talking about it on the community pages and it took on a life of its own."

"I hate that fuckin' thing," my dad replied in disgust. "Just a place for assholes to bitch about each other."

"It used to be, the neighbors would just bitch to each other until they'd worn themselves out," my mom said dryly. "Now they've got a whole fucking audience."

"I'm not sure how I'm going to fix it," I said quietly, taking a sip of my beer. "How do you prove that you don't have mold and rats and shit? Take pictures? Invite customers inside?"

"Just don't get into it on the community page," my mom warned. "That'll just add fuel to the rumors."

"I know," I said in frustration. "Do you have any idea how hard it is not to call people liars? Some of them are saying that they saw shit when they came through. Uh, no, you didn't. That never fucking happened."

"That's why I don't have any social media," my mom said with a laugh. "I know that I wouldn't be able to keep my mouth shut. I'd be fighting with people all day long." She shrugged. "If I want to see someone's shit I just sign in on Callie's accounts."

"Smart," I said with a nod. My dad was quiet, but I knew he was paying attention. I knew that expression. He was thinking, looking at the problem from all angles as he figured out a solution.

I was just grateful that we finally knew the problem and actually had something to fight against.

"Ignore it," he said finally. "Ignore all of it."

"That's your solution?" my mom asked flatly.

"If you'd let me talk," he said, looking at her in exasperation. "We're gonna rebrand you."

"Rebrand her," mom said, unconvinced.

"Yep," dad said, smiling comfortably at me. "You were already plannin' on movin' to the new location. We'll just move up the timetable. You're gonna finish out the week, then we'll move the cart Friday night. Bring it here, change the signs, paint the outside, get her all spruced up. Monday mornin' you'll be in your new spot with a new name, in a shiny as shit cart, drawin' people in."

"You think she can just change the name?"

"I think that people have short fuckin' memories," Dad said. "And as long as no one keeps stokin' the fire, the talk will die out. They'll be talkin' about the old name on the community pages—that cart is no longer there, it'll quiet down."

"You really think that will work?" I asked in disbelief.

"I do," he said, nodding. "Hell, Charlie, I bet half of the people commentin' on those bullshit posts haven't even been to your shop. They just wanna be in on the action of tearin' someone down. Once Coffee Now is gone, they'll shut it."

"Unless someone mentions that I've moved the cart and renamed it," I muttered.

"You should advertise that you have," my dad said, leaning back in his seat with a grin. "New place, new look, new name, new drinks. They'll be crawlin' all over you to see what you've done."

"This seems like a Hail Mary," my mom said with a laugh. "But I kind of like it."

"Doesn't stop those girls from badmouthin' the new place though," my dad said thoughtfully.

"Oh, I think I handled that," I said, my lips twitching. "I called their boss."

"Oh," my mom's mouth dropped open in awe. She toasted me with her beer bottle.

"Narc," my dad joked.

"Hey now," I said defensively. "Mal gave me his number for a reason—I just didn't realize I'd actually need it. All I did was ask him to make it known that they weren't allowed to badmouth other businesses."

"Did he say he would?" my mom asked.

"He was a little reticent—"

"Good word," my dad interrupted.

"But he said he would."

"Nice," my mom said, nodding.

"And then," I grimaced. "Bishop showed up with one of them tonight, and when we kicked her out of the house I'm pretty sure we got our point across."

"He did what?" my mom yelled.

"Bishop," my dad said, pointing at mom. "That's who you're killin'."

"They'll never find the body," she replied darkly.

"I don't want you to kill him," I said in exasperation, leaning down to thump my head against the table. "Maim, maybe."

"What the hell was he thinking?" my mom asked in disbelief.

"He was thinking that he wanted to bring his date home with him," I replied around the knot in my throat. "He didn't know that we knew her."

"His date," my mom spat.

"It's fine," I said, leaning my head on her shoulder. "I told him that I had to much going on to date him—"

"Which one?" my mom asked. "Redhead or brunette?"

"Tabitha," I replied, still leaning on her. "Brunette."

"Ugh," she said in commiseration. "Pretty but mean."

"In a nutshell," I agreed.

"Stupid," my dad said, shaking his head slowly.

"He didn't know," I argued tiredly.

"He knows he's hung up on you," my dad said simply. "Takin' someone else out is stupid."

"Can't argue with that," my mom agreed.

"He's obviously not," I retorted.

"Please," my mom said with a laugh. "If he was any more into you he'd be following you around like a lost puppy."

"He's dating other people," I countered.

"Thought we already concluded that he's not firin' on all cylinders," my dad pointed out.

I didn't want to talk about Bishop. Not with my parents or anyone else. Not while the burn of betrayal still tingled under my skin.

"He'll come running back," my mom said reassuringly. "They always do."

"Maybe I don't want him to," I replied.

Both my parents started laughing. It was both annoying and infuriating.

"Charlie Bear," my dad said, reaching out to pat my hand. "Don't lie to yourself."

"He's banging other people."

"You love him," my mom said, rolling her eyes. "And you already know that he hasn't actually done anything wrong."

"One," I grit out through my teeth. "I never said I loved him. And two, he's clearly not in love with me if he's been banging Tabitha of all people."

"Men are idiots," my mom said, making my dad huff with laughter. "They'll bang anything when they're lonely."

"Low hanging fruit," my dad added. "If things are hard, we gravitate to what's easy."

"Watch it," my mom said, raising an eyebrow.

"Not sayin' she's easy," my dad clarified. "Don't even know her. I'm sayin' the situation with her was easy. No feelin' or stress. No commitment."

"I don't care," I said, smacking the table. "I don't care if he *technically* wasn't doing anything wrong. He can't stick with *easy*. Fuck him."

"Alright," my mom said firmly. "Fuck him."

"Fuck him," my dad repeated.

"I'm not bringing him coffee tomorrow," my mom announced.

"I'll spit on him," my dad replied. "What's he gonna do about it?"

"Ooh, that's a good one," my mom said, nodding. "I'll pretend like he's not even there."

"We won't even acknowledge him," my dad agreed. "Except the spitting."

"Just stay out of it," I ordered. "Both of you."

My parents both smiled.

"You're not funny," I grumbled. "None of this is funny."

"I know," my mom said, kissing the side of my head with a loud smacking noise. "But it'll all work out. I promise."

"Come on," my dad said, standing up. "Shit'll seem easier after you get some sleep."

"He's right," my mom said as she followed him.

A few minutes later, I was tucked in next to my mom. They hadn't even mentioned making the kitchen table into a bed, just got into their queen at the end of the trailer and scooted over so I could slide in next to her. It reminded me of when I was little and I'd crawl in with them after a nightmare. I always climbed in next to my mom, never my dad, because I'd needed them both but I'd always needed her more. I'd wanted her to know I was there so she'd wrap her arm around my waist and curl around me, protecting me from everything.

That night, even with the smell of my mom's hair in my nose, I couldn't find my way to sleep. I thought about how I'd revamp the cart, what colors I wanted to paint it, what supplies I needed to buy for the list of new drinks that I hadn't had a chance to make yet. I refused to let my mind wander to Bishop.

I wasn't ready to think logically yet. Thinking about Bishop was like prodding at a sore tooth, I couldn't seem to help myself and then as soon as I let my mind wander in his direction I remembered exactly why I didn't want to touch that particular soft spot yet. It was too raw.

I'd let myself believe that neither of us was interested in anyone else. That he'd wait. That it would all work out. It was my own fault, really.

I'd been so sure about us that I'd walked away, believing it would be temporary.

I was almost as angry at myself as I was with him.

I watched the sun come up behind the curtains and smiled as I heard my dad quietly get out of bed. He cursed under his breath as he dropped something heavy on the floor, and then I heard him curse again.

"I'm awake," I whispered, keeping my back to him.

"You get any sleep?" he whispered back.

"A little."

"Meet me outside in half an hour," he ordered, giving my foot a squeeze through the blankets. "I'll get us some coffee."

"Shit," I said, sitting straight up.

"Texted Kara for you last night," he said, reading my reaction. "She's openin' today."

"Fuck," I muttered, falling back on the bed. My mom huffed and rolled away from me, reaching for my dad's empty place in bed.

"Just relax," my dad said. "She's got it."

I nodded and stayed where I was as he left the trailer. I tried to relax, I really did, but within a few minutes, I was up and reaching for my phone. Kara answered on the first ring.

"You okay?" she asked, without bothering to say hello.

"I'm fine," I replied quietly, letting myself out of the trailer. I sat down on one of the lawn chairs out front and stared at the newly built house. "I just needed to get out of there. Sorry I didn't let you know."

"I don't blame you," she said flatly. "I heard you leave last night. Your dad texted before I could get worried."

"You're cool opening for me today?" I asked apologetically.

"Yep," she replied. "I didn't really want to stick around there either."

"Has it been busy?" I asked, holding my breath.

"Not really," she said quietly. "Steady, but not normal."

"I didn't really expect otherwise," I mumbled.

"I think we should start spreading it around that they spit in the drinks," Kara said conversationally. "Fight fire with fire."

I choked on a surprised laugh. "No way."

"I'm serious," she said. "I'm done letting people fuck with us."

"Bring it down a notch," I said, smiling. "I don't think they'll fuck with us anymore."

"Wanna bet," she said darkly.

"If they want to keep their jobs, they'll shut the fuck up about us," I pointed out. "Plus, Tabitha looked like she was going to shit herself last night."

"She showed a little backbone for a second," Kara said grudgingly. "And then she was trying to hide behind Bishop." She cackled. "Did you see that?"

"It's burned into my memory," I replied dryly.

"Yeah," Kara said with a sigh. "That whole situation was fucked."

"I told him I didn't want a relationship," I reminded her… and myself.

"Still," she said. "He didn't have to go out fucking crazy bitches."

"That's fair."

"And he brought her to our house? On what planet did he think that was going to go over well?"

"He lives there, too."

"Then he should move the hell out," she grumbled.

"Calm down," I said, comforted by the fact that she seemed even angrier than I was about the whole thing. "He can do what he wants."

Kara was quiet.

"My dad figured out how to save the cart," I said after a moment. "Well, sort of."

"Yes," Kara hissed. "He's going to scare the crap out of them, right?

Please tell me he's planning on going in to their work—no! He's going to their houses, isn't he?"

"Neither," I said, laughing. "We're going to move the cart and rebrand."

"Oh."

"We'll be at the new location starting Monday."

"Damn, Casper doesn't mess around," she said with admiration. "Well, put me to work. What do you need me to do?"

We talked for a few more minutes about how she could help and we hung up when my dad stopped by the cart for our coffees. I stayed in my spot, enjoying the sun on my face until he pulled back up in front of the trailer driving my mom's SUV.

"It's weird to see you driving that thing," I said as he strode toward me.

"Hard to pick up coffees on the bike," he replied with a grin. "I had Kara make you what she thought you'd want."

"Thanks, Pop," I said, taking the coffee cup.

"Your ma show her face yet?"

"Nope," I said, taking a sip.

"Figures," he replied. "If I didn't get her coffee she'd be up bitchin' that I hadn't, but since I did, she'll sleep until it's cold."

"I was just enjoying the quiet," I said, tilting my face back toward the sun.

"Yeah, it'll be nice to have the work finished around here," he replied, sitting in the chair next to me. "Boys won't show up for another hour, just so you know."

"Thanks," I said, glancing at him. "Not really ready to see him yet."

"Relationships are hard," he said, nodding. "Don't matter if they're just startin' or thirty years in."

"We're not in a relationship," I reminded him.

"You wanna be?"

"I don't know."

"Bullshit."

"It's not bullshit."

"It is," he said calmly.

"He was screwing around with other people," I said in frustration. "How am I supposed to just overlook that?"

"He cheat on you?"

"Not technically."

"That's right."

"I still don't think I can get past it," I snapped, getting to my feet. It didn't feel like a conversation I could have while sitting down. "When I think of him, all I think of is him screwing around with Tabitha. Where's the goddamn loyalty? I didn't want to be with anyone but him. I still can't imagine being with anyone else!"

"You told him you were too busy for a relationship?" he asked, waving me off when I looked at him in surprise. "I hear shit. No one around here can keep their trap shut. You give him a time frame? Tell him to wait?"

"No."

"You just expected him to read your mind, then," Dad said calmly.

"I expected him to not want to be with anyone else!" I practically yelled.

"Not a fair expectation, yeah?" my dad asked, a sympathetic smile on his lips. "You were expectin' the man to hang around alone while you figured your shit out—but you didn't tell him that."

"I know it's not logical," I spat. "That doesn't help how I *feel*."

"Guess you gotta figure out if feelin' betrayed and punishin' him is more important than actually bein' with the man," my dad said with a shrug. "Can't have it both ways."

"I hate having conversations with you," I said, dropping back down in my seat.

"Next time you and your mother can sit out here bitchin' about men and how horrible we are," he said, sipping his coffee.

"We can do that with you present," my mom joked, coming out of the trailer in her robe.

"Ladybug, workers are gonna be here in less than an hour."

"And?" she asked, taking her coffee.

"You gonna get dressed?"

"No one is going to see me in my robe, Cody," she said, rolling her eyes.

"Uh huh," he grumbled. "That's why you're already wearin' makeup?"

"You worry about you," my mom said dismissively, making dad chuckle. "How's my youngest and favorite this morning?"

"Tired," I replied. "Still mad."

"Yeah, I heard the last bit—"

"Were you eavesdroppin', Ladybug?" my dad asked in amusement.

"You weren't exactly quiet," my mom replied. She looked at me. "I get it."

"Thank you!" I said, sending my dad a pointed look.

"But your dad's right," she said with a shrug.

"Mmhmm," my dad said in satisfaction.

"You don't have to get past it today, kid," my mom said, grimacing. "But if you want to be with Bishop, you'll have to let it go eventually or you'll both be miserable."

"Could you both stop acting like I'm being crazy?"

"I don't think you're crazy," my mom said instantly. "I'd feel the same way you do. I'm just saying, don't wallow in it."

"I'll wallow if I want to," I joked.

"Change of subject," my mom said, smiling big. "What are you going to name the new cart?"

"Buy My Fucking Coffee," I joked.

"Hippies, Stop Here," my dad said.

"Not a Health Hazard!"

"Clean as Fuck, We Promise."

"Very funny," my mom said. "But really, any ideas?"

"Yeah, but it's nothing fancy," I said with a shrug.

"Hit me," my mom said, leaning forward.

"Charlie's Coffee?" I said with a self-deprecating laugh. "It's basic, but—"

"I like it," my dad said, cutting me off. "Simple."

"I do, too, actually," my mom said thoughtfully.

"Really?"

"Really," she said. "But, I mean, I named you."

"I should've thought of that," I said with a laugh. "But I also thought, I don't know, it's so close to the club and stuff, and it was your dad's name, too."

"Namin' it after the former president," my dad said with a smile. "Smart."

"Aces will *have* to stop by for their coffee," my mom said with a snicker.

"Well, I wasn't trying to be that sneaky," I said defensively as I laughed. "I just thought it was a nice thing to do."

"Sure," my mom said, drawing the word out.

"You guys are impossible."

"Where'd you think you got it?" my mom asked, reaching over to poke me in the side. "Charlie's Coffee—the alliteration is good. Plus, your dad's right. It's simple and the boys won't mind having it written on the sides of their fancy coffee cups."

"I'm going to have to order new stuff," I said with a sigh.

"We'll figure all that out later," my dad said.

At the sound of a vehicle on the gravel, we all turned to look down the driveway.

"Looks like Bishop couldn't sleep either," my dad said, getting to his feet. "Ready or not, Charlie Bear." He and my mom went inside, abandoning me before Bishop had even parked his truck.

Since I didn't feel like letting them eavesdrop, I walked toward the truck, meeting Bishop halfway. "I left for a reason."

"I told you I was sorry," he replied. "Not much more I can do."

"You're right," I said with a laugh. "So what exactly are you doing here?"

Looking at him hurt. Standing close to him hurt. The fact that he'd come to find me before work, hurt. It all hurt.

"I didn't know she was talkin' shit," he said with a sigh. "You know I wouldn't have gone near her if I'd known."

"I don't know how you could go near anyone," I blurted, frustrated. It wasn't just the fact that it had been Tabitha, though that had made it worse—it was the fact that he'd wanted to date anyone else at all that I couldn't see past.

"You wanted me to be alone," he said with a half-laugh. "Alright."

"I was alone," I pointed out.

"That was your choice," he bit out. "It wasn't mine."

"I'm sorry that I was overwhelmed and your little girlfriend—"

"I went on two dates with the woman."

"And your little *girlfriend* was trying to tank my business," I continued, ignoring him. "But here's the thing, I wasn't dating other people. I didn't want to see anyone else and clearly, you did."

"You know how fuckin' lonely it gets—"

"Oh, give me a break," I scoffed.

"No," he said flatly. "You've got a ton of family that you can hang with when you're bored. You've always got shit you could be doin' and I don't. I'm not from here, Charlie. I don't have never ending shit to occupy my time. I moved here because Draco's here and once I did, I was stuck."

"You're not stuck."

"My parole officer is here," he argued. "I'm here. My job is here. I'm here."

"How exactly is that my fault?" I asked.

"It's not your fuckin' fault." He looked up at the sky in frustration. "I'm sayin' that you told me you didn't want to spend time with me and now you're pissed that I was hangin' out with anyone else!"

"Well, *I* didn't want to hang with anyone else!"

"Jesus Christ!" he snapped. "Neither did I!"

"Could've fooled me."

"You were super fuckin' clear, Charlie."

"You're right," I said, throwing up my hands. "You're totally right. I was. Go, do whatever you want. Fuck your way through town."

"You're a fuckin' head case, you know that?"

"Cool," I snapped. "Then you're lucky you escaped while you could."

"For fuck's sake," he mumbled under his breath, walking away from me.

I stood there with my arms crossed as he walked to the end of his truck and back again, muttering the entire time. When he got back to me, he leaned down until we were nearly nose to nose.

"To be clear," he said precisely. "I didn't fuck anyone."

"Give it time," I shot back.

"You're actin' pretty fuckin' jealous for a woman who blew me off."

"You know exactly why I didn't want to start a relationship," I argued.

"That change?" he asked, his face still close to mine.

I wasn't sure how to answer him.

"Well?" he asked, unwilling to let me off the hook.

"We're moving the cart this weekend and rebranding," I said, dodging the question.

"You want to be with me, Charlie?" he asked flat out.

I couldn't even find the self-preservation to lie.

"Yes," I bit out. He reached for me, but I shied away without thought.

"What the fuck?"

I swallowed hard. It felt like there was a lump in my throat the size of Texas.

"All I see is you with her," I said quietly, shaking my head as I laughed at myself.

"We went on two fuckin' dates and one of those was with other people."

"It doesn't matter," I replied with a helpless shrug. "I look at you and I see you defending her. Getting in my face last night and calling me a bitch."

"Fuck," he said, looking down at his feet.

"My parents think I'm in love with you," I said, scrubbing my hands over my face.

"And what do you think?" he asked quietly.

"I think if I wasn't, this wouldn't hurt so bad."

"Honey," he said softly, reaching for me again.

"I'm not—" I put a hand out to stop him. "It doesn't change anything."

"It changes everything," he replied simply.

"Not for me," I said, taking a step backward. "Cause see, pretty sure I loved you before all of this." I laughed, the sound coming out broken and wrong. "But I thought it could wait until I had shit figured out." I closed my eyes. "But it wasn't the same for you. You didn't wait."

"What the fuck do you think I'm doin' here right now?" he asked, his tone making my eye pop back open. He was angry.

"I have no idea," I replied honestly.

"Charlie, you kicked me out of your room and said I stunk last night—"

"You did."

"And I still got my ass out of bed at the ass crack of dawn to come lookin' for you." He pointed at me. "You're actin' like a lunatic, and I'm still standin' right here."

"I'm not acting like a lunatic."

"Why do you think I'm here, honey?"

I stared at him.

"I love you," he said in exasperation.

"And dating someone else was how you decided to show it. Makes sense," I replied. Now I was angry again. How dare he say that to me when the night before he'd been with someone else?

"Jesus," he said, shaking his head as he glared at me. "We're just gonna keep goin' round and round."

"I guess we will," I said in defeat.

He wanted everything to be better, and I did, too, but I wasn't there yet. It was all too fresh. As much as I wanted to just step into his arms and let it all go, I couldn't.

"Listen, you know where I am," he said, finally. "I'm not goin' anywhere."

I bit back the words on the tip of my tongue asking how long he would wait this time before he gave up. As he headed toward my parents' new house, I stomped back to the trailer.

"That went well," my mom said dryly, leaning up from where she'd unashamedly been watching us from the window.

"Poor kid," my dad said from his seat at the table.

"I'm not even sure which of us you feel bad for," I replied. He just shrugged.

"You'll figure it out," my mom said as she strode toward their little bedroom area. "It always takes you kids a while to get your heads out of your asses."

I was so full of nervous energy that I rolled up onto my toes a few times.

"Hey, dad," I said, looking down at his shaved head. "Do we have to wait until the weekend to move the cart?"

"What are you thinkin'?" he asked, looking up at me.

"Can we get it today?" I asked, curling my fingers together under my chin. "It would give me more time to get it all set up and ready for Monday morning."

"That's actually a good idea," my mom called.

With a sigh, my dad pulled out his phone. "I'll call Grease and see if he can move it today. I think he's the only one with a truck big enough to haul it."

"You're the best," I said, leaning down to give him a hug, wrapping my arms completely around his head.

"We know what you're doing," my mom said, walking toward me as she buttoned her shorts. "And we're more than happy to help. But just saying, distracting yourself so you don't have to deal with Bishop hasn't worked all that well for you up to this point."

Chapter 16
BISHOP

I FELT LIKE an absolute asshole. There was no getting around it and I'd stopped trying to reassure myself that I'd done nothing wrong. If we were discussing technicalities, I guess I was in the clear, but that didn't really change shit.

I'd known in my gut that I shouldn't be taking anyone else out. Sure, it was fun in the moment, but all that time I'd known that if Charlie would've crooked her finger at me, I would've dropped Tally in a heartbeat. So, I hadn't been fair to either of them.

Taking Tally to the house had been such a moronic idea that half of me wished that Uncle Beau was around to thump me on the side of the head like he'd done when I was a kid and did something stupid.

Bottom line, I'd hurt Charlie, and that's what made my guts twist in remorse. Charlie, who'd never done anything to me except be honest about what was going on in her life and why she didn't have enough time to spend with me. Who'd gone out of her way to make sure that I had furniture, and bedding, and one of the best homes I'd ever lived in.

Instead of punching a hole into one of Casper and Farrah's new walls, I picked up a broom and started sweeping. It would be a while before the rest of the crew showed up and I had too much energy to sit there doing nothing. I needed to figure out how I was going to fix things.

I thought of the way Charlie had shied away from my touch and cursed, throwing the broom across the room.

"Hey now," Farrah said, stepping through the front door. "Careful in here, we're almost at the finish line."

"Sorry," I mumbled, slicking my hair back from my face.

"It's getting long," Farrah said, nodding toward my head. "I can cut it for you if you want, or my Cecilia can."

"Thanks," I replied cautiously. Didn't she know that I'd fucked up? Why was she being nice to me?

"I told Charlotte I'd ignore you," she said, leaning against the window ledge that faced the driveway. "But I'm pretty sure she didn't expect me to follow through."

"She's pissed at me," I replied with a sigh.

"With good reason," Farrah said easily.

I gave her a short nod. I wasn't willing to get into the details of what had happened between me and her daughter, and even if I had been—was I really going to tell her mother that I'd done nothing wrong when I knew that wasn't exactly true? Did I really think that I had room to defend myself?

"People don't realize how sensitive Charlie is," Farrah said conversationally. "They take her at face value, most of the time. Snarky. Strong. Tough. But my girl feels things deep even when she isn't showing it."

"I know that," I replied quietly. I'd seen it.

"She'll forgive you," Farrah said, looking around the room. "I doubt she'll even make you work for it. Charlie's always been quick to anger and even quicker to forgiveness. It drives me nuts most of the time."

"Not sure how to work for it when she doesn't even want me around," I replied.

"I'm sure you'll figure it out," Farrah said kindly. "And hey, if nothing else, be glad that you dodged a bullet with that girl you brought home. From what I've heard of her over the last couple of years, she would've sucked you dry and then told everyone how bad you tasted."

I choked on my own spit as she laughed.

"She didn't—I didn't—we—"

"She still might," Farrah said thoughtfully. "That one's never been good with the truth."

"Is Charlie okay?" I asked. "Kara said that the rumors are everywhere. I didn't really have a chance to ask them about any of it."

"Too busy shielding your soft parts, I'd imagine," Farrah said, raising her eyebrows. "Yeah, she'll be fine. She just went with Casper to move the cart. We're gonna bring it back here and spruce it up before we take it to the new location."

"She's moving it?" I asked, leaning against the wall. This was the first I'd heard of it.

"She's bringing it to that property that Tommy bought," Farrah said, waving her left hand toward where I guessed the property was located. "The new store is opening up next week and Charlie's *new* coffee cart will be all set up and waiting for customers."

"Nice," I replied. I tried to ignore the disappointment that Charlie hadn't told me the news herself. "Bonus, that cop won't have an excuse to stop by all the time now that she's halfway across town."

Farrah looked at me intently, like she was trying to make a decision. Finally, she smiled, but there wasn't anything happy about it. "Casper took care of that," she said calmly. "He won't bother her again."

I barely kept my mouth from dropping open in surprise at the implications of that. "What—"

"Oh, it looks like Harry and the boys are showing up," Farrah said, glancing through the window behind her. "I'm gonna go ask him where my carpet is."

"Carpet guys will be here tomorrow," I replied, still a little stunned.

"Shh," she said jokingly. "I want to bug Harry about it. See you around, Beauregard."

I jerked in surprise at the name.

Farrah smiled. "I just wanted to use it once," she said with a chuckle. "Bitchin' name, dude."

Harry gave me shit about how he wasn't paying me overtime because I'd shown up early without being asked to, but he slapped me on the back as he did it. I wondered briefly if Farrah had said something about my eventful night but forgot about it as the day moved on like normal. By the time we broke for lunch, Charlie's coffee cart was sitting pitifully on the edge of the wide driveway like a lost puppy. It looked so different when it wasn't all set up in its usual spot. I walked toward it, curious.

"Son of a bitch," Casper said as he crawled out from under it. He looked over at me and scowled as he got to his feet.

"Everything alright?" I asked as I got closer.

He looked at me like he was trying to decide something, then shook his head. "Floor's damn near rotted out," he replied, putting his hands on his hips. "The fuckin' fridge has been leakin' and it's gonna need to be replaced, but the floor has to be fixed before we can do anything else."

"Damn," I breathed. Charlie was going to lose it.

"I told her it was probably an easy fix," Casper said with a huff, reading my expression. "That was before I climbed under and got a good look. She's off with her mother choosing paint colors. Goddamn it."

"You mind if I take a look?" I asked, dropping down to my knees when he nodded. I scooted under the trailer and put my hand out. "You got a light?"

When Casper handed me the flashlight, I saw exactly what he'd been talking about. I reached out and used my thumb to push at the flooring. The outside was dry but stained from where the water had been leaking, but the entire thing was soft. Shit.

"You're right," I said as I crawled back out. "How the hell didn't they notice?"

"Where they're standin' when they work isn't real big," Casper said with a sigh. "Hardly noticeable when you're in there unless you know what you're lookin' for."

"The entire floor will need to be replaced," I said with a grimace. "You can't even patch it."

"Yeah, I know," he replied, staring at the cart.

"I'll do it," I said, reaching up to scratch at the back of my neck. Casper looked at me.

"I know what I'm doin'," I said wryly.

"I sure as hell hope so," he replied, glancing at his newly built house I'd just walked out of.

"It'll take me a day, max," I said with a chuckle. "But we'll need to take everything out. You have anywhere to put shit?"

"Give me half an hour," he said, pulling his phone out of his pocket.

I walked back to the house and told Harry I needed the rest of the day off, and he didn't even blink. It probably helped that I hadn't shown up late or missed a day since I'd started working for him.

"Cavalry's on the way," Casper said once I was back outside.

"Alright," I replied. "I'm gonna head to the hardware store and get the shit I'll need."

"We'll need," Casper corrected. He pulled out his wallet and I took a step back, raising my hand to stop him. He smiled. "Ah, it's like that, is it?"

"Don't need your money," I replied firmly.

As I drove to the hardware store I mentally made a list of the shit I'd need. Repairing what was essentially a shed built on top of a trailer was very different from repairing the floor of a house, but I had a pretty good idea of where to start. The axle was perfectly fine, it was just the flooring that needed to be repaired.

An hour later, my truck bed was full and I headed back to Casper's place. When I got there, three cars sat at angles around the cart, the trunks wide open.

"I'm taking the appliances," Cecilia called out over her shoulder as she went inside the cart.

"I'll carry out the espresso machine, Cecilia," Casper ordered. "Don't even try to lift that thing."

"I've got most of the pantry stuff," Lily called from the back of her car. "Do you think these glass bottles will be alright if I don't wrap them?"

"With the way you drive?" Kara's mom Rose asked. "Yes."

"Oh, hey Bishop," Lily said as I walked toward them. She looked beyond me at the truck. "Is that a refrigerator?"

"This one won't leak," I replied jokingly.

"Hey, our dishwasher is on the fritz," Rose said as she grinned at me. "Help a girl out?"

"Sorry," I said, laughing. "I'm all tapped out."

"Charlie's gonna kill you," Lily said with a whistle.

"Don't tell her," I muttered out of the side of my mouth.

I walked toward the cart to help carry out whatever was left inside, and the two of them continued the conversation like I couldn't hear them.

"He must've really fucked up," Rose said, her voice not as quiet as she thought it was.

"Oh, yeah," Lily replied. "Definitely."

"Almost done in here," Casper said, popping his head out when I reached the doorway. "You wanna help me with this fridge?"

We finished emptying the cart, and as soon as the women had left, taking all of Charlie's supplies with them, I went back inside. As soon as I'd pulled up the linoleum, the massive water spot was visible.

"Fuck. They're lucky no one fell right through it," Casper said in disgust. "How the hell didn't Mal's husband notice this shit?"

"Maybe he did," I said, staring at the plywood. Casper was right, it was an accident waiting to happen.

"He better steer clear of me," Casper muttered, stepping back outside.

We worked the rest of the afternoon, pulling shit apart. The pile of garbage next to the driveway was knee high when Casper left without a word. Half an hour later, he and Charlie's brother Cam came back and set up lights.

We'd just switched them on and were getting ready to start rebuilding when Charlie's car came up the driveway.

"What in the everlasting *fuck*?" she yelled, jumping out of her car the minute she'd parked. "Holy shit, what did you do?"

"The entire floor was fuckin' soup," Casper barked. "It had to be replaced."

"What?" she turned to me, wide eyed.

"Nothin' for it," I said, keeping my voice level.

She turned to her dad. "You said it wasn't that bad," she said accusingly.

"Turns out it was."

She looked between us, then down at Cam who was halfway under the trailer and then back at her car as her hands moved restlessly.

"Dad," she said hoarsely. "I just bought all the paint and ordered the new signs with the last of my graduation money."

"Good," he said with a nod.

Her voice was even quieter when she looked at the supplies lying around the trailer. "I can't pay for all this."

"It's taken care of," her dad said simply.

"What?" she said, looking at him. "No, you can't—"

"Wasn't me," he said as he walked back around the other side of the cart.

Charlie turned to look at me, and just like Lily had earlier, she looked beyond me to the bed of my truck.

"Beauregard Augustus Bishop," she said, her voice almost a whisper. "Tell me you didn't."

I followed her as she stomped toward my truck and climbed into the bed.

"You didn't," she said, her eyes wide as she ran her fingers over the refrigerator box. "I can't believe you—I'll pay you back. Soon, okay? As soon as I have it, I'll—"

"Nope."

"What are you talking about?" she asked, looking down at me in confusion, her hand still gently pressed against the refrigerator box. "It might take a little while, but I swear, I will."

"I don't need you to pay me back," I replied.

"You can't buy me a fridge!" She looked around. "And—and wood and—" She crouched down and looked at the roll of rubber flooring in the bed of the truck. "And flooring!"

"When someone does somethin' nice for you, honey," I replied, reaching out to touch her cheek. "Just say *thank you*."

I walked away before she could argue with me about it.

"Hey, Bishop, can you give me a hand?" Cam asked as I got closer to the cart.

"This conversation isn't over," Charlie called from the back of the truck as I scooted under the cart again.

"Can't hide from her down here," Cam said jokingly. "But you're welcome for savin' ya."

"You two are the worst," Charlie snapped, looking down at us from the doorway of the cart. Her face was drawn with worry. "And also kind of awesome. Holy shit, my entire floor is *gone*."

"That's what happens when you have to replace the whole floor," Casper told her, physically moving her out of the way.

"Where is all my stuff?" she asked slowly, looking at the empty walls and counters.

"Your sisters took it all to the club," Casper replied distractedly. "It's got the most storage space." He looked around. "Thankfully these counters weren't full cabinets or we woulda had to take them out, too."

"Won't take us long to finish," I told Charlie, hating the stricken expression on her face. "And then you can load it back up."

"The hits just keep on coming," she said under her breath. "Thank God we decided to move it today and we didn't wait until the weekend."

"Why don't you find somethin' to do," Casper said kindly. "Where's your ma?"

"She stopped at Aunt Callie's," Charlie said with a sigh. "She found a bunch of ugly lawn ornaments on clearance and she was going to put them in the yard and see how long until Aunt Callie noticed them."

Cam chuckled beside me.

"Go find Kara, then," Casper said. "We'll call ya when we're finished."

"Fuck that," Charlie said stubbornly. She looked around and then bent down. When she stood back up, she was holding a wrench from my tool belt. "Put me to work."

"What are you gonna do with that?" I asked, my mouth twitching as I tried to hold back a smile.

Charlie looked at the wrench. "Turn something," she answered, glaring at me. "A screw or something."

"I taught her how to change a tire," Casper told me apologetically. "And I don't even think she was payin' attention then."

"Fine," Charlie said, tossing the wrench over her shoulder.

"Hey," Casper barked, dodging out of the way.

"Tell me what to do," Charlie ordered, looking at me.

"Fuck," Cam said, letting the back of his head thump against the ground. "This is gonna take twice as long."

"Shut it, Ca-moron," Charlie shot back.

"Come here, honey," I said, grinning. "You can hand me tools."

"That sounds like a pity job," Charlie said, disappearing out of the door. "But since I want to help, I'll take it."

I spent the rest of the night with Charlie shadowing my every move. It didn't take long to rebuild the floor since we'd already had everything all pulled apart, and as I grabbed the rubber flooring out of the back of my truck, Farrah came tearing up the driveway.

"Jesus, Parnelli," Casper called as she climbed out of her rig. "You think you could drive any faster?"

"I wasn't driving that fast," Farrah yelled back as she closed her door.

"You know, I got two of your kids out here, layin' in the gravel," he pointed out. "You'd think their mother would take a little more care."

"They're adults and they're standing in the spotlights," Farrah replied with a chuckle as she strode over to give Casper a kiss. "The only one who's standing in the dark like a creeper is Bishop."

"Just grabbin' somethin' from the truck," I replied, even though she wasn't talking to me.

"Have you spit on him yet?" Farrah asked Casper.

"Mom!" Charlie snapped, glancing at me.

"Nah," Casper said, laughing under his breath. "I needed his help."

"You're both assholes," Charlie said in exasperation.

"We're just teasing him," Farrah said with a grin. She looked at me. "We like Bishop."

"Yeah, we all love him," Cam said flatly. "Now, can we finish this shit? I'd like to have dinner at some point tonight."

I carried the flooring into the cart and started the process of rolling it out while Charlie and her family bickered. It was kind of nice having their conversation as background noise. I'd never had a big family like that, one that was easy with each other. I'd lived in a few foster homes that had a bunch of kids, but it hadn't ever felt like a family—more like a bunch of strangers sharing a house.

I'd gotten to the point where I was trimming down the edges of the rubber to fit the space when Charlie stepped in behind me.

"Oh," she said softly.

I looked at the floor and my stomach sank. I'd found some gray rubber flooring at the hardware store that was thick enough that I knew we wouldn't have to replace the subflooring if there was another leak, and I'd been pretty proud of it until I saw it inside the actual cart. It was ugly.

"Fuck, honey," I said, sitting back on my heels. I'd been able to get the supplies I needed, but I wasn't exactly rolling in cash. There was no way to return it now that I'd started cutting and I couldn't go back and buy something prettier. "I'm sorry."

"For what?" Charlie asked in confusion, her eyes meeting mine.

"I didn't think about how it would look," I said apologetically, gesturing at the floor. "It's—"

"It's perfect," Charlie said, cutting me off.

"It's ugly."

"No, it's not," she argued, wrapping her arms around my neck from behind. "Are you kidding?"

"Honey—"

"Look how thick it is," she said happily. "And it's all textured, so I won't slip if I spill something."

I looked at the ugly pattern on the floor.

"Are you serious?"

"It's so much better than what was in here before," she said happily, her voice breathy in my ear as her arms tightened. I froze in place as I felt her lips against my neck. "You're the best."

As long as she kept her face against my neck like that, I was happy to stay kneeling on the floor.

"You need any help?" Cam asked from behind us.

"Nah," I said, still as Charlie continued to hug my neck. "It'll only take a few more minutes to finish."

"Alright," he said in amusement. "Come out when you're done and I'll help you unload the fridge."

"Thank God my behemoth of a brother is here," Charlie said with a sigh. "I'm guessing that fridge is heavy."

"They used a forklift to get it in the truck," I confirmed, reaching up to run my hand along her forearm.

"Why did you do all this?" she asked with a quiet sigh, pressing her forehead against the side of my neck.

Because I'd hurt her. Because she needed it. Because I didn't want anything else to sidetrack what we could have if she'd give it a chance. Because I'd known how devastated she'd be when she realized how bad it was. Because in this small way, I'd been able to make her life a little easier.

The answer was as complicated as it was simple.

"I take care of my own, remember?" I said, kissing her arm.

"Dammit," she whispered, her body going slack against my back.

I waited.

"I love you," she said with a small shudder.

"Love you too, honey."

"I'm still mad at you," she replied softly.

"I can work with that," I said, pulling on her arm until she was practically in my lap. Her hair was a mess, pulled up into a high ponytail, but at some point she'd put on a full face of makeup that hadn't budged even when she was crawling around in the gravel with me that night.

"I can't believe you built me a floor," she said, her lips curling up at the corners.

"I'm good with my hands," I replied, making her laugh. "And you helped."

"For the first time in a while," she said, laying her forehead against mine. "I'm feeling a little hopeful."

"Good," I replied, tilting my head so I could kiss her.

When her mouth met mine, I swear to God, every muscle that had been tightened into a knot since the night before seemed to relax at once.

"Okay, lovebirds," Farrah said in amusement from the doorway. "Super excited that you've made up, but we need to unload this refrigerator."

"My dad's not going to let her unload anything," Charlie whispered in amusement. Before she'd even finished her sentence we could hear Casper outside, telling her mom exactly that. "Told ya," Charlie said as she climbed off my lap.

Cam and I had underestimated how awkward unloading a full-sized refrigerator from the bed of a truck would be, and we ended up having to wait around while Casper called in the troops. Bike after bike pulled up, some of them trailing a car or SUV, and soon, Charlie's sisters and their husbands, Draco and Kara, and Kara's parents were there in the driveway.

"You know, we could use the tractor to get it out," Charlie's brother-in-law Mark said easily. "Why didn't you just call me?"

"That tractor's cursed," Draco said, sounding only half serious. "Last time we borrowed it the entire house burned down."

"That logic is frightening," Charlie said, smiling at me as she handed me a beer and walked away again.

She was the happiest I'd seen her in months. The tight way she'd held herself, even at her graduation party, had disappeared. As the crowd gathered in small groups and beer was passed around, she flitted from person to person, smiling and laughing. Her excitement was palpable.

"I don't know what you did to make it come back," Kara said, stepping close to me. "But if you do anything else to take that smile off her face, I will end you."

"I won't," I said, my eyes on Charlie.

"We'll see," Kara muttered, walking back into the darkness.

"Kind of hard to believe," Rose told me from a few feet away. "But my kid is usually the sweet, quiet part of that duo."

"Charlie's the mean one," Lily agreed. She smiled reassuringly when I opened my mouth to disagree. "Rose is the mean one in our duo."

"Truth," Rose said, toasting me with her beer.

Eventually, we got the fridge out of my truck and onto a dolly that we parked right outside the door of the cart, but we didn't put it inside because Farrah started ordering everyone around. Within half an hour, there were people inside and outside the cart, paint brushes and rollers in hand.

Painting the coffee cart in the dark.

"This probably wasn't our best idea," Charlie said with a laugh as she found me in the shadows.

"Can't say I've ever seen paintin' done by moonlight before," I replied, wrapping my arm around her shoulders as we watched everyone painting. "Well, I've seen people taggin' shit at night, but that's different.

Charlie chuckled as she leaned against me. "I'll probably have to touch it up, but it was a good idea to try and finish it while everyone is here."

"You've got an awesome family," I replied as we watched Leo pinch Lily's ass, making her jump and splatter paint all over herself.

"They're not too bad," Charlie said. "I better go help."

I watched her walk away, her ponytail swaying from side to side, and took a deep breath of the cold night air. We weren't solid, not yet, but I figured we'd made a good start.

It was late by the time the walls were freshly coated in paint and people started leaving.

"We're gonna grab some food on the way home," Draco told me, dropping some unused lumber in the bed of my truck. "Any preferences?"

"Didn't have lunch, so I'd eat grass at this point," I replied, making him chuckle.

"Salad it is," he joked. "We'll grab you something. See you back at the house."

He and Kara left with Charlie not far behind them, and I walked around the cart making sure that I hadn't left anything behind. I almost missed the wrench Charlie had thrown over her shoulder earlier.

"Can't thank you enough for all you did," Casper said from his seat across the driveway.

"No worries," I said, walking toward him. "I was happy to do it."

"I can reimburse you," he said seriously, taking a drag off his joint. "Had to set you back quite a bit, especially the fuckin' fridge you brought back."

"It's all good," I told him, shaking my head. It had. I'd used a good chunk of what little I'd been able to save—but it was worth it.

"Feels a little suspicious havin' you buy all this shit after you fucked up with my daughter so bad," he said easily, watching me for a reaction. "You tryin' to buy your way out of the doghouse?"

I jerked in surprise and stopped in the middle of the driveway.

"It's a legit question," he said, still leisurely enjoying his smoke.

"No, I'm not," I said, tightening my fist around the wrench.

"But you can see how it looks," Casper continued.

"I'm investin'," I said after I got my temper under control. He'd waited to say this shit until we were done with the coffee cart, and while I respected how wily the old fucker was, it still irritated the shit out of me.

"Investin'," he repeated thoughtfully.

"Yes," I grit out. "In the future I'm plannin' on havin' with Charlie."

"Oh, is that what it was," he said, his lips twitching.

"Leave him alone, Cody," Farrah said from inside the trailer. I looked up in surprise to see her face in the window. "Let the boy make his grand gesture in peace."

"She needed it," I said to Charlie's mom, not wanting her to think I was shallow enough to try and buy her daughter's affection. "And I had it to give."

"Good boy," she said to me. She put her hand against the screen in a gesture that surprised me by how sweet it was. Then she turned to look down at her husband. "Cody, save some of that for me."

After I'd tied down all the odds and ends in the back of my truck, I headed for home. For the first time in a while I was anxious to get there, to just be in the place where I felt most comfortable, to walk in and know Charlie was somewhere inside. When I pulled into the driveway, Draco's truck was still missing but Charlie's car was parked in the usual spot.

I was looking forward to the fact that she didn't have to work the next day and I'd hopefully be able to wake up next to her, and I wasn't paying attention as I let myself inside and swung the door shut behind me. I probably should've noticed how quiet the house was, or the fact that every single light in the house was on, but I was too distracted. I kicked off my boots and jogged up the stairs in my socks, wondering if we had enough time for a little cuddling before Kara and Draco got home—and nearly fell back down the stairs when a softball bat swung toward my head.

"What the hell?" I yelped as it barely clipped my forearm.

"Thank fuck," Charlie gasped, her body slamming into mine.

Chapter 17
CHARLIE

I WAS BRAVE. I was strong. I could take care of myself.

But when I realized that it was Bishop's head that I'd nearly clobbered with my bat, I was so relieved that I almost knocked him down the stairs.

"What the hell is going on?" he asked, pulling the bat from my hand as he wrapped his other arm around me securely. "You okay?"

"Someone was in the house," I stuttered, still freaked way the fuck out.

"What do you mean someone was in the house?" he asked, straightening. He pulled me closer. "Who?"

"I don't know for sure," I replied. God, he felt good. Solid. Safe. "But I have a pretty good idea."

I started to pull him toward my room, but he wouldn't budge.

"I'm gonna check the downstairs," he said, dragging me behind him as he took the steps two at a time. "You stand right here."

"You're not leaving me here," I argued, gripping his hand.

"You're standin' by the front door," he said, leaning down to give me a quick kiss. "You hear anythin' or see anythin', you go outside and get in your car."

"I'm not leaving you either," I argued.

"Charlotte," he said, his voice low. "Stay."

"I'm not a dog," I hissed as he strode away, disappearing into the kitchen.

I was on edge as I waited for him to take the same route that I'd taken the minute I'd walked in the door a little while earlier and realized something was wrong. I'd already searched every room in the house, but I wasn't about to dissuade him. I was pretty sure that I'd heard someone downstairs *after* I'd done my search.

"Stay there," he told me quietly as he passed me to jog back up the stairs. He grabbed the bat where we'd dropped it on the landing and rounded the corner out of sight. It must have taken less than a minute, but I swear to God, it felt like ten before he came back around the corner.

"Nothin'," he told me as he came back down the stairs and set the bat back in its spot behind the front door. "You sure someone was in here, honey?"

"Positive," I said darkly, grabbing his hand so I could tow him to my room.

I stopped in front of the entertainment center and looked at the wall that I'd spent so much time on, waiting for him to see it.

"Son of a bitch," he breathed, reaching for the frame in the center of the collage. "That fuckin' cunt."

Inside the frame of what should've been my brother Cam holding the twins when they were born was a photo of Bishop and Tabitha. They were smiling at the camera.

"She came into my room," I said softly, looking around us.

I hadn't left out anything that would embarrass me, and the room was clean, but I couldn't help but feel violated that she'd been in my private space. My little piece of home that was perfectly mine. She'd seen the couch that me and Kara had picked up at a garage sale, the bed that my parents had bought me when I was a teenager, the quilt that my grandmother had made before I was born. She'd seen the size of the weights that I'd used when I worked out and the bag of makeup sitting on the floor in front of my mirror. They were little pieces of my life that didn't really matter unless I knew someone had been looking at them without my permission. It felt gross and invasive. It made my stomach churn with nausea.

"I'm goin' over there," Bishop said, stomping out of my room with the frame still in his hand.

"Beauregard Augustus Bishop," I yelled as he started down the stairs. "Don't do it!"

"Looks like the truce didn't last long," Draco said as he stepped inside the front door. "Where's the fire?"

"Tabitha broke into our house," I said, hurrying down the stairs. "And Bishop thinks he's going to defend my honor or something."

"Whoa," Draco said, putting his hand out to stop Bishop just as Kara came in the door. "You don't wanna do that, man."

"I really do," Bishop replied. I wouldn't have been surprised if smoke started billowing out of his ears. He held up the photo. "This was on Charlie's wall."

"Holy crap," Kara said, swinging her head toward me. Her eyes were so wide they seemed to take up half of her face. "*She came in our house?*"

"Take a second," Draco said calmly to Bishop, even though I could see he was barely keeping a handle on his own temper. "You can't go rushin' over there. They'll call the police so fast, you won't even be able to talk to her before they're slappin' you in cuffs."

"Worth it," Bishop said, taking a step forward.

"It's really not," I said.

Bishop didn't even seem to hear me. He was too stuck in his head. Draco looked up at me, his eyebrows raised, waiting for me to do something.

So, like an idiot, I leaped from the second stair and clung like a monkey to Bishop's back. To say he hadn't been expecting me to do it would be the understatement of the century.

He staggered in surprise, and I started to slide downward, unable to get a grip on anything.

"Jesus, he's going to drop you," Kara screeched in panic, like I was dangling off a cliff instead of being able to reach the floor if I'd just put my feet down.

"I'm going down!" I yelled, digging my fingers into Bishop's shoulders as I slid. Apparently, Kara's panic was contagious.

"For Christ's sake," Draco muttered as Bishop reached under my legs and boosted me up on his back.

"The hell are you doin' up there?" he asked, looking over his shoulder at me.

"Um." I glanced at Kara and then back at Bishop. "Stopping you from doing something epically stupid?"

"She was in your room," he said, lowering me to the floor.

"I know that," I replied, circling him until we were face to face. "But don't make it worse by going over there half-cocked—"

Kara snorted.

"I don't need you to defend me," I said, reaching up to put my hands on Bishop's cheeks. "But I love that you want to."

"You don't need me to defend you," he said with a smirk, glancing at the top of the stairs.

"Okay, when I think there's a crazy person in the house, feel free to let your protective instincts run wild," I replied. "But not when we know she's not *here* and you're just pissed."

"I'm just supposed to do nothin'?" he asked me in disbelief.

"Not tonight, okay?" I said, leaning against him. "Let's just eat whatever Draco brought home and then go to bed. I'm tired, aren't you tired?" I was rambling, but it seemed to work.

He let me drag him into the kitchen after he made sure the deadbolt on the front door was locked, and we all just kind of sat staring at each other around the table. I met Kara's eyes and quickly looked away. But she was like a magnet, and within seconds I was looking at her again and we were both trying to hold back laughter.

"What?" Bishop asked, looking between us.

I looked at Kara and she stared back at me. Then I looked at the table. The ceiling. The bag of food. The kitchen sink. Nothing worked. My eyes met hers again and we couldn't stop the explosion of giggles that burst out of our mouths.

"Nervous laughter," Draco said, smiling.

"What?" Bishop asked in confusion.

"It's nervous laughter. The scare is over." He looked at Bishop's blank face. "It's like a pressure cooker. Someone hit the valve and now the pressure's escapin'."

Bishop looked at us, still giggling. "Okay."

"Just be glad they're not throwin' shit," Draco said with a shrug as he started handing out meals to each of us.

The laughter eventually tapered off and the four of us dug into our meals, nothing breaking the quiet until Bishop spoke.

"I fuckin' read her wrong," he said, leaning back in his chair. "How the hell did I miss it?"

"She's been like that for years," Kara replied before I had a chance to. "And she's always been good at hiding it, at least for a while. You would've noticed it eventually."

"I've been readin' people since I was old enough to talk," Bishop said with a grimace. "I should've seen it."

"People are always on their best behavior at the beginning," Draco said around a mouthful of food.

"Except me," I said with a shrug. "What you see is what you get."

"Puhlease," Kara said, tossing a french fry at me. "You act all tough."

"I am tough," I said, throwing the french fry back.

"I'm gonna check all the locks," Bishop announced abruptly, getting up from the table.

"He feels bad," Kara said, tilting her head to the side as she watched him walk away. "He should."

"He didn't know," I replied quietly. As soon as I said it, the words sunk in like talons, all the way to the bone. "Thanks for dinner, guys."

I got up and followed Bishop and found him checking the window locks in the living room.

"I don't even think we've opened those since we moved in," I told his back as he pulled to make sure they were secure.

"Just wanna be sure," he said, turning to face me. "I can't find how she got in."

"Maybe one of us left a door unlocked," I said with a shrug. "It happens."

"I can't believe she came in our house," he said in disgust. "What the fuck is wrong with her?"

"She feels like I've won," I said simply, shrugging my shoulders.

"That's bullshit," he spat.

"It's not though," I replied. "I did. I bought the coffee cart. I got the guy."

"Who does that kind of shit? She's got a new job and we'd only been on two fuckin' dates and they weren't even good ones."

"A narcissist," I said dryly. "A mean girl."

"I'm sorry," he said, shaking his head as he walked toward me. "I can't even tell you—"

"I know you are," I said with a sigh, wrapping my arms around his neck as he reached me. "I am too."

"What the hell do you have to be sorry for?" he asked, pulling away.

"For making you wait," I mumbled, dropping my head against his chest. "For blowing you off while I tried to figure shit out."

"You were just doin' what you thought was right."

"So were you," I replied. Bishop huffed.

"No I wasn't," he said, tightening his arms around my waist. "Knew it was stupid and went out with her anyway."

I looked up at him in surprise.

"Told myself it wasn't a big deal," he said. "That I shouldn't feel guilty about it. Fuck if that worked. I felt like an asshole the minute I brought her into the house."

"You sure didn't seem contrite," I joked.

He laughed. "I was feelin' a bit defensive," he muttered apologetically. He sighed. "Damn, it's been a long day."

"And a long night before that," I agreed.

"You get any sleep?" he asked softly.

"Not much," I admitted.

"Me either."

"Kara, we're going to bed," I yelled, making Bishop smile.

"Thanks for the update," Kara yelled back.

"Stop fuckin' yellin'," Draco yelled. "We've got neighbors!"

I followed Bishop up the stairs and let him lead me into the bathroom, where without speaking we both started to undress. Climbing into the shower after him, I took in the broad expanse of his shoulders and the narrow flex of his hips. He really was the most beautiful person I'd ever seen.

"Let's start now," he said to me, pulling me into the spray.

"What do you mean?" I asked, letting him pull the ponytail out.

"I loved the beginning, honey," he said, running his fingers through my hair. "But when we look back, I'd rather remember this. The feel of you here, happy and calm. Not the shit last night or even the last couple of months that I barely saw you even though we've been livin' in the same house."

"Oh, I don't know," I replied, turning to face him. "I don't think I want to forget any of it."

"Oh, yeah?"

"If we skip to now, we'd have to skip all those nights we stayed up late talking," I whispered, kissing the center of his chest. "And the crazy good sex we had in your bed—"

"And in yours," he said through a grin.

"That one, too," I agreed. Thinking about my bed made me think about how Tabitha had been in my room, and that led to the look on her face when she'd walked in with Bishop the night before. I pushed it all away.

"I'm sorry," he said, leaning down to kiss me softly. "Fuck."

"Stop saying it," I replied, reaching up to tug his hair. "I know you are."

"I wouldn't hurt you for the world," he said, his brows still drawn in contrition. "You know that, right?"

"It's over," I acknowledged.

"You know I wouldn't hurt you?"

"I know it wasn't your intention."

"I won't hurt you again."

"You can't promise that," I responded, smiling at him.

"I sure as fuck can," he argued.

"Fine," I conceded. "You will never hurt me ever."

"Now you're just bein' sarcastic," he muttered, leaning over so the spray of the shower hit me directly in the face.

"Hey!" I sputtered, ducking away.

The rest of the shower was quick as we soaped up and took turns rinsing off. Our shower really wasn't meant for two—was there such a thing? But we made it work. I don't think either of us was willing to let the other out of our sight. We didn't bother grabbing anything to sleep in, and without any discussion, Bishop led me into his room.

I crawled beneath the covers as Bishop pulled the blinds closed and turned off the light. Once we were cocooned in the darkness he turned to me.

"This is where I've wanted to be since I met you," he said, pulling me into the curve of his body. "Can't explain it." He paused for a moment. "Just spent the day helpin' you with your dream and now I get to fall asleep next to you."

"Naked," I whispered back.

"Naked's a bonus," he said, kissing my bare shoulder. "Sleep, honey. I'll be here when you wake up."

Epilogue

CHARLIE

"Wake up," a quiet voice murmured in my ear, pausing to bite it gently.

"Beauregard Augustus Bishop," I groaned, swatting at the air. "Leave me alone."

"Nope," he said, pulling the quilt and top sheet all the way off the bed. "Up."

"You are the worst," I mumbled, curling into a ball. Sleeping naked had not been my brightest idea.

"Honey, I gotta get to work."

"So, go," I muttered. "Bye."

"Charlie," Bishop snapped, not unkindly. "Please get up and get dressed."

"Why?" I whined, sitting up in bed.

"Because I wanna take you somewhere before I go to work."

"It's the butt crack of dawn," I bitched, climbing out of bed. "This can't wait until after work?"

"No, it can't," he replied, tapping me lightly on the ass. "Get ready. I'll meet you downstairs."

I hurried through my morning routine, slapping on a little makeup and throwing my rat's nest of hair into a high bun. Sleeping on wet hair had also been an epically bad decision. By the time I got downstairs, Bishop was waiting for me at the door.

"Beautiful," he said, grinning as I tiredly flipped him off.

I followed him to the truck and climbed inside, only half curious about where we were going. I'd trained myself to wake up early after years of taking the morning shift, but that only worked if I was expecting to get up early. If I'd been planning on sleeping in—which I had—then waking up fully was a challenge.

"Thank you for comin' with me," he said as we drove. "I wanted to see you this morning before I left."

"A little morning nookie would've been better," I said, leaning back against the seat as I turned my head to look at him.

The morning sun was coming through the window, outlining his face in a light so bright I had to squint, and I almost laughed at how angelic he looked. Not like one of those chubby baby angels, but like one of the avenging ones, all chiseled lines and strong bones.

"I'll be sure to wake you up for that tomorrow," he said, reaching over to squeeze my thigh. "How's the leg?"

"You've seen it," I replied, reaching down to run my finger along the scar beneath my jeans. "It's pretty gnarly looking."

"I heard you tell Kara that it was infected," he said quietly. "I wanted to ask you about it, but—" He shrugged. "Wasn't my place."

"It's all healed now," I assured him.

"Good," he said, shooting me a smile. "I worried a bit."

"No," I gasped theatrically. "You?"

We pulled onto the freeway, and I looked around in confusion. I had absolutely no idea where he was going, and I opened my mouth to ask when he pulled off at the next exit.

"Bishop," I said, realization dawning.

"This'll only take a minute," he replied.

I sat like a statue as we pulled into the line at Morning, Joe.

"Smile, honey," he said, lacing his fingers through mine as he pulled up to the window.

I wish I would've been prepared. If I'd known what was happening beforehand, I would've pulled out my phone and taken a picture.

The look on Tabitha's face was one of the best things I'd ever seen.

Bishop was all business as he ordered our coffees, somehow remembering exactly what I preferred. He waited, glancing over at me to smile while she prepared the drinks. Then, he took them from her hands politely and handed her a twenty.

We waited as she made change, but as she tried to hand it back, Bishop shook his head.

"Keep the change," he said easily, handing her the photo she'd left in my house. "Just wanted to give this back to you."

Tabitha gaped at us like a goldfish as she struggled to think of something to say.

"I doubt I'll see you around," Bishop said, putting the truck in gear. It was somehow both a promise and a threat. He pulled away before she'd uttered a word.

I lifted the coffee to my mouth as I savored the memory of Tabitha's face.

"Don't drink that," Bishop snapped, taking the hot coffee out of my hand. "Jesus, she probably spit in it."

"Oh, god, you're right," I said, wiping the back of my hand against my mouth, even though I hadn't even touched my lips before he'd taken it.

I started to laugh as he turned into a gas station and immediately threw the coffees into the trash can outside.

I was still laughing as he opened up my door and leaned inside the cab.

"I bet she won't fuck with you again," he said, grinning as I giggled.

"And you didn't even get arrested," I said, wrapping my arms around his neck. "My hero."

"Love you, honey," he said sweetly, leaning in to kiss the smile off my lips.

"I love you, too," I murmured. "This was totally worth getting up early."

"Tomorrow will be better," he said against my lips.

"Can't wait," I whispered back.

ACKNOWLEDGEMENTS

To the bloggers and readers – thank you for continuing to read about this little world I've created. This has been such a wild ride! Cheers to another nine years.

Mom and Dad – Thanks for listening to me complain. Love you guys.

My kiddos – I love you! Thank you for taking care of each other while I wrote this story. I could have never finished it without your help.

My fella – you make me crazy and happy in equal measure. Love you.

Ellie-dude. Thank you so much for squeezing me into your editing schedule when I texted you in a panic. I hope your poltergeist stops messing with your electronics – for both our sakes.

Toni – Peas and Carrots, dude. Always.

Letitia – nailed it again. Thanks for finding my perfect Charlie and putting her on a beautiful cover.

Michelle, Pam and Beatrice – You guys are the best reader group admins, beta readers, and friends a girl could ask for. I'm so thankful for you.

Amber, Melissa, and Ashley – you've always got my back, reading the minute I send you the book before anyone else has seen it. I'm not sure what I'd do without you.

Donna – here's another acknowledgement for the chance you took on a brand new writer and the difference you made in my career. Nine years later and I'm still as thankful as the day you agreed to read Craving Constellations.

www.ingramcontent.com/pod-product-compliance
Ingram Content Group UK Ltd.
Pitfield, Milton Keynes, MK11 3LW, UK
UKHW031430161224
3699UKWH00056B/2175